PAINTER OF SILENCE

PAINTER OF SILENCE

GEORGINA HARDING

BLOOMSBURY

LONDON · BERLIN · NEW YORK · SYDNEY

First published in Great Britain 2012

Copyright © 2012 by Georgina Harding

The moral right of the author has been asserted

Bloomsbury Publishing, London, Berlin, New York and Sydney

50 Bedford Square, London WC1B 3DP

A CIP catalogue record for this book is available from the British Library

ISBN 978 1 4088 2112 1 (hardback)
10 9 8 7 6 5 4 3

ISBN 978 1 4088 2446 7 (trade paperback)
10 9 8 7 6 5 4 3 2 1

Typeset by Hewer Text UK Ltd, Edinburgh
Printed in Great Britain by Clays Ltd, St Ives plc

MIX
Paper from
responsible sources
FSC® C018072

www.bloomsbury.com/georginaharding

Augustin

Though he has seen photographs of cities he has never been in one before. In the dusk as the train came in it looked monochrome as the photos: black smears of road, grey walls, grey buildings angled across the sides of hills. The buildings appeared singly at first then massed, most of them solid but some hollow so that he could see through them to the sky as it darkened. Between the buildings there were the bare outlines of trees – still there were trees – but the forest was gone. He had been sitting with his back to the engine so he had had a sense of the landscape receding rather than of the city approaching. He had seen the land become forest, and then the forest became city, and then he closed his eyes. That way he could keep the land with him for longer. He held the memory of that land in his mind and he pictured himself disappearing into it, vertically, not moving his limbs but only standing like a post, sinking down into some long brown fold between the tracks and the wide horizon.

He had known all along that the train would not be stopping there. In land like that trains do not stop. They only pass through pouring out clouds in ribbons above them.

He has taken this train because this is where he means to come, to this city.

He does not open his eyes again until the last of the other passengers has gone. The carriage is quite different now, devoid of motion, a hollow space filled with stale grey air. He looks about him at the floor littered by the journey, the bottle stilled at last that had for so long rolled back and forth beside his feet. The emptiness seems etched with a grime that matches that on his fingertips. He rubs the length of each thin hand on the rough cloth of his trousers but that does not make them any cleaner.

There are two objects left on the rack above his head: his rolled-up coat and a small bundle. With an effort he draws himself up, reaches for the coat and puts it on, knotting the belt where it is far too big for his slight figure, then takes down the bundle. He starts to go. Stoops a second before the next row of seats and picks up a crumpled paper from the floor. It is a label from a packet of biscuits, a scrap of waxed paper printed in yellow. A sunflower, a ring of petals, bright yellow lettering. He pauses to smooth the paper out, to fold it precisely into half and half again and put it in his trouser pocket. Then he goes on to the open door, down the steep steps to the platform.

So many people there are in the world. The tracks run together line upon line and people pick their way across the lines or huddle on narrow platforms where they divide. There are many people going different ways. The passengers from his train, spilling away along the platform. Others coming from the opposite direction, where the train on the next line stands with steam building ready to leave.

There is a great hall. Its roof is so high that the people seem small and dark and animal within it.

There are soldiers breaking through the crowd, running. He shrinks back beside a kiosk. The soldiers must be running after someone. No, they are running after the steaming train. The person they are after must be on the train – or perhaps, possibly, it is the train itself that they must catch. They jump on. The last one is pulled up by the arms and they are gone. They are not the kind of soldiers he is used to. It is some years since he has seen such uniforms. He is glad when they are gone because he does not like the images they brought back to mind.

He goes out from under the roof. The smell of the city is sooty and bitter as that of the station. There is a dark height of sky but no stars, and the people split off in different directions. He selects a street at random, walking along at the side of it with his shoulder close to the walls. Sometimes the walls break down into rubble and he hunches lower and feels an urge to scuttle across the space. He comes to a crossing, a street that goes up a hill. Though he is beginning to wheeze with the effort, some instinct makes him choose to climb. He comes to a monumental flight of steps, starts up one step at a time. Halfway he stops to rest. No people here. He drops his bundle and sits, hollow with fatigue, holding with one hand the cold stone of the balustrade.

A cough rises in him. He tries not to cough because he knows that it will hurt. After he has tried to hold it down the cough when it comes hacks at him all the more.

He stands again, bending slowly back down for his bundle. When he reaches the top of the steps he is still in the city. If anything he seems to be deeper into it since the buildings are larger and more imposing, the air as coarse, the stars as hidden. Streets fan out before him. Once more he selects the one that continues most to rise, as if in climbing he will find more to breathe. And here he seems to be right in his choice. This way there are big buildings but clear spaces between them, openings for cars to be parked or people to walk, grass and sometimes trees. It is good to step on to the softness of turf, on to rotted layers of another year's leaves. He finds a bench and lays himself down with the bundle beneath his head. Tomorrow he will start his search. When it is light he will write out her name and get one of all those people to show him where he might find her. He pulls his coat tight about him. He does not so much sleep as fall into a suspended state, body and breathing slowing, time fading, like a small creature chilling for hibernation, the chill broken at points through the night by fits of coughing that come with an internal searing heat but make his outer body shiver.

Consciousness returns with the dawn, with a vague yellow streak in the sky that his eyes catch like a hope.

With deliberate effort, as if it were some object apart from himself, he lifts his body to an upright position on the bench. Just as he does so a girl walks before him. The girl wears a dark coat, a nurse's white cap. She appears to look his way for just a second as he moves. He has only a glimpse of her but he retains the image: a glow to her, the long eyes of an angel.

Is she real? If she is real, then did she not see him? He has the feeling that she did not so much as see him. If she had seen him her eyes would have shown it somehow. She might have come to him with care in her eyes, lips moving. Or she might, seeing him, have run away. Perhaps nobody in this city can see him. Perhaps he can no longer be seen. Perhaps that is what this numbness is, that spreads right across his body and into his brain.

A thread of determination pulls him to his feet. His coat is sodden with dew. Such a weight of dew. The coat was always too big and now it is too heavy. He unties the belt, shrugs it off him. It is so stiff with the wet that it sits up on the ground like some half-melted figure of wax. He feels light without its load. He does not attempt to pick up his bundle but leaves it there on the bench. Eyes to the ground, arms across himself, he shuffles the way the angel has gone.

They find him on the steps of the hospital just as the nurses are coming in on their morning shift. It is clear by the dampness of him that he has spent the night out but it might be anyone's guess how many previous nights he has spent outdoors. Certainly it does not appear, from the state of him, that he has lived a settled life or even fed regularly for a long time. He is frail as a fallen bird. Did somebody bring him or did he find his own way? In these days it is best not to question such things. However the poor man has got here, he has come just in time.

The first few days they do not even attempt to ask him who he is. For most of those days he is either unconscious or so feverish that they cannot expect to get sense out of him. In his delirium he moans and cries out with strange animal cries, covering taut eyes with hands that seem too big, out of proportion with his emaciated body, scrabbling bone fingers across the sheets. But then the fever passes. His horrors appear to abate and give way to vacancy. The nurses come to his bed and see his eyes open and calmly staring beyond them, where there is no more to see than the cracks in the paint on the ceiling or the motes in the sunlight. Good morning, they say, or how are you today, but his eyes do not budge, as if the ceiling or the motes were of more interest than they themselves. You're looking better now. You were in a bad way when you came in. It was touch and go there. We were afraid for you. But he does not appear to care, does not so much as shift his stare towards them. Where's your family? Is there someone we can contact?

His clothes were burned because of the lice in them. All that he has left are the boots he was wearing, holed, broken-laced, the leather worn with his history or possibly the history of some other man who had them before him. They look as if they were good military boots once but this man does not look like a soldier. He carried nothing else that could tell them anything about him but only a number of pieces of paper folded into a trouser pocket.

It was the ward sister Adriana who supervised his admission. When she found the papers they were so neatly folded and bundled that she thought at first that they must have some value, as if they were money or letters. But when she opened them she saw that they were nothing – no more than old tickets and labels and torn scraps – so she threw them away. In the other trouser pocket she found an acorn and a purulent rag that he had used for a handkerchief. That, too, was nicely folded, even though it was gummed together with phlegm. The handkerchief was the first thing to go into the incinerator. The acorn she put down on to the duty desk.

Adriana had completed the details on his admission form as best she could. Name: unknown. Address: unknown. Comments: carries no identification documents. No possessions, not even a coat. Date of birth? Hard to tell when a man was in his condition, but a young man still. By the things in his pockets she would think him only a boy. She rolled the acorn beneath her fingers. Recalled the pockets of her son's trousers when he was eight or ten: how when she did the washing she would turn the pockets out, the intimacy of the action like feeling into a burrow; and then if there was anything that mattered she would put it down beside the rest of the laundry and try not to forget to give it back.

* * *

Adriana stops beside his bed when she passes on her round. He is asleep, wheezing softly but breathing better than he has in days. Or perhaps he is not asleep, or he has been woken by her presence so close by. He opens his eyes and looks at her.

'Can you tell me your name?'

'Do you have a mother somewhere?'

'Don't you think you could eat a spot of lunch today?'

By the look in his eyes she thinks that he understands yet he makes no attempt to speak. He seems to watch and yet his lips are clamped tight as if they were only painted on his face.

This man will be about the age of her son. She has seen his body as once she used to see her son's, every inch of it. Two of them had washed him after he came in, when she was showing a student nurse how to wash a man. They had shaved him and disinfected him of lice. Then with soap and water they had gently sponged his neck, his chest, his back, his crotch, his frail limbs one by one, as if he were a baby or a corpse. His thinness was pitiful. There were sores and bruises on him, but these were superficial marks that would heal before long and disappear. Nowhere on his body was there a scar. She had noticed that. That has been a rare thing for her, in her profession, to see a young man who has got through all of the war and these years after without one scar.

If she had time, she thinks, if there were not so many here demanding her attention, she would sit on the bed by his feet and talk to him a while so that he got used to her voice, and give him time to talk to her.

'Tell me if you need anything, won't you? I'll be back later.'

At least she has made the offer but he is quite motionless. She cannot picture him asking for anything.

She puts her hand on to his. Really he is like a boy there, huddled on his side as they had laid him in the narrow bed.

When it is her night shift Adriana sits at her desk and knits. There is enough light to knit by but no more. Sometimes when she comes into this ward at night she feels that the air is heavy with diseased breath, as if it is the sick themselves who are the source of darkness; as if that is what they exhale when they cough and even when they lie still, the dark exhaust from used bodies. Sometimes there are patients who die in the night, quietly, their souls slipping away in the darkness with their breath. She finds them after dawn. Thin light penetrates through the half-curtained windows, and the atmosphere in the ward seems to thin with it like an escaping mist, and she finds a body laid out with a face pale as paper.

This night the stillness has been broken by the young man's nightmares. Every now and then she feels she must go to him. She puts down her wool and needles and goes to calm him with soothing words and with a cool touch on his brow that seems to soothe better than any words. The cries he makes in his sleep sound to her like moans from a time before speech. They resemble no language that she can understand.

An idea comes to her.

*   *   *

In the morning at the end of her shift she stops at the doctor's office along the corridor. The doctor has just come in, a stout man trim and freshly shaven, putting on his white coat.

'The man in bed number 43, the one who does not speak –'

'What about him?' The doctor has a thousand things to see to: the sick that he already knows, a failed suicide, new admissions undiagnosed.

'Do you think he could be mute?'

'It's possible. I wouldn't know.' If it is so, it is not his sphere. Not a medical condition.

There is a nurse standing at the door. She is a new nurse here. She is slight, dark, young, and yet she says that she has been a nurse since the start of the war. That is hard to believe as she seems just a girl.

'Excuse me for interrupting. I couldn't help overhearing what you said just then. I have not seen this man. I wonder, if he is a mute, might I perhaps go and see him? I might help, perhaps. I have some experience you see of mutes.'

When Safta goes to the ward she is carrying some blank sheets of paper and a pencil.

'What are those for?' Adriana asks her.

'In case he can write. Has anyone tried to see if he can write?'

'Shouldn't think so.'

'Or draw. He might like to draw.'

She puts on a mask. She has not been into this ward before. It is on the south side of the hospital and long. A long high cold white room, the light in it like chalk on a winter's day. A chilly order to this ward, more order than she has seen elsewhere in the hospital. There are no visitors here, no milling about, no patients sharing beds, only herself in white gown and mask walking down the line looking at the numbers on the metal frames.

His bed is against the wall facing the open windows. He is curled on one side with his back to her so that she must go round to see his face. Somehow it does not surprise her that she knows it. It is no less than she had expected. She had come on an impulse, because as she said she had once known a mute, but also out of a kind of superstition that she would barely have admitted even to herself. She stands a minute looking. His face is known to her though it is so long since she saw it last. Not a muscle in it moves. It is thin, awfully thin, like the stripped skull of the boy she used to know. His eyes are closed, either because he is asleep or because he has chosen to cut out the world. How complete the blackness must be when a deaf man closes his eyes. The world exists then only by touch and smell: the smell of the hospital that tells him what kind of place he is in; her shadow falling on him; her finger now so lightly touching the hand that clasps the edge of the sheet.

He opens his eyes but there is no sign in them that he remembers her.

Of course he will not know her in the mask. She takes it off, places it in her apron. Then she bends and takes his hand close to her lips. 'Tinu,' she says, speaking almost without sound, the long second syllable a blowing of air across his skin.

There is no sign that he knows his name.

'I can't stay with you long. I have work to do. I'll come back. But I've brought you these.' She puts the pencil and the paper on the locker beside his bed.

'Maybe you're not well enough yet, but I've brought them anyway.'

She ensures that her face is in full view all the time she speaks.

'I'll come back later if I can, or tomorrow.'

When she leaves the ward she feels the whiteness of the room still inside her, as if she is bleached out inside. It is the shock, she tells herself. She feels the whiteness like a dam holding back all the coloured flood of memory. She walks down the flights of stairs, one after the other, without seeing the people on them. She holds the whiteness to her. Out through the gates and on to the street.

That evening she writes a letter to his mother. She has heard no word about his mother since early in the war. She does not know where to find her now, only that she can no longer be at the house. So she addresses the letter to the priest, assuming that if Paraschiva is alive she must be somewhere in the village. It is a short, simple letter, a practical administrative letter from a nurse directed to a priest. The priest will surely be able to find Paraschiva and read her what it says.

*   *   *

14

The doctor places the cold disc of the stethoscope on the young man's chest to listen to his lungs. He is thin to an extreme. His chest lies bare as that of a small plucked bird, every bone in it showing. But there is a wiry strength there. Sometimes it is like that: those who are thin to start with, built like birds, have a better chance of recovery than the bigger men. Their slighter bodies seem to have less need for food. They are thus less broken by the malnutrition and have more resistance to the disease. Yes, this man is tougher than he looks. If he is rested, and fed, he has a chance of recovery, even if they cannot get the drugs. The doctor is pleased, rolls back on to his heels, puts the stethoscope away.

Adriana helps the patient to sit up. She lets him lean forward on to her as she firms up the pillows behind him, in the small of his back and behind his head. Her arm reaches across his chest, his head falls to her shoulder, and she smells the sourness in the nape of his neck, the hollowness of him there. He is still so feeble that there is a long way to go.

When he is upright she brings the food. She places the bowl on the blanket and puts her arm around him as she feeds him.

Still he has made no attempt to speak. The girl Safta is probably right. He is a mute. Perhaps he is completely deaf, since he does not turn when she speaks to him or look when one of the other patients in the ward cries out. If he is deaf, that will not prevent her from talking to him. She talks to him all the time that she is with him, as if he is a baby that must be talked to if it is to become attuned to the human voice and learn the patterns and the sounds of

15

speech. It does not matter what she says any more than it would matter what she were to say to a baby that she was feeding. The message is there in the tone of her voice – or if it is really as she thinks and he cannot hear her voice, then it is in her touch and her manner, in the shapes made by her lips and the warm breath from them so close upon his cheek.

'You should have a name. We still do not have a name for you. May I call you by my son's name, would that be all right? I am sure that he would not mind. He would not mind sharing his name with you. He would not mind at all. Yes, I'll call you Ioan like my son. It's a plain, true name. There are lots of Ioans. Perhaps you were even called Ioan before? Wherever you were. Whoever you were with. Wouldn't that be strange, if you were Ioan before and then we named you that again?'

She is talking rubbish, she knows that. But she is speaking softly. Even from the next bed it would sound as no more than a murmur. And the patient is gone now from the bed on the other side. He has pushed aside his lunch and shuffled off to roll a cigarette in the stairwell. She has often seen him there, skulking in the stairwell in his pyjamas. His lungs are so bad with the disease that the smoking seems to be no more than an idea to him. He rolls the cigarette and lights it, and then he coughs and can do no more than watch it burn between his shaking fingers. When it dies he pinches out the end and puts the stub in his pyjama pocket for the next time. She sees that all the same it is some kind of comfort to him.

'One day I'll tell you about my son, Ioan. I don't have anyone to talk to about him, not now. My husband said I should stop talking about him, that it didn't do any good to talk – well I don't see that not talking did him much good either. What do you think about that, Ioan? Anyway, my husband's gone now. He said I should stop waiting for the boy to come back. He wanted me to throw out his things. How could I do that? How could that be right, when I don't know? With the world as it is nowadays, with people coming and going like they do, and coming back and you don't know where they've been. Even now you hear about people come back from the war when they've been gone for years, and they've been in Russia all that time, and nobody's ever heard anything about them, but there they are again, all of a sudden. No, I keep everything for him. That's right, isn't it? Isn't that what you'd expect your mother to do? You'd think that, wouldn't you? Or maybe you wouldn't think it. Maybe you don't think. If you don't have words, how do you think anyway? How do you remember things? Maybe you don't remember things. Can that be so? Then you're just here, now, and here I am speaking to you, but you can't hear me or understand what I say, and that's all there is.'

The horror of the thought runs deep into her: that experience can be held down to this moment, this hospital ward with its hollow faces and its odour of disinfectant and illness, this bleak March day and the used-up sky beyond the windows, the aching city outside which seems only an extension of the ward.

She stops speaking and looks into his eyes, which are alert, staring directly into hers. No, she is wrong. Of course he has memories. Only they will not take the shape of words.

'It was terrible of me to think that, wasn't it? Of course it's not so, it's not like that, just because you can't say. I don't know what you must think of me, Ioan. I am sorry, Ioan, I'm just a fat old fool. Don't pay any attention to me.'

That is how he becomes known in the hospital, as Ioan. It is a name. Better to have a name than not. It is understandable to Safta that the mother should choose to make his silence hers and to take him as a silent son. After all, he is still like a boy. He still seems a boy despite his stubble, despite the lines, the appearance of ageing brought on by his suffering.

Safta has told no one that she knows who he is. It would be little help to him and none to herself. There is no one here who knows where she comes from. She has told only the immediate truth: that she has come from Bucharest and that prior to that she was with the army in Ukraine and Crimea. There is anonymity to that, to the city and the war. If anyone guesses as to who she is or what she was before – and her background must surely reveal itself in her voice and manner, even after a decade – if anyone has guessed, then she is grateful that they have been silent about it. Perhaps there are things about themselves also that they would prefer not to be known. Who they used to be. What they think. What memories they carry inside their heads.

She brought him paper that first time she came to see him, and a pencil, but he has not touched them. Has he, too, learnt the lessons of these years? Does he also choose to keep things closed away?

Whenever she has time she comes from the part of the hospital where she works and sits with him. She takes up the pencil and paper from where they lie on the locker. The lockers of other patients have food and books and photographs on them. His has nothing inside it except for the worn military boots.

'They're calling you Ioan now. See, I'll write it out for you.' She writes the word and points to him. Writes her own name, indicates herself. Once he could read that. There were just a few words he could read: his own name, hers, the name of the village. Poiana. He had learned to write *Poiana* and wrote the word beautifully, with that same care he gave to all the letters he wrote so that they seemed like the work of a calligrapher, and then he had held out his two rounded arms as if they contained the whole globe, and Safta thought that he understood its meaning, for the village was then the whole world to him.

She writes out his new name again, then passes him the paper. She has it resting on the stiff board that holds his medical notes. He looks, no more. He looks at what she has written and then he lifts the papers to look at the notes beneath, the record of medications given, temperatures taken. He hands it back. It is as if they are all of equal value: the page, the record, herself, the pencil she had offered him which lies untouched on the blanket.

She takes up the pencil and begins herself to draw. Her hand is clumsy, the lines unsure, overdrawn. She was never so good at drawing as he was.

It is a clumsy sketch but he knows its subject from the first few lines. The house. The long span of it, the wide porch with the fountain before it, the drive with its acacias. She has some details wrong. She has too few windows on the façade, too many columns in the porch. His memory is precise. He would not have made such mistakes himself. Then the dogs are not there, the long pale dogs that used to spread themselves on the porch between the shadows of the columns. He would like her to have put in the dogs. The sun shone sidelong across the porch some days and the dogs would lie there in the bright patches on the stone floor until they were hot and shift then into the stripes of shade. Her drawing is like the house he knew as she is like the girl he knew: recognisable, but altered. Her name though, as she has written it, over and over again these past days, is unchanged. He wrote it himself when he was looking for her. He had walked up the avenue to the house and found no one there but the dogs, and they and the house were changed, and the dogs had shown their teeth and come at him to drive him away. He had gone to the priest by the church and again he had written her name. *Iaşi*, the priest had written, the name of the city. Then he had drawn the sign for a hospital. And a cart gave him a lift to the station and he had come to Iaşi and he has found her. Now she is asking him to draw. He has drawn nothing in a long time.

Poiana

The house at Poiana was imposing at first glance. There was its whiteness, the long neoclassical front, the pedimented porch and ranks of green-shuttered windows. It looked larger than it was because it was only one room deep. If a person came up the drive and looked in he might see right through the glimmer of glass to the garden beyond.

It was a place that light passed through, the light of successive windows thrown on to fine parquet floors in rooms that opened one on to another, the doors of the rooms always open – save when great and irritated effort was made to close them during the coldest stretches of winter – since this was a house which people moved through freely, like the light: family, servants, visitors, villagers who came on errands or to make a request or seek advice, the children of the house and the children of the servants, who were left to roam along with the dogs.

Some days there were wild moments when the children ran from room to room, skidding on the polished wood. Or they hid themselves in cupboards and behind long curtains where only a quiver in the damask or a peeping toe revealed them. They jumped out from behind settees and when no one was looking they climbed on the furniture, not so much on the Biedermeier in the drawing room but on the heavy wooden chests and tables in the hall which for them were galleons to be boarded and fought for, one after the other, when the wooden floor was sea and the bearskins and scattered rugs an exotic archipelago. It made the game the more exciting that it was played beneath the painted eyes of ancestors who wore fur hats and robes with jewelled daggers and the long dark faces of mourning pirates. This game came to an end one day when Safta's brothers got angry with one another and tore two crossed swords off the wall above the fireplace and fought with them. The other children watched in horror. Augustin cowered beneath the oak table and Safta screamed for help but by the time Stanislaw and Fräulein Lore arrived there was a gash four inches long on Gheorghe's leg and the fight had ended of its own accord. They all looked at the cut and it was so sharp and deep that time seemed to stop for a hard shocked moment before the blood welled up.

Augustin and Safta were both born at Poiana in the same year, six months apart. Safta – a name like a quick breath, for her full name Elisabeta was hardly ever used – was born on a still late-winter's day in the great bed in the room upstairs that had seen the birth of at least three previous generations of her family. It was right at the end of the house, a high panelled room that had windows on three sides to the bare trees and the wide white distance like porcelain beneath the snow. The bed had tall wooden posts at the corners and was covered in an embroidered turquoise silk from China. Safta's mother had been shown into the room when she first came to the house as a bride, and she thought it was beautiful until the housekeeper opened a deep panelled cupboard where the instruments of birth were kept. Marina Văleanu was a slender impressionable girl of barely seventeen, dark as the boyars in the portraits on the stairs and with eyes that could be as passionate or as sorrowful. She had just come back from a honeymoon in Venice and was so in love that she could not think of her husband without lust. Mama Anica was old and dried up, well past the age of gynaecological fears. She pulled out from the recesses of the cupboard pans, forceps, towels boiled and dried hard as bark, scissors, thread, a knife of unthinkable purpose. And the ugly sight quite unnerved the bride. When she had sex in the bed that night there was an underlying touch of dread, a premonition in the act, that took away her ardour. What is it, her husband said, still loving her. Aren't you happy coming home with me? She could not tell him of the horror that lay hidden in the cupboard. From that moment on she understood that she was to be no longer his lover but the mother of his children. The first of these was already in her, born within eight months of that night but dead in his cot within a year. Safta, then Gheorghe and Mihai followed in too swift succession, but her spirit stayed apart. Making love and giving birth to

four children in that great bed were the cause of a separateness that was to last all the rest of her marriage.

The boy was born in August in one of the servants'
cottages beyond the stable yard. There was a terrible storm
that night, crashing thunder and a stroke of lightning that
struck one of the tall acacias close to the house. His mother
Paraschiva was aware of the great clap of thunder just at
the moment when she pushed him from her, so aware that
she did not know if the noise was inside or outside of her.
He will have heard it, she thought. That's the first sound he
will hear in the world. But later she was to wonder if that
single burst of sound, the thunder and the almost simultaneous crack and fall of the tree, was simply too much for
newborn ears.

Or perhaps it was a judgement. Because she was alone.
Because the baby's father had not stayed long enough to
make him whole. Because he was what they called a child
of the flowers, though in his case it was not flowers but a
crackling bed of autumn leaves. Because he had no inherit-
ance and she could think to name him only for the moment
of his coming.

She could not have said exactly when it was that she
might first have realised that he was deaf. He was a quiet
baby. He cried rarely and when he did there was some
different quality in his crying, which seemed less loud, less
insistent than the cries of other babies, and less sustained.
Safta could cry fit to drive everyone in the house to a

frenzy, a cry that reverberated off the walls and went on and on until the only solution seemed to be to take her outside where there was space and silence and no echo, just for a moment, until the cold or the night made her gasp and there was silence and relief. But Augustin's crying was level and brief, without drama. Or he did not so much cry as moan and writhe and thrash about. When she saw him do this it disturbed her deep and urgently as any mother with her firstborn, but often she did not see just because she did not hear him. Often he must have thrashed about for a long time without her knowing. From those early days he had learned to be undemanding of attention.

He was slow to smile, she noticed that. In the first few weeks and months after he was born she noticed the restraint in him. His eyes seemed to focus and to alight on her face, but he did not respond as other children did. His head did not turn towards her when she spoke. She did not make much of it at the time. The world about him was busy. Often she was in the kitchen where there was always talk, or sometimes she would take him along to the nursery where she went to help look after Safta. The girl burbled and sang to herself most of the time, but she was six months older. She had quick dark eyes and was so lively that you could see she was listening to everything you said. It came about naturally that Paraschiva fell into the habit of talking to the girl more and to him less, of taking his quietness for granted.

*   *   *

He was almost four years old before she admitted what she had in a way known all along. He was up in the nursery in the house. He was playing with a toy train, one that had been given to little Gheorghe who was not old enough for it and Augustin had taken it for his own. He loved the train. It was made of wood with a red-and-green engine, and carriages that hooked on behind. He could play with the train for hours, pushing it up and down, so intent on it that even the other children could not get his attention. Sometimes this annoyed Safta. She would give him a kick or a punch to get a reaction to make him stop his game and look at her while she paraded or told a story. And he would raise his little face beneath its dark mop of hair and smile placidly and do as she wanted. He would forgive Safta anything, even at that age, and watch her dancing movements as if she was some flickering, endlessly absorbing film running before his eyes. This day Paraschiva came in and saw that clearly. It was a film for him, like the films the travelling cinema brought. A silent film. The little girl was a tiny dark silent actress: oval face, mouthing lips, eyes full of feeling. On this particular day Safta had made him her audience as usual and pranced before him and told him a story, and he appeared to listen as he always did, but she was only moving her lips. She was playing her own game with him. She was pretending to be talking to him but she wasn't actually speaking, and he didn't know the difference. The girl knew what Paraschiva had not admitted to herself: that he could not hear a thing.

That evening in the kitchen she told Mama Anica what she believed. It was hard to find the words. She thought she had known them for a long time and yet she could not have brought herself to speak them before. She looked at Mama Anica and wondered if she already knew, if she too had guessed as much. If each of them had known in silence. The discovery was the kind of news that did not fit easily into words because it was concerned with wordlessness. Once it was spoken she had the feeling that she was looking down into a deep black well.

'If it is so,' Mama Anica said, 'then we should do a test. It will be easy to test. We should have thought of doing this before.'

The boy was on the floor playing. He did not look up when his mother went to stand close before him where she could see his face. He did not look when Mama Anica came and stood behind him. She had brought the handbell that hung in the passage beside the back door, that had a high clear ring that called men in when they were needed from across the grounds. She rang it from positions behind the little boy's head, close first to one ear and then to the other. Then she took a saucepan and a wooden spoon and beat the pan as if it were a drum. Each time his mother watched his face. She saw no reaction on it, not even a blink, until the saucepan was close enough almost to touch him.

'So that's it. It's true. He truly cannot hear.'

All her simultaneous hearing world rushed in on her then, all the things she heard in that moment: the spoon beaten on the pan, Mama Anica speaking, the chatter of children in the yard, a horse and the wheels of a cart coming in, the chickens and the geese, the rooks in the

29

trees, someone calling from the door of the house. All the things that she heard that he did not hear. Yet he looked such a bright, normal boy as he took up the pan and began to beat it himself. First he beat its side with the spoon as Mama Anica had. Then he turned it over and began to stir with the spoon as if he was cooking. He picked up a walnut that had fallen on the floor and began to stir that round. Paraschiva gave him another walnut from a bowl, then a potato. She let him sprinkle some salt into the pan. She played his game yet felt very far away from him. She wanted to call him to her. He stirred the pan again, and again looked up to her for more ingredients. She looked about, found some herbs for him to throw in. There was so much that he was missing, and yet he seemed quite complete in what he was doing. Alongside her pity she felt a sudden anger. She felt it like a rejection that he did not hear or speak to her.

'Talk to him,' the doctor said. 'He's stone deaf, that's for sure. I can't let you hope anything else, but he can learn to read your lips. Speak to him whenever you can. Make sure you face him when you talk. Speak clear and slow. Use simple words and repeat them often. You say that it's always been so, that he was born like this. Those cases are the hardest because the child who has never heard speech doesn't know what it's for. I've seen children a few years older have scarlet fever or somesuch, or some injury that caused them to lose their hearing, but they had language already, and they learned to lip-read so well you'd hardly know it.'

She went to the priest and stood holding the little boy by the hand at the door of his house. The priest was a big man and bent low towards Augustin. She was sure he meant it in a kindly way, but the boy took a step back in fear at his height and the blackness of his robes and bushiness of his beard. The priest gave his blessing none the less. He told her of the miracle in which Jesus made a dumb man speak.

'But was the man deaf? Did he make him hear? The doctor says my Augustin's not dumb but only deaf. He does not speak because he does not hear.'

The priest replied that if Jesus could make a dumb man speak then surely he could make a deaf one hear. But there were particular saints to whom she might also pray for intercession. He mentioned certain icons and relics in the churches of the region. And he asked on what saint's day the boy was born.

It was the feast of John the Baptist, she said, the 29th of August.

'But that is not simply the feast of John the Baptist, that is the feast of his decapitation. You must certainly pray to him, most of all. Yes, you must pray to the saints I mentioned but you might especially pray to the Prophet John.'

She did all of that. She bought fine white flour and baked cakes and plaited loaves of bread in offering, and travelled to the various icons. At each church she had someone write down her plea and left it there, and lit a candle and prostrated herself in prayer. To celebrate his anniversary when he

31

was five, she took the boy with her on a journey to a famous church of the Baptist, a whole day each way by cart, and they slept before it. In the morning she took him into the church and lifted him up to kiss the icons and to gaze at the wild saint's head bleeding on its platter. She prayed for a miracle. A saint who had lost his head would surely understand.

She did all that everyone said she might do but she came to believe that the doctor was right from the start. It was already too late. Augustin lived without words. His way in the world was set. Sometimes she suspected that he did not feel the need to hear or to speak. Most of his wants were simple and generally she understood and could satisfy them. On those occasions when she did not understand, his tantrums could be silent but dreadful. He punched and kicked and slewed about, and rolled over and over on the floor and drummed with his fists. Sometimes Safta was the only one who could work out what was troubling him. He has a pain, she would say, there, where you would not know it. Or simply, he is angry because Gheorghe took his pencil. Sometimes Paraschiva wondered if it was by telepathy that Safta knew. Was it that she could actually read his thoughts or was there some signal he made that only she could understand? The truth was that, growing up beside him in the days even before she herself learned to speak, little Safta had come to know him with a quick intuition as if he was the silent side of her self.

When Safta and Augustin were eight a governess came to teach the children in the house. Fräulein Lore came from Germany. She was tall as a man, with red hair of which she was proud and a smooth still face that was hard to read and harder to age. She came recommended as being firm with boys which was thought a necessity, with Gheorghe and Mihai born so close together and both so quick to fight. The lessons were stiff and tetchy. The nursery up beneath the roof was cold in winter and stiflingly hot in summer. The Fräulein made the children sit up straight and keep their elbows off the desks, taught the three of them to write neat letters in endlessly repeated rows, and drilled them in their times tables so that Mihai had these parrot-fashion almost before he could make the simplest addition.

The boys groaned and shifted in their chairs, and when they did some work as likely as not it would have to be redone. Often Safta worked on ahead of them or read a book to herself. Sometimes while the governess explained some tricky piece of arithmetic to Gheorghe, Safta sat across the desk from Mihai and had him read to her, pointing to each word with a pencil and reading his page upside down. When the morning's lessons were over she ran off and took her freshly acquired skills down to Augustin in the kitchen. She got for him an exercise book with carefully spaced lines finely ruled in blue. She gave him a pencil, sharpened by Fräulein Lore to a fine point, and demonstrated the formation of each letter of the alphabet, one by one. The lines on the page dictated the height of each letter, the position of each tip and curl and tail. She imitated the governess. She stood behind him as he painstakingly followed her lines. She breathed over his shoulder as Fräulein Lore did – though her breath was sweeter. When he made a mistake she rapped the table top with a ruler, or sometimes his knuckles, and when he did well she showed his work to her mother.

Marina Văleanu was impressed with the boy's efforts. She asked to see him and he came shyly and stood quite still before her with his head bowed and his two hands held down before him. Something in him, the muteness, the enigmatic eyes, the fine baby smoothness of his face, brought to her mind the image of her lost first son. It gave her an idea. She had been intending, anyway, as soon as she had time, to do something about promoting literacy in the village. As the children got older she meant to take on the responsibilities of her position. This deaf boy, she thought, might be the beginning of it. She suggested to Fräulein Lore that he come every morning and share the lessons.

*   *   *

A small wooden chair and desk were found for Augustin and placed beside the others. At first the Fräulein made no effort to teach him besides planting him there and putting paper before him and a tin of coloured crayons. The first morning he sat with his arms clamped to his sides and watched. The second morning he came in and began straight away to draw. His lines started tentatively but grew bolder as the days and then the weeks progressed. On the lined pages he drew the letters that Safta had taught him, again and again until the pages were filled. On squared pages he copied numbers like those written by the other children. He arranged the numbers horizontally or sometimes vertically with rules between them as if they were sums. On plain pages he drew pictures. He drew deliberately and precisely, with the same control of his hand as he had shown in his letters. He drew first the objects before him in the room, chairs and tables, walls and doors. Then he drew the things outside, things like trees that he could see through the window, then the things that he knew were there that he could not see, carts and ploughs and horses, and the car. When he had made the outlines he coloured them in with neat shading that never spilled over, but he chose the colours by whim so that the trees might be pink or blue, the sky orange and the horses green.

At first Marina was pleased with the pictures, but then she began to question his progress.

'But what are you teaching him?'

The Fräulein pursed her lips. 'If he's deaf and dumb, what can I possibly teach him?'

The schoolmaster Grigorescu had long ago said much the same, though in stronger terms, to Paraschiva. Grigorescu was a thin sallow man already defeated by the children of the village. He wouldn't take the boy on. It would be like teaching a stone, he had said. As if he didn't have enough thickheads in the school already.

Marina Văleanu had more sense of purpose.

'If he can write letters, then he can write words. Begin with that.'

There were many languages in the house. The family spoke Romanian first but the children were expected to acquire some proficiency also in German, French and English. Fräulein Lore spoke generally in her native tongue but gave lessons in the others. And when she began reluctantly to teach the mute boy to write she let him use whatever words came to hand. Since he had no language at all it did not seem to very much matter to which one the words belonged.

Augustin learned to write the word *chat*, and how to draw a cat beside it. *Haus*, and a picture of a house. *Der Hund*, *das Pferd*, *l'arbre*, *le soleil*, *la lune*, *l'arc-en-ciel*, *rainbow*. He wrote the words with as much care as an old-fashioned clerk at a high desk, so beautifully that Safta, who expected to excel in everything, was jealous. He made the drawings that went with the words. In some of the drawings the word and the object became interchangeable. He

drew the schoolroom, the desks and the chairs, the wall
with the map of the world on it, the door opening to the
passage, and *le chat* slipping out around the door jamb just
as the cat might have done.

This proved that he had intelligence.

'See,' Marina Văleanu said to the governess. 'He understands that the writing is a symbol for the thing.'

The Fräulein had come all the way from Darmstadt
to teach the children of the upper class, not to waste her
time on a dumb peasant boy. 'Yes, the words are pictures
for him, but only that. He has only these few nouns, and
they might as well be drawings. He cannot connect them
together. He has no verbs. These words are not language
to him. They are things. There is no point in teaching him.
You might as well teach a bear to dance.'

'But that's just it,' said Marina, who had become deeply
religious since the loss of her baby. 'He is not an animal.
He is human. He has a soul. It is our duty to teach him
language. Without language, how can he know God?'

The governess did what she was told. She had teaching
materials sent out to her from Germany. She studied them
in her free afternoons. She learned how the alphabet might
be spelled out in the fingers of two hands, how the letters
of which words were made divided up in different kinds of
sounds, how vowels might be classified as gutturals, palatals
and labials, how consonants might be open or closed, and if
closed, they might, curiously enough in the circumstances,

be termed 'mute' or 'semi-mute', then how patiently and painstakingly these must be taught and learned, letter by letter, sound by sound; how these letters and sounds must then be reconstructed into words. All for an odd slip of a boy with watchful eyes and a mess of dark hair on his head. His mother was a servant and his father seemed to be no one at all. She didn't see the point.

The boy couldn't see the point either. But it was his habit to be amenable so he smiled his fine-lipped smile and drew the letters she had taught him before. He drew the room. He drew the Fräulein's hat without her head. He drew her, a tall rectangular form with a dress that buttoned all the way up to the collar and all the way down, a squared face above it with orange hair and two narrow eyes and a downturned line for a mouth. He drew the map on the wall, in such detail that each continent, and even the bigger islands, Iceland and Madagascar and the chain that formed Japan, were clearly recognisable. He drew the heading *Le Monde*, serifs and all, precisely as it appeared in the typeface.

She took his picture away.

She held his exercise book in the air before his eyes, then slammed it down on the bare desktop before him.

On a clean page she drew the single capital letter 'B'.

She put the pencil into his hand and took hold of it in her long white fingers and drew the letter once more, making the sound of it as she did so.

Then the letter 'u'. Then 'c', and 'h'; the sound of the two combined.

It took sympathy and enthusiasm, the textbooks said, to teach the deaf to speak. It required kindness, affection, individual rapport, long intercourse. Such intercourse was hard when cold little eyes looked out at one day after day from a face blank with incomprehension.

'*Buch*,' she said, the explosion of the word so close to his face that he felt the faintly vegetable blast of her breath. She bent lower. She took his face in her hand to make him look at her, digging her fingers deep beneath the cheekbones, but he dropped his eyelids and held them down. She squeezed his lips into the form for *Buch*. That was what the experts told her to do. The oral method of teaching the deaf to speak. You first demonstrate yourself, and then show them how it feels: holding their lips to shape, pushing their tongues in place, holding their hands on the vibrations of the larynx and before the plosions and exhalations of breath.

His teeth clenched. With her other hand she held his nose so that he could not breathe. His lips finally spat out the opening consonant with a spray that showered her cheek. Her pale face went red. Her fingers dug in harder. The boy went all tight for a moment, then suddenly lunged and writhed himself from her grip, and fixed his teeth into her arm.

The other children watched in astonishment, the boys with a gleeful vengeance dawning on their faces, Safta angry as she would have been for an animal mistreated. Augustin

39

ran out. The open door gaped on the black passage where he had gone and the Fräulein turned about to face them.

'Get back to your work, all of you.'

Safta stood up. 'Fräulein Lore, I've finished my work.'

'Well memorise this poem then.'

She felt the hurt deep down in him, the incomprehensibility of it. She stared at the governess's arm where she had rolled back her sleeve to expose the wound. She hoped to see blood where he bit but there were only white indentations.

'What do you think you're looking at, Elisabeta?'

'Nothing.'

'Nothing?'

And the Fräulein sent her to her room.

She found him in the stables. As soon as the Fräulein closed the door to her room, she climbed out of the window. There was a piece of flat roof above the verandah, an aged wisteria with branches she liked to think were tangled pythons. She climbed out and down, and ran to the stables. She knew that was where he would be. The stables were shady in summer and warm with bodies in winter, and nobody bothered him there but he had the horses for company. For him horses must be not very different company from people. Sometimes he climbed up and sat on the high iron hayrack in the stalls where they nudged him with their soft noses and their hot breath. Sometimes he went to the loft above.

He liked to sit with his back to a wall. That meant no one could come up behind him without his seeing. He was sitting in the far corner of the loft where the sunlight could not reach. She could barely see him but he would see her coming at him out of the light. She heard a dull thudding sound as she came up the ladder that was not like the thuds made by the horses in the stalls below. He was banging his head on the wall, but slowly, in such a way she thought that he would feel a hard sensation but not a pain, and yet it hurt her just to see it. Stop it, Tinu. He did not stop. He did not seem to feel the hand she put out to calm him. So she grabbed him firmly by the shoulders and pulled him, pulled hard so that he moved at last and came with her into the light, before the high open door of the loft where the hay was pitched in. Usually he liked it there, where there was a long safe sniper's view of the yard and the drive and comings and goings. A shaft of sunlight, golden hay, motes dancing; but he sat dully, arms by his sides, eyes to the floor. He would not look up, even for Safta. He had this ability, that when he did not look the world did not exist.

She took one of his hands in hers. He let her take it, hot, limp, passive.

She heard the rustle of hay, the snort of a horse, the sound of a car in the distance.

She resolved to teach him herself. *Ti-nu*. First of all she would give him his own name. Other words could come later. She lifted the back of his hand close to her lips.

A light 'Ti' spat from between her teeth, the first sound of the first word. The soft blow of 'nu'. There.

He felt it. He raised his head and looked into her eyes. And just as he did so, she looked away.

In Safta's world there were sounds, layers, distractions. There was more than Tinu.

There was the sun shining beyond the loft door.

The glint of a car coming between the trees.

There was the moment that was occurring inside the loft but there was also the moment that was occurring outside, all the moments there. A car coming to a halt outside the house, a voice calling that was her father's, a single note of her mother's voice coming from the house.

Papa! She raced down the ladder, out into the sunshine.

Her papa was back after weeks in Bucharest. She would run to him and he would pick her up and swing her round. He would have a present for her. When he caught her his arms were strong. He smelt of the city and tobacco and of dust and the road.

The boy in the loft had seen her go. Then closed his eyes once more.

Again Safta breathes his name upon his hand. Does he know it? In this hospital he is not Tinu any more but Ioan. If she were to breathe this new name on to his hand there would be no movement to it. No plosion in it, nothing to feel. The word Ioan exists only in the throat and in a subtle twist of the mouth. Does he remember who he was?

The white light of the ward is stark on his face. His oddity is more noticeable now that he is older. In the boy it was only at moments that one saw that he was different from others, and one saw it in the expressions rather than in the form of his face. These expressions have fixed now into lines and into the set of the muscles around his mouth. His muteness and his experience have become written on him. He is a little stronger than when he first came. He is taking food. Yet there seems to be no change in his mental state. He is passive. Even his eyes do not engage. It is a strange exile, an iron bed with chipped white paint lined up alongside so many other identical beds, and yet the man seems like an exile to her: one who has been cut off from his world, from names and things.

His silence becomes catching.

She used to be able to natter away at him all the time, tell him everything she thought about, what she felt about everyone, every trivial thing. She was utterly without self-consciousness with him; but now his eyes throw her back into herself.

Each day she comes into the ward and sees him there doing nothing, looking at nothing. She has to grope for words.

There is this ward, then there is the hospital, and beyond the hospital, the city. There is the stillness of the ward and the idea of the city beyond the open windows: that life is happening there, outside. But when she gets out into the city, life is not there either but somewhere else, beyond. As if she too is an exile.

'I wrote a letter.'

The meaning falls away.

'I'm trying to find your mother.'

If she could find the words she would talk to him about that time when they were children at Poiana. So much growing apart there has been since then. It is as if they had grown and gone to other countries and now they meet far from home. She had almost forgotten him. But Tinu had a way that let you forget him. Even when he stood right in front of you there was no insistence to his presence. He appeared always at a remove, contained within himself. He had been easy to abandon. She had done it often, abandoning him lightly, carelessly, as children abandon one another, living in the present, moving on from one moment to the next and letting go of the moment just passed. Things are different now. Time is different. The present is less vivid than it used to be. She tells herself that she will not abandon him now.

'You're very dedicated,' Adriana says, seeing her again at his bedside.

'I thought it would do him good to have a visitor.'

There has been no reply to her letter. She thinks she will write to the priest a second time, just in case the letter did not arrive.

In the wards where she is used to working there are always visitors about. Wives, mothers, family, bringing food, supplementing the hospital's care, camping out even beside those they love. In the dreariest of them there is an echoing life. This ward is different, filled with absence. The patient has gone from the next bed. She assumes that he has died. She cannot imagine that he can have left for any other reason. The last few days she has been aware of the erratic nature of his breathing; periods of wheezing and then pauses as if he did not breathe at all. As if he was passing through voids.

This nurse must think it strange that she should come like this and sit here beside the mute's blankness, and leave beside him pencils and blank pages on which he does not draw. Yet her look has sympathy.

'How is he? He seems a little better. What does the doctor say?'

'He needs drugs. There are drugs that would cure him but the hospital does not have them.'

'Do you know anywhere I can get them?'

'They're foreign. They'll be very expensive.'

What else should she spend her money on?

Each morning after the cows were milked Paraschiva gave the boy some of the warm milk to make him strong, then wiped the white foam from about his mouth and brushed his hair. However hard she brushed it sprang back up as oddly as before about his little pointed face. She did not know why they were so interested in him at the big house. He was intelligent, they said. He had a special talent for drawing. Certainly she had never seen any child, or adult either, who drew so much. He drew when he went up to the nursery, and when he came back to her he drew again, drawing what was before him and also the places where he had been, clearly so that she would know them, and other scenes and views that she believed he must have invented. At first he had drawn only in pencil, but at the house they gave him paints and colours, and if these were not the colours he wanted then he made his own pigments by grinding stones and mushing berries and things from the kitchen, experimenting with them, shading the powders and juices with chalk or soot, wetting them with water or with his spit to make them flow on the paper. He brought his pictures back to their little cottage, pages and pages of them, more paper than she had ever possessed. József the groom who was his friend made him a box in which to keep his pictures and he spent much time sorting and arranging them. He folded them and piled them by size, or sometimes he tied them into bundles or folded them into books. At first Paraschiva stitched the books for him, but then when she saw how handy he was with a needle she let him do it himself, bothering her only for string or a length of wool, then stitching on card from packages or sometimes scraps of cloth for their covers. He wrote on the covers in big letters so regular in form that they might have been printed. The writing at least made her proud. Since she could not read herself she could not have known whether his letters spelled words or not. He made pictures of the little house where they lived, first the outside of it and then the rooms inside, so precisely that she would look at them and recognise even the corner of a window or a table leg. The rooms he made empty of people. He made people separately, cut from pieces of thick paper or card so that they stood on their own. The people were strange to her. If the rooms were real, then the people were not. They were only symbols of people. They had no smiles. Didn't children's drawings of faces always have mouths and smiles? Hands? Waving arms? Augustin's people were always made in a similar way, their basic form a simple rectangle but with divisions across it or occasionally separate pieces that conformed to the normal human proportions of head, torso, legs. Some of the heads had all the features of a face but some had only eyes or nose. There were others that were entirely blank or had just one or two horizontal lines or random patterning across like postmarked stamps. Did he not care about people? He put more ingenuity into their clothes than into their faces, laboriously drawing and colouring shirts and waistcoats and all kinds of hats, and sometimes adding scraps of fabric or stitching patterns like embroidery on to them. He made horses better than humans. He knew the form of horses well from all the time he spent with József around the stables. He made horses and cows and chickens. Once he made a bird that pleased him very much. It was made from pieces of card. The beak was bright and shiny orange, separate but fixed, and the wings were a softer grey card and loosely threaded so that they could be moved up and down.

Paraschiva could see that it was clever but such strange cleverness disturbed her. She could see no use for his skill. He would be better off working on the land or somewhere else about the place. There was an old man in the village who whittled spoons. Augustin might have gone to him and learned to make spoons also. There was a clever thing the old man did, making a spoon with a hole in the handle and a ring passing through the hole, all from a single piece of wood. If Augustin was so clever with his hands he might have learned to do that, and then decorated the spoons with patterns of his own. But no, they had decided up there in the house, and each day she must make sure his clothes were clean and brush his hair and send him to the German lady. She could have told her from the start

that she was wasting her time. The Fräulein was trying
to teach him things that he would not learn. She did not
know what his mother knew: how hard he was inside.
There was something in him that was hard, fixed, black,
like the black buffaloes on the farm. A buffalo was the sort
of animal that you kept but that was never entirely yours.
It was docile only to a limit. It would seem to go along, and
then could stop, just when you least expected it, and drop
its sullen head and stiffen its back and legs. That was how
he could be. A mother knew that sort of thing. Mothers
know the ugliness in their children even as they love what
is beautiful in them. Paraschiva could see his stubbornness
in the way he stood and in the set of his lips and the separateness of his eyes.

Paraschiva did not know it but Fräulein Lore was coming
to the same conclusion. What was required, the textbooks
said, was patience, repetition, focus. She had put her best
effort into it, she told herself, despite her initial scepti-
cism. She had given him all that, and more. She had gone
beyond the usual requirements of her work, and she had
received viciousness in return. Never in all her career had
she met a child with a nature so entirely closed to her
as this elfin peasant boy. She briefly considered handing
in her resignation but professional pride held her back.
She had never resigned from a post before. And in so
many other ways this was a good position: the family was
eminent, their land stretched to the horizon, the girl was

clever, the boys manageable, the conditions reasonable, generous even.

She went to her mistress in the study where she sat every morning to write her letters.

'I must tell you, Madame, that I can make no progress with this boy. Words are nothing to him. He does not see the point of learning them.'

He is obstinate and difficult, she wanted to say. He has a devil in him. She chose rather to retain a position of professional objectivity. 'There is something missing in him. There is something that is assumed in all the books I have studied that in this boy is entirely missing, and that is the will, the simple desire for speech.'

Marina Văleanu's voice was dark and musical, like a viola. 'You told me he took to it so well at first. He was so amenable. There are all those lovely drawings, all the lettering he has done.'

'That's all they are, Madame. Drawings, pictures. He does not mean them to be anything more.'

As she spoke she thought of him drawing. How fixed he was. How he sometimes hummed with concentration. How tight-lipped he was, frozen inside himself. Once he was concentrated on his drawing he had no awareness left for anything else. She had come to think that he would not speak so long as he could draw.

'I think that may even be the root of the problem. The drawing, I mean. The wretched boy is making pictures instead of words. Don't you see? He won't so much as try to speak so long as he's allowed to draw.'

'But his pictures are beautiful.'

'If he did not have them, then he might be taught to speak. To write at least.'

'That would be hard.'

'Sometimes in education one must be hard.'

Marina looked at the governess and felt a quick dislike of her. She sensed the anger beneath the Fräulein's smooth and regular face, the resentment there. Was it possible that the governess might even relish depriving the boy of his ability to make pictures?

'No, I will not have you do that.'

The Fräulein was well qualified and came with the best references but her fastidiousness and her intuition suddenly rebelled against the woman. She was so deliberate, so ugly, so down to earth. If the mute boy could learn to write, then what would she teach him? What words would they be? And if he were to learn to speak? She thought of what she had seen in his face: something fine, ethereal in him that was not like the other peasant children; some still solemnity that was there also in what he drew. When the deaf spoke they groaned and made strange sounds that might have come from underground. That was not what she wanted for him. She wanted for him something altogether higher.

Marina loved art almost as much as she loved religion. To her the two were inextricably linked. On the wall above the desk where the governess had come to her was a very precious and beautiful icon, an antique image of Our Lady of Saint Theodore, richly framed in gold. The black-veiled Virgin was a daily inspiration. She was so sombre and yet so tender, her hands long, her head angled so gracefully against the head of the finely made child who seemed almost to stand on his own tiny feet on a fold in her robe. Marina would feel that serene look on her even as she wrote out lists and invitations and made household payments, and now as she put an elbow thoughtfully on the desk and addressed the tall governess who stood before her. For herself, the presence of the Virgin raised even the most trivial activities a little above the level of the mundane. And she was not unaware of the effect the icon had on others coming to her at her desk, the dark compelling eyes on the wall behind her echoing her own eyes and adding to her dignity. A woman who has grown up knowing that she is beautiful has always an awareness of how she is perceived.

'No, I will not have you do that. The boy has a gift. Such gifts come from God.'

And she continued, turning away from the woman and addressing the icon, 'From now on I shall teach him myself.'

The impulse of a moment became a mission. It had been a mistake to try to teach the boy words, she saw. His path to God must lie in his art alone.

There was a monastery a few hours' drive away that was famous for the beauty of its paintings. She visited it often. The church was ancient and revered. It held relics of many saints, the toe of an apostle and the skull of Saint

Simeon encircled in a crown. The air within the monastery walls was calm with centuries of contemplation and intoned liturgies. The monks within it moved in unhurried order. The Abbot was a cousin of her husband's, a man of broad shoulders and slow dignity who would make them welcome and who might besides advise her what to do with the boy.

They went there in the car one blowy November day, herself, the two young children and Ilie the driver. Augustin had sat in the car often but he had never been driven anywhere before. Ilie let him sit in the car sometimes when it was in its garage or even – and that was better – when it was parked before the house. He would sit in the driver's seat with the smooth ring of the steering wheel in his fingers and imagine that the car was moving, around the fountain and the turning circle, between the shimmering trees and down the drive. Now he sat in the back and watched Ilie's hands in leather gloves, the wheel turning. The wind had blown the last of the leaves from the trees, and was blowing them again where they had fallen, swirling them up across the road. He watched Ilie's hands on the wheel and on the gear, and only after a long time did he look out to see the land go by. They had already left the village behind them, the church and the school and anyone to whom he might have liked to wave. The road went on, and they passed horses and carts and oxen and carts and men on donkeys but hardly ever another car. There were trees along the road, tall trees widely spaced. Because of the lines of trees you could see where the road went a long way ahead, where it crossed rivers and wound up out of valleys. The land was wide and rolling, most of it dull brown and gold, rising away into a shining purple distance where there were mountains unlike anything that he had ever seen.

The monastery lay just before the forest and the mountains. In the foothills and valleys there were other monasteries and hidden hermitages but Augustin knew nothing of them. To him this was the last building before the wilderness. And it was the biggest building he had ever seen. The tall white walls of a fortress, a great gate that might have opened on to a city. Within, the space of the courtyard, all the more wide and bare beneath the November sky. In the centre of the courtyard, the church. Within the church, another sky and a crowding coloured mass of forms and figures that set up a clamour in his mind. He looked up and gaped, and turned round and round like a country boy come to the city for the first time.

The pictures he made that day were full of colour. He worked his crayons until there was a polish to the surface of the page, and the colours were those of jewels: emerald and ruby and amethyst and turquoise and sapphire and gold. He drew ladders of angels and saints with haloes about their heads; and a man that was Jesus walking in sandalled feet on scalloped waves, and another that was Peter falling into them flat on his face. He took pages from his sketchbook and joined them one after the other in concertinaed lengths. He made vertical lengths of the damned tumbling layer upon layer amongst the black demons in hell, and on a horizontal he made orderly lines of the saved, figures that repeated again and again. In the sapphire skies above them he painted golden stars shooting, and flying golden words in Cyrillic letters that he copied precisely, that were like but also unlike any letters he had drawn before. The November day was short and it began to grow dark. The colours faded about him but he went on working. The lamps were lit. A mass of points of light glowed like stars in the great brass chandelier that hung beneath the tower. Black-robed monks gathered for the evening liturgy. When Marina Văleanu finally pulled him away he dragged after her like a dreamer, turning and looking back.

She went to dine with the Abbot and showed him the pictures. She told him how she meant to bring this boy to God.

'He does not understand what he is depicting.'

'There must be something there though, don't you think? He is learning something. The meaning is in the pictures themselves.'

They went out from the Abbot's residence into the courtyard and up an open staircase in one of the towers. At the top he took a key from a niche in the wall and let her in to the workshop where his monks painted icons. She thought the room beautiful, the order of it, with the high stools of the monks, the easels covered over with cloths, the paints and brushes laid out beside them. The Abbot carried a lamp and lifted the covers on the easels one by one so that she could see the icons in progress.

'Every detail is prescribed by tradition,' the Abbot told her, 'recorded in the manual which the copyists use. The form of Christ's fingers as they are raised in blessing, which contain the Greek letters "IHS", formed not for their elegance or expressiveness but for their meaning. The composition of the Dormition, where the Christ carries the Virgin's soul depicted as a baby as once she carried him. The colours too are prescribed, even the order in which the elements are painted: first the gold leaf is laid on, for the background and the haloes, and then the architectural detail, the clothes, and only finally the hands and head. The painting is a ritual, undertaken in a spirit of contemplation.'

The gold of the unfinished icons on the easels glowed beneath the light he held. The windows reflected the forms of the icons and their shadowy figures moving between them.

'For the monks who work here the making of icons is a form of prayer.'

'I thought about that. I thought, perhaps, you would consider . . .'

'Taking the mute boy here? What do his parents say to that?'

She did not mention that she had not asked his mother. In fact, in all the time that she had had an interest in him, she had scarcely spoken to Paraschiva about him. Paraschiva was his unlikely root, that grounded him. She preferred to think of him as some kind of changeling, as independent and separate of any others as if he had sprung of himself.

'It would suit him. Such a life would suit him. The silence of it. He would learn the icons and painting them would be his prayer.'

57

The Abbot's pause indicated some weight of reluctance in him.

'There are some you know who say that a deaf man, a man entirely without words, can have no sense of God.'

'What, do you mean that God is only a word?'

'That isn't what I said.'

'Well, will you take him then?'

'When he is older perhaps. Perhaps we might speak about it when he is older.'

She went back to the guest house. The night began blustery, restless. She went to her room which was beside that of the children but she could not sleep. The wind crashed in and blew about the courtyard and shook the glass and the doors and once swept something from the roof that she heard fall on the ground below. Rain followed, surges of it like waves dashed against the walls. She lay and listened to the wind and the rain, and imagined other lives she might have led. She imagined that she was no mother but a nun, painting icons in a convent, walking in a heavy black gown that rustled about her legs. Or when the storm at last dropped, in the bitter stillness of the last moments before dawn, she imagined that she might have been one of the kind of women her husband had come to love, with their sleek hair and high heels and half-wrapped furs, coming out of a city nightclub with metallic laughter that carried like cock's crowing through the air.

For a long time Augustin also did not sleep. It was the first night in his life that he had slept in a house other than his own, here in the great monastery, in a narrow bed in a strange room. If he did not hear the wind he felt its disturbance of the air. He felt it inside him and saw what he felt as the waves on the Sea of Galilee, sharp little waves that carried a boat balanced on their tips. Then he smelled the dampness of the rain. The waves were blue and the boat was brown and its sail was white. The men on board wore cloaks the colours of rust and verdigris, and held out their arms to the mast to save themselves from being tipped into the sea. In the blackness of his sleep the boat itself was tipped, and broken on the sharp points of the waves, and everything blackened and the men drowned. He saw them drowning about him, slim naked figures pale as worms, men and women too, a mass of them, more people than he had ever seen, tumbling and falling.

All that he had seen in that day came back raw to his eyes, turned and twisted within him. The serried ranks of humanity and angels. Ladders of men; men tumbling off down black ravines and into fire. Shamed sinners cowering in lines, shivering in their nakedness, covering themselves with long hands. A line of beheaded martyrs, saints bowed over with their haloed heads rolling on the ground; slim executioners beside them, black tights and red tunics, pointed toes and pointed helmets, swords raised high over their bloodied necks. Augustin moaned in his horror, softly at first, but then he cried out, and Safta woke. She was afraid. She did not know this terrible voice was his. She left her bed and came to him, groping for him in the dark which was dense now that the rain had come. His arms flailed about him when she tried to touch him. His eyes did not seem to see her at all. She could feel the heat of his terror coming off him like a fever. Since she could not soothe him any other way she tried to cool him down. She stripped off the bedclothes, found the water pitcher in the room and brought a wet towel and laid it on his hot forehead. All this she did in silence, and gradually he became silent also, returning to himself. When he was still and cool, she got into his bed beside him and pulled the blankets over them, the bed so narrow that the two of them lay in it like pins, side by side.

The next day was a festival. People came to the monastery from all the villages around. The church was full when they went into it, people crowding at the back, grey-bearded monks like statues in the stalls against the walls, other monks milling about, their raven forms prostrated in the corners or grouped about the lecterns to chant the liturgy. Marina Văleanu led the children in, took Augustin's hand in hers and pulled him forward. He felt faint at the press of people, the smell of peasant pilgrims mingled with the heaviness of incense. He felt the pull of the tower over his head like a black vortex into which he would fall upwards, not down, an inverted well where smoke swirled grey across the light and the soot of endless years clung to the walls. He felt that he would fall, like a stone or a feather. But she tugged him on until they stood at the front before the iconostasis. They got there and she let go of his clammy hand, and at the same instant the icon-ostasis doors opened and the priest was suddenly revealed. His apparition came like a conjuring trick, a man appearing with a confusion of gold and smoke and lights about him. Big as a bull he seemed, the blackness and the thickness of his beard fearful in themselves. It was too much for Augustin. The image was too strong. At the same moment the congregation surged forward. His nightmares came back to him and he sensed an awful power in the bearded man. He panicked. He turned and ran – or tried to run, forcing himself between the press of people. There was no clear way. He had to push and elbow himself out, even putting down his head and butting like a goat. Out from the smoke. Out from the black well. Out into the glare of the day. He ran out of the church into the great courtyard, out beneath the painted tunnel and the great wooden doors of the gate.

When they found him later he was already sitting in the car. He did not sit in the driver's seat where he liked to play but in the passenger seat behind, stock still, eyes looking directly ahead, hands rolled into fists at his sides.

It was late in the day when the car got back to the village, the time of day when half the population was out along the road, come in from their work in the fields, waiting as the cows returned from pasture. The homecoming herd came in at just the same time as the car, so that for a while they were forced to wait while the flow of the animals parted about it, muddied rumps rubbing past its shiny metal sides. Any other day Augustin might have been proud to have been seen in this way, travelling so grandly in the Văleanus' car. This day he did not seem to be aware that anyone at all was watching. When they got to the house, Ilie went round and opened the boot, and he took out his bag and his drawings, and it was a private act. He walked off without looking at any of them, not even Safta. He carried his little bag in one hand, his sketchbook in the other, with the folder of drawings he had made slipping awkwardly beneath one arm.

Once he was inside the cottage he let what he was carrying drop. He closed the door and leant his back against it. Then he took up the folder of drawings and went out again, this time into the yard. To the side of the woodpile there was a hole in the fence, roughly blocked with a plank to keep the chickens from straying. He moved this aside and went through, propping it back behind him. He walked through the mud along the edge of a vegetable patch, out to the fields that led down to the river. There were only a couple of old women still at work that time of day, and they saw him pass with urgent steps, walking a straight fixed line. They saw his back recede and knew that he had some deliberate intention; but the boy was strange to them, his ways were always strange, and they did not question his direction any more than they would have questioned that of the wind.

The water was high, heavy and muddied after the storm. He walked down the bank and stood on a gravel shelf beside the shallows, where there was a wide flat rock to which the women came to beat their clothes. On the far side of it the water ran in a fast and tangled current. He stepped out to the rock and knelt on it, then untied the folder. One by one he took each picture he had made in the church and tore it, and scattered the coloured pieces on to the water and watched them swirl and rush away.

In the stillness of her study, Marina Văleanu prayed before the tender Mother of God. Dusk was falling across the garden, the hills, the view of the village. In the river, darkening scraps of colour grew sodden and began to sink unseen. The boy walked home across grey fields. All colour was gone now; the plank fence about the yard, the barns, the woodpile reduced to a smudged charcoal blackness. In the icon there was still a glimmer of light, in the gold behind the Virgin's veil, in the ring on the finger of a long hand raised in peace. Everything else fell into shadow – the pale oval of her face, the long almonds of her eyes, the head of the woman praying. Marina Văleanu prayed away her shame and her disappointment. She crossed herself and kissed the cool metal. Her mind went over other things that the Abbot had said. How God might be found in the performance of simple tasks. How he might be found in silence itself.

Recently he has begun to look at her pictures. He still hasn't touched the drawing things she has given him but he looks at the pictures she brings. He takes them from her one by one and looks at them very seriously, and then he folds them away according to some incomprehensible logic of size or subject or colour, on to one pile or another in the locker beside his bed. Sometimes his interest is in the image on the reverse of the page she has intended to show him, some odd detail or simply the form of a word that appeals to him. One day she brought him a matchbox with a hammer and sickle and a slogan on it in broad red letters on white: *TRĂIASCĂ 1 MAI*. Now whenever she sees a matchbox with a new slogan she brings him another. In white on red: *TRAIASCA PRIETENIA ROMANO-SOVIETICA, 7 NOIEMBRIE; Citiți „Scânteia"*. She is happy to think that for him these words have no significance whatsoever.

It was not difficult to find the drugs. One of the doctors helped her.

'They'll be expensive,' he said.

He thought she would not have the money but she still has a few pieces of jewellery she can sell.

'That's all right.'

'He must have the full course. No point him starting if he doesn't have the full course.'

'I'll get him the full course.'

It was clear the doctor could not see why a nurse like her should help this one mute patient among all the others. People don't do things like that. He suspected something unsaid, some connection.

'He reminds me of someone. He reminds me of my brother.' It wasn't true. It was only something to say, and yet she felt that it was true in the moment that she said it. There was feeling in the way she spoke.

The doctor softened. 'OK, I'll get them for you.'

He seemed a good man. He was tall and wore his clothes loosely and his hair fell across his forehead. He had sympathy for some imagined tragedy of a lost brother. And there were so few people she knew in this city. She smiled, switching on her brightness for him, feeling his attractiveness. But the possibility lived only for a moment, then she closed the shutter. She had already lied to him anyway.

She asked only, 'How long must he stay in hospital?'

'A month. Six weeks perhaps, we'll see.'

'And then?'

'And then he can go home.'

She did not say that he had no home.

This day she has a whole magazine for Tinu, an old illustrated magazine from before the war.

'Look, it has a Lipizzaner on the cover. Like my grandfather's. There's a whole article on Lipizzaners.'

She had been browsing a stall in the market, heaps of books and lace tablecloths and bric-a-brac, and the magazine happened to catch her eye. A beautiful white horse rearing, a soldier in hussar's uniform on its back. She didn't know what she was doing there really, what she was looking for. She has so few needs beyond the immediate, living as she does in a hostel with twenty others, living day to day with little to call her own. And yet she finds herself poking through the stalls, full of nostalgia for other people's discarded things.

'There are more pictures inside, I'll show you.'

In the Spanish Riding School in Vienna, a line of white horses like a *corps de ballet*. The building where they perform like a vast ballroom with chandeliers and high white Corinthian pillars and a floor of golden sand.

'They teach the horses to dance and people go to watch. They used to make them dance for the Austrian emperors.'

She has his interest now. She leans across him and turns the page. The next picture shows a dappled grey horse with four feet high in the air, high as its trainer's chest. It looks as if it's flying.

'I thought you'd like it. It's like Grandfather's horse, only Grandfather's was whiter, but maybe that was partly age. The foals are born dark, that's how they are in the pictures here, and then they go whiter and whiter as they grow older.'

Soft sentences, pauses between them.

'Since you came here I've been remembering things. Things I hadn't thought about in ages. I wonder who's left, what's left.'

She is speaking for herself, not for him.

He has taken the page from her and traces the images with his fingers. There is a series of a single white stallion performing its steps. *Capriole*, *courbette*, *pirouette*, *passage*, *levade*: neat, white, perfect in the photographs as if it was not a real horse but a statue carved of marble. She looks at his face that also might be made of stone; mouth and eyes and expression so still and fixed. And she sees that there are tears on it.

'You were happy there with the horses, weren't you? It was better than with us. The horses liked you. All the animals did.'

It comes back to her. The warmth and smell of the horses, their eyes like molasses.

'If only you could go there now. That would make you well.'

After that trip to the monastery Marina Văleanu decided that he should learn a job of work. There was discussion about what this should be, and József the groom was getting old and needed help so he ended up in the stables. That was all right, Safta had thought. Tinu liked to be in the stables.

She did not see him so often after that because it was the start of winter. The weather was cold and kept her indoors. She was a girl and there were many things a girl could do indoors. Her cousins came to stay. There were games. Only sometimes there were rides, on fine days. They rode out and up across the hills that were dusted with snow. If she glimpsed him in the yard when they came back she was too full of the ride and the hot smell of horse and the bite of the cold on her cheeks to notice him. She sat high in the saddle and talked over his head to her cousins. And then she dismounted and gave him the reins to lead the pony away, and the pony shook its head sharply up and down and breathed steam into his face.

*　　*　　*

When there was no work to do he sat and made his drawings at the bench in the tack room amid the smells of leather and saddlesoap and wax and horses. Mostly he drew in pencil, sometimes shading and polishing till the graphite shone black. He had no need of colour here. The tack-room walls were white. The tack was brown. He did not draw any more angels or demons or people who walked on clouds, but real things: the stable; the stalls where the horses were kept, with wooden partitions and hay-filled mangers and a floor of herringboned bricks with the dark runnel of a drain down the centre; saddles mounted one beside another on poles stuck out from the wall; bridles with looping reins hung alongside; harnesses. Sometimes he stole just a word from the life at the big house, some letters memorised from a book or from the nursery wall, and added them to the drawings. He drew their forms with the accuracy almost of print but he let them slide their positions around and across the rest of the work. His favourite image, one that he worked on over a series of days, depicted the wide archway that was the entrance to the stable yard – an arch columned and pedimented, almost as grand as the portico of the house – and within this frame all the inanimate elements of the yard were crammed together in rows: the doors to the stables and coach house, the mounting block, water trough, carts, muck rakes and tools and buckets. When he had completed this picture he folded it in half and half again and put it into his pocket. After that, he could

69

bring it out and look at the yard even when he wasn't there.

At first he only mucked out the stables and cleaned the tack but József taught him to wash and curry comb the horses and plait their tails and manes, and saw that he had a knack for it. He seemed to have an understanding with the animals, that he communicated by touch and by the movements of his hands, even by eye, but also by the closest that he ever came to speech. He blew through his lips as the horses did. Sometimes he made a clucking sound by touching his tongue to the roof of his mouth. It was a gesture that seemed to come to him out of instinct.

It was his father in him, people said when they saw it. It was so long since his father had left Poiana, and his existence there had anyway been so light and brief, that the villagers had almost forgotten who he had been. The stolid Paraschiva and her slight mute son had been taken as they were, without history or requirement for paternity. Now they saw the boy at his work they remembered how his father had appeared one day bringing a horse from a famous stud in Transylvania. The man spoke little enough himself, but they did not know if this was only because his Romanian was so poor. His name was István Szabó and he was Hungarian, and there was no one around but József who could speak to him in his own language. His eyes were steely blue but otherwise he was wiry and dark, and his way with the horse was that of a Gypsy.

They had seen how he could crouch on the ground, tiny and low, before the elegant creature, and focus all of its attention. How the animal's eyes would fix on him, its ears pricked to every minute sound he made, the connection between man and horse taut as if there were threads stretched between them. From his position on the ground, close and trusting and within range of the horse's hooves, István Szabó would hold up his hands. He held them up loosely, palms gently cupped, and his fingers moved as if they pulled in the invisible threads. Like a puppeteer, he pulled ever so slightly one way or another, and the horse would walk or step neatly sideways or backwards as well as if he rode it.

Like father, like son. When Paraschiva saw the talent her son had inherited it made her uneasy. She would have preferred that the boy work in the gardens or on the farm, where he might be bound down by the touch of the soil and its weight on his boots. Even when she saw how firmly he sat on the Lipizzaner's bare back when he brought it in from the field, how happy he seemed to be, she was not entirely reassured.

Marina Văleanu would not have said it to her cook but she realised that Paraschiva had been right from the start. He'll not learn anything, Paraschiva had said. He's what he is, and that's all. There's no point teaching him. No changing a thing like that. She saw the boy go by with the horses or the hay and regretted her mistake. It had been an error of her charity, however well meant. She realised that his remarkable drawings should be taken simply as they were, as the work of an innocent, and of God.

As the years passed she had become more remote and more devout. Her face had set in solemn lines so that she seemed always at a distance. Plans were made for the boys to be sent away to school in England, and for Safta to be 'finished' in Paris or in Switzerland after a final year with a new governess. The prospect of her children's departure did not affect her as much as it would have in the past. She had removed herself even from these arrangements. She left them to her husband, and when he was away, as he so often was, to his father who lived with them at Poiana.

It was old Constantin Văleanu who had decided that England was the place to send them. He said that for the times ahead the boys would need the most reasonable minds, the broadest and most liberal education available.

Constantin Văleanu carried himself still with the authority of his past distinction. He had a diplomatic career behind him, a fine bearing, white temples, a malachite head to the cane he carried. While most men of his class looked to France for culture, Constantin was Anglophile. He admired England's tailoring, its politics, its sport and particularly its gardens. He had laid out the gardens at Poiana in the English style. He had visited gardens in England, consulted the works of Gertrude Jekyll and come back with plans and lists of plants. Beds of lavender were put in along the terrace; herbaceous borders cut out of the formal lawns; exotic trees planted in the distance, a catalpa, a *Ginkgo biloba*, a black locust tree. The Moldavian climate was so much harsher than the English one that he had to adapt the English plantings. There were species that were too tender, that must be cajoled through the hot summer and mulched or lifted entirely in winter, or relinquished from his plan. He saw, but wished he did not see, a metaphor there: that Britain's moderate climate fostered a democratic variety of plants, far more than the extremes of his homeland.

'England's so far,' his daughter-in-law had said. 'What if there's a war?'

'If there's a war then what place could be safer than England?'

Much as he admired the spirit of the British, he pitied them just a little. He was invited to England every year to shoot grouse in the north. The scale and the form of the land up there, the dales and the moors, reminded him of his home, but the weather was dreary. Beyond that was always the knowledge that he was on an island that was small and damp and tamed. That harboured no wolves, or bears, or wild boar even. That lacked the drama of his homeland – melodrama, some might have called it – the heat, the storms, the vividness; the sense of continental vastness which he knew whenever he looked out towards the River Prut and the eastern horizon.

Though he was over seventy, he went himself with the two boys to London. He took them to Harrods for their uniforms. He bought them trunks and tuck boxes and cricket bats. Then he entrusted them into the hands of an experienced housemaster, personally recommended to him by a shooting acquaintance, in a rambling red-brick house, all stairways and panelled corridors, that was part of a famous English school.

After that he spent two days in a Mayfair hotel with a view of grey streets and interviewed replacements for the tiresome Fräulein Lore, who seemed to have grown ever bonier and more strident as her country did. It rained endlessly. The pavements outside were black with umbrellas and taxis, and the governesses came in variously damp and dishevelled. He met them wearing a Savile Row suit and carrying his stick, and yet his bearing and his dark features were unmistakably exotic even before he spoke a word in his precise but accented English. He chose Clare Sanders because of her freshness which, he thought, made the drops of rain rest lightly on her like dew. She had qualifications in French and in art and the history of art, which he thought ideal for the teaching of a girl. He thought that Safta, lonely without her brothers for the first time in her life, would warm to the young woman's smile and prettiness. And she really was pretty, like Queen Marie when she was young.

Augustin saw the yellow-haired governess the day that she arrived. The car stopped in the village and she leant out of the window to look about her. He saw her again the day after. She was wearing a blue dress the colour of the sky.

Constantin Văleanu had on his usual linen suit. He was a tall man and with age had developed a way of looking draped, even when he was walking, slightly creased like the suit itself. He was holding his cane up in the air, pointing at this and that, and the two slim beige dogs that followed him everywhere hovered beneath the stick as if it was about to be thrown. The dogs were agile enough to have reached and snatched the stick but it was only a game that they were playing with their master. Beside him walked the governess and on her other side was Safta, and now and then one of the dogs ran an impatient circle about the three. Safta looked sleek and dark beside the blonde woman. She was almost the same height but girlish still, her hair tied back, smooth and dark as if it was polished, her plain red skirt slim about her like a tulip. To Augustin she seemed slender and distant, the old connection between them smoothed away. He observed the three of them blandly and without self-consciousness, as a photographer might watch through a camera. They entered the yard and went to the stable where the Lipizzaner was kept. The horse came to the door of its stall and ate the sugar lumps that the old man produced from his jacket and held out on the flat of his hand. The governess reached to stroke its nose, tentatively as someone would who was not used to horses.

When he went in that evening Augustin made their shapes. He coloured them with some stubs of chalk which the schoolmaster had given him. He chalked the figures blue and scarlet and bone.

'Who's that boy?' Clare Sanders asked. 'I've seen him at the stables.'

'It's only Augustin,' Safta said.

'Why does he watch us?'

'Augustin watches everything.'

The summer days were so hot and beautiful that the governess had thought she would bring the girl down to do her work on the verandah. The verandah stretched the whole length of the house that faced the garden and the various chairs and tables scattered along it allowed spaces for privacy. Every morning Constantin Văleanu took coffee at one end, where he had a chair with a faded cushion and a small table beside it with an ashtray and the newspaper – the previous day's since Poiana's remoteness meant the news was always a day late – set out upon it. Clare Sanders arranged another table at the furthest end, where the morning light fell green through the overhang of wisteria. Even there there were distractions, movements, people coming by, flights of swallows slipping past. Now the men had come to mow the lawn, and Augustin had been sent to help.

The men, five of them, were mowing the lawn with scythes, working in a diagonal line across the width of the terrace. Augustin stood behind with his rake looking vacantly towards the house.

'He used to come and play here and do lessons with Fräulein Lore. Until my mother decided he was stupid and let him work instead.'

'Shouldn't he be at school?'

'He's deaf and dumb. No point in him going to school.'

'I think he was there in the village, the day I came.'

In this country she had every now and then the sense that she had strolled into some picture that she had seen, that she did not know was real. She had taken a train across all of Europe to get here. In Paris and Venice she had stopped for a day or two and seen the sights. She had seen the Corots and Millets in the Louvre, the Renaissance paintings in the Accademia. Then there was the Danube and Bucharest, and another long train journey of a day and a night. She looked out of the window of the train and saw living scenes from the paintings, and when she arrived at the station Constantin Văleanu was there to meet her, and there had been a dusty drive past pale oxen pulling carts and men walking with scythes on their shoulders, and they came to the village and stopped, and a man with a face from a Duccio came to kiss their hands. There was the ploughman from Brueghel's *Icarus*. There was this boy, standing aside like Brueghel's shepherd. And now there were these men mowing, all dressed in white, the sweeps of their scythes moving in slow waves across the grass.

Constantin folded his newspaper and took up his hat and stepped down on to the grass. His dogs got up from the floor and followed him, brushing against his legs. They were Weimaraners, hunting dogs with sleek coats of the softest mushroom grey. One and then the other stretched, stood, rubbed against his legs. When they went out into the sunlight their colour seemed almost no colour at all. 'Come, Spitzy, Heinz.' The dogs were a German breed. He loved the dogs and had given them German names, though he did not much care for Germany nowadays.

He stopped before the mowing men. They did not look up but went on working. Their rhythm held, passed down the line: a stroke, a step forward, a geometric passage across the lawn; a pause every now and then to whet a blade. Such a slow, medieval process. He watched and shook his head and idly put out a hand to stroke a restless dog.

'Grandfather's getting a lawnmower.'

Safta was meant to be working on her English grammar. Her English had a long way to go before it would be as good as her French or her German.

'The mower's coming from England.'

'I know. I helped him to buy it.'

'He says the lawns in England are very green and mown in stripes, and Gheorghe and Mihai will play cricket on them wearing white shirts and trousers like the peasants.'

Clare Sanders wondered if they had really better go and work indoors. Yet she had found the old nursery unbearably stuffy. Heat gathered up there beneath the roof and the sun slanted in just so much as to make the two of them feel caged. She had felt the atmosphere there of the past: the rigid teaching of her predecessor, who had put up the world map on the wall and marked on it the major European capitals and pinned and arrowed facts and photographs beside them; the fidgeting of the boys who had scratched their names on to the desktops. Sometime she would add to the map more notes and pictures describing Romania itself, which seemed to have been neglected, but she would have to learn about it first. That could wait until the summer was over.

'Do you know how to play cricket?' Safta asked.

'Of course.'

'Can girls play?'

'I don't see why not. But you need lots of people to make a team.'

'We could get some of the children from the village.'

The boy in the garden was watching them again. There was something that distinguished him from others. He was thin, small, a little abrupt in his movements. She pictured him fielding, standing out in the deep field looking on.

Imagined the boy inside the still body suddenly flinging himself into the air, birdlike, to take a catch.

She spoke to him despite knowing that he was deaf. She spoke in the soft tone she would use if she were talking to an animal. You would speak to an animal knowing that it could not understand, so why not a deaf boy? She spoke first in English, then used the few words of Romanian she had learned. Perhaps he could lip-read; there was no one to tell her. She enunciated the words slowly, aware of the forms of her lips. She put her smile into her eyes as she invited him forward, sitting back herself, not moving her position. If you move towards an animal you risk frightening it away. The thing to do is to make it come to you.

She was sitting in the garden painting. She had a little canvas-bound sketchbook and a watercolour box suitable for travelling, that she had out on the grass beside her. She was making a painting of the house. The light of the late afternoon was long and brought out all the yellows, the lemon in the acacia leaves, the cadmium and golds of flowers in the border. She heard him come and stand behind her, and had the sense that since he did not hear himself he would not know that he was heard. He gave the impression when she smiled at him of being caught in a secret.

He did not look at her so much as at her paints. He looked at them greedily, the square colours in the box shining where her wet brush had touched them.

'Do you know how to paint?' Somehow she thought that he did. She held out her sketchbook to him and he looked at it very closely, page by page, then he went away.

The next day he came with some work of his own to show her.

A book the size of her own sketchbook but home-made; cardboard cover and brown-paper pages stitched together with blue thread.

A title page with letters on it grouped like words, no words she knew but only letters shaped like print, regularly and rigidly formed, seriffed and spaced.

Ten pages of pictures, charcoal sketches that had smudged when they were folded. All of them showed flat and empty spaces: the stables, the tack room, a room without furniture, a room with a table and a chest, with a window, a doorway, a chair alone; a ladder set up against a wall in the yard; a fence, an open gate and a rounded hill behind. The forms were precise, carefully shaded with regard to their texture and all pretty much to scale.

Clare Sanders gave his drawings as much attention as he had given hers. There was something special, strange and still in the work. She thought she would have noticed that even if she had not known who had made it.

'You draw beautifully,' she said. She was wearing the blue dress that made her eyes bluer. It was strange to him to be looked at by such blue eyes. 'But I wonder if there's something that I can teach you.' She spoke the English words softly and if he did not hear them he saw by her lips that her meaning was soft.

She tore a page from her own sketchbook and put it beside the first drawing. She copied the room that he had drawn, just as he had drawn it, and then alongside she drew the room with the correct perspective. 'See, that's how it's done. That makes the room look deeper. More real.' She did not know if he saw what she meant so she drew it again, and did the same with one or two of his other subjects. He watched intently but without expression. She repeated the simple drawings a number of times, wondering why she was bothering with it. 'I don't know why I'm doing this. I just thought I'd show you. Of course it doesn't really matter how you draw things. Your pictures are lovely as they are.' She smiled and offered him the pencil and a couple of clean pages. 'Take these anyway. Draw whatever you like.'

He took the pencil and the page, and the sketchbook on which to rest it. Then he began the drawing of the room again, copying her lines this time. When he finished it, he showed it to her with satisfaction. She was astonished that he learned so fast.

He drew frantically in the days after that. He redrew the rooms and the stables and the barns, all the subjects he had drawn before. Their forms were already so precise in his memory that he did not need to go out and sit before them, but he could draw them at the table in the kitchen while he waited for his dinner, bent low over his work while the women worked about him, Mama Anica helping to peel potatoes or chop onions, Paraschiva before some boiling pot at the stove. He shielded the page with his spare arm so that they could not see the pictures as he made them. Then when he had finished he drew a blank page across as if for decency.

The women were used to having him there like a lone person in the midst of them. Most of the time they ignored him as he did them, only pushing him aside, or his pages if they spread too far on the top of the table and took up cooking space. When they put food before him he would put his work away and eat. Now they noticed a change in him.

'What's got into him?'

'He won't even stop to eat nowadays. That soup's getting cold.'

His mother tapped his shoulder, offered him the spoon.

'It's that girl. She's turned his head.'

'Who's that? Someone in the village?'

The women laughed together and he noticed the commotion and looked up with his strange separateness. His hair stood in a tangle. His shirtsleeve was flopping into the soup bowl.

The Romanians called her Domnişoara Clara. They thought the English Clare too simple and plain a name. And as the days passed she felt less and less English, even though she knew that it was her job to be English, to teach the language but also the ideas, the qualities that were considered special to an English education. As if to remind her of this, Constantin Văleanu persisted in calling her Miss Sanders as he had done that morning in Mayfair. And Mama Anica, who was quick to see trouble coming, just called her a surly Miss Clare.

The first moment she had arrived at Poiana Clare Sanders had been shown into the drawing room to meet her charge's mother. It was a long light greenish room. There were vases of flowers and landscapes and mirrors on the walls and formal chairs stood about like people on a country platform waiting for a train. Marina Văleanu sat on a green silk sofa. When Clare went forward to shake her hand she saw that she had a sombre beauty like that of the cloaked and bejewelled boyars in the portraits in the hall. The elderly Polish butler served tea from a samovar, and gooseberry jam to eat from a tiny saucer, and she thought that she had wandered into a Russian novel. She answered a string of courteous but searching questions about her age and education and family and religion. She answered precisely as if this was the interview and she hadn't yet got the job, and felt as she listened to herself that her answers all sounded disappointingly flat and suburban and twentieth century.

She did not meet Safta's father until he came up from Bucharest a week or so later. Alexandru was standing in the hall with the staircase winding up behind him and the boyars looking down on him so like his wife. He was taking a cigarette from a silver case, a man in his forties,

not as handsome as probably he once had been but power-
ful in his presence. She wasn't naïve. She recognised the
look he gave her and knew in that moment that she should
keep her distance. If as the summer went on she failed in
this, she put it down not only to his charm but to the exotic
nature of the place, the heat, the Gypsy music whose sound
carried in the nights, the ease with which these people with
whom she lived slipped from one language, as from one
identity, to another.

Augustin saw it in her face when he brought her his drawings. He saw that she paid less attention to them and had
less time to sit with him and teach him. Her own sketchbook, even when she carried it with her, did not fill up in
the way it had before. He was alert to details in the behaviour of the people he knew. One day he sat beside her on
the white bench beneath the catalpa and Alexandru
Vălcanu came across and spoke to her. Though the man
stood back some distance in the sun, and she who sat in the
shade had to frown and raise her hand above her eyes to see
him against the dazzle, Augustin knew as if he had heard
the words that they were intimate ones. He saw her eyes
run after him as he walked away, sensed the rush in her.
All those summer weeks he watched the governess
and saw the lines she made through the garden and the
grounds, and the lines made by her lover, and where they
intersected. There were people staying, men in straw hats
and women in print dresses coming in and out of the house,

putting hands to their eyes as they walked from the shade into the sun. He did not know who these people were but he saw that their faces changed from time to time; that some came and others left, but it did not matter because life at the house went on the same. The boys were home and sometimes Safta went out riding with her brothers in the early morning when it was cool, and came back hot as her horse, wet and shining with the heat. Sometimes her father rode and he looked on horseback like the statue of a hero in the town square. Clare Sanders who did not ride looked up with admiration.

Then one morning very early he saw her go.

Sudden movements were rare at Poiana. Comings and goings seemed always to be attended by long greetings and partings, decorous circlings, nothing so abrupt as this. Augustin saw the car taken out and brought up to the front. Marina Văleanu was standing between the columns of the porch, stiff as a pole. She did not move her body but only turned her head. The governess came out through the open door and went into the car as if she was blown by a gust of wind.

He worked all the day and watched out for her but she did not come back. That evening he made another figure. He cut it from card. He needed yellow for the hair but he had no yellow – no yellow crayons or paint or chalk, or cloth or wool either. There was only the yellow of the flowers in the little garden Paraschiva tended before the gate, and the colour of them was too strong. He had blue though. He had a piece of blue silk that had come to him from the house, that he kept in the box with his treasures. It was just the right colour. Nothing else that he or Paraschiva owned was that shade of blue except for the walls of the rooms in which they lived. He cut the silk and pleated it in fine folds about the figure, and tied it round and round with a thread.

From his bed he has a clear view of the doors to the ward, a view down the length of the room along the lines of floorboards that he knows narrow with the distance. There is a certain time of day when he looks down this perspective of the boards and watches the doors. It is the time when Safta comes. They are double doors but usually only one of them is opened at a time; one is enough for her to slip through. But today the doors open together. She is pushing a wheelchair. She has pushed it against the doors so hard that they go on swinging long after she has passed. It is a bright day. Since morning when he woke the ward has been streaming with light. It seems to him that some of the brightness of the day has gone into her and made her eyes darker.

The other patients lie still in their beds. It is as if the whole ward is still, or its motion slowed, before the dark speed of her. She comes down the aisle between the beds, directly to him. Her eyes are on him, communicating without the need for words. He knows that she is smiling beneath her mask.

* * *

She had decided as soon as she woke: she would take him outside this day for the first time. Only she had to do her shift first, and find the wheelchair because he is still so weak. She will take him out like a newly washed sheet that she would hang high in the breeze and the sun. Hold him up and let the sun run through him. She comes straight to his bedside, and all in one movement she picks up the coat she has found for him and turns back his bedding.

His face is pale as his pillow, the discoloured grey of white cotton long used and roughly laundered. When he raises himself he leaves the greyer indentation of his head there behind him. He edges forward, turns his body and puts his legs over the side of the bed, lets his quivering weight down on to them. He puts on the old coat she holds out for him, first one arm and then the other, and she buttons it right up as if he were her child. Yet it is she who seems young, the girl Safta. He is an old man before her, sitting now, the chair wheeled rapidly, if not so fast as before, out of the ward and along dark systems of corridors to a creaking lift, down then and through more and darker corridors and along a ramp and out into the yard, where the sun hits him full face and hot like a slap.

He closes his eyes against the first dazzle of it. There is colour still beneath his eyelids: yellow, a burn of magenta running through. He opens them to blue sky and the green of new leaves. The yard is shaded by tall trees, limes and chestnuts. It is enclosed on three sides by the hospital buildings but on the fourth there is a high iron railing and beyond it the street.

It is like a public garden only the people in it wear pyjamas, dressing gowns, white coats. There are men on benches, old women shuffling, a young woman rocking a pram, sleeping dogs. Safta pushes the wheelchair along the paths until she finds a place where it catches the sun. She sits beside him for a while.

There is a patient who is a barber and has set up shop on a bench beneath a tree. A patient barber with patient customers. An old man takes off his pyjama top, has a robe put around his thin white shoulders, holds his head erect to have the barber snip at wisps of hair.

She looks at her watch.

'I'll be back later,' she says to his eyes. 'I have to go now.'

As she leaves the yard she takes a look behind her. Another patient has come up to him, an old fellow she knows by sight. He has been at the hospital as long as she has worked there. He has some chronic condition that keeps him there as if it is his home. When the old man approaches, Augustin puts his index finger up to cover his ear and then passes it back and forth before his mouth. It is the first piece of communication she has seen him use since he came to the hospital.

Each day after that he spends some time in the sun. Once he is strong enough to walk on his own he can go out whenever he wants. The fine weather continues. The leaves on the trees have fully unfurled so that the yard is washed about with green. There is a bench where he particularly likes to sit, in the corner of the yard where he can watch people come and go through the gate. He sits very still. His hands that seem too big for the rest of him lie flat on his lap, fingers rising and falling now and then, faintly twitching like leaves in a breeze. Sometimes other patients come and sit beside him. They know now that he is deaf. Some sit and are happy not to speak. Others use the opportunity to talk. They begin with random words or casual pleasantries. Then sometimes they let go, talking, telling, confiding in a flood of almost whispered words. He knows the urgency in them by the tension in their bodies and he turns his head and put his eyes on them. He understands that he must sit like that impassively until whatever flood it is has ebbed. In times like these it would appear that a deaf mute may be ideal company.

He sees that people's faces have changed since he has come back into the world. In the place where he has been there was a particular kind of face. Before that, in the village, there was another kind. And now here again they are different. The features may be similar, but the differences between them are as profound as the differences between a summer and an autumn and a winter landscape.

He expects that he will be leaving this place soon. The fat nurse has brought him clothes to wear. She is a kind woman, he can see that. She has tried to teach him her name. She points to herself, denting the broad white front of her nurse's apron into the deep valley between her breasts, opens her mouth wide and speaks her name. Four movements to it: lips wide, then drawn, wide, drawn again, tongue coming forwards. He does not read the shapes but he knows that she is good. The clothes she brought were too large so she measured them against him and then took them away, and when she came with them again she had shortened the trousers and taken them in at the waist. So now he has the shortened trousers, and the shirt and the jacket that also are a little too big but which she does not alter, neatly folded in the locker beside his bed, ready for when he leaves.

Most of the time he does not think about where he will be going. He expects only that men will come for him as they have the other times. There will be men, uniforms; of that much he is sure. Only sometimes when none of the nurses are about him, or at night when he is awake and there is nothing to see and he might be alone in the ward, floating in the dark, only half-conscious, his thoughts come to him in pictures, pictures in which memory and nightmare are combined. There will be a transport of some kind standing at the hospital gates, black, rectangular, like a square black hole cut out of the city street. He knows how it will be inside: hard floor, hard walls, darkness, judders running through him, the bitter smell of men, the blindness of knowing nothing because it is always others who get to sit at the back or by the barred window and have the chance to see where they are going to or where they have been; men to whom he is chained but with whom he has no further connection, each one of them shut away within himself, not so much as looking him in the eye. And he lies very calmly and sees the pictures through and ignores the faces of the men and then they go away. He has experienced fear before. He knows that the pictures will dissolve in the end if he is calm.

In the morning it gets light and he looks out of the window and they have not come. He watches for them coming through the doors. He is ready to put on his clothes. But there is only breakfast and the doctors on their rounds, and lunch. And still wearing his pyjamas he takes his stroll in the garden, and sometimes he goes right to the gate where there is a kiosk selling flowers and he can see the people who pass on the street.

'I think he has someone,' Adriana says. 'I think he's waiting for someone.'

'How can that be?'

'Haven't you seen how he stands about the doorways? He stands around, waiting. And I've seen him standing on the stairs, where they bend round above the lobby and you can see everyone down below and they don't see you. He watches, as if he's expecting someone.'

His case is no longer acute. If he had someone to care for him he might have left the hospital already. But Safta has received no reply to her letters.

'What if nobody comes? What will happen to him then?'

'If he's not in the hospital then I suppose they'll say he's a vagrant.'

'What happens to vagrants?'

'I don't know. I think they arrest them, don't they?'

Safta seats herself beside him in the garden.

'What are we to do with you, Tinu?'

There is a cat that has attached itself to him. He does not appear to have sought its friendship any more than he has asked for the confidences of the other patients. Only the cat comes to where he is sitting and rubs its back against his legs. 'I thought that perhaps I should go to Poiana and see who I can find. It's risky. I'm not allowed there. None of us are allowed back. But I wouldn't be there for long.' She watches the cat as she speaks, listening to herself. Her voice seems clearer than her thoughts, a light, fresh, clear voice. The cat is thin and mangy but Tinu doesn't seem to mind. He drops his hand as if to stroke it but it doesn't quite trust him yet and pulls back, stays just out of range watching the hand which he leaves dropped there, open for approach. 'I'd just see a couple of people, that's all. I don't know who's left. If there was no one to answer my letters, then I can only imagine your mother's gone. If I go there then perhaps I can find out where she is. And then of course she might be there, after all. Maybe it was just that the letters didn't arrive. Maybe it's all there, like it was.'

Speaking to someone who cannot hear is more than thinking aloud. The words make a trail of their own.

One summer a young man came to Poiana in a long green car. It was clear that he had travelled a great distance to get there because the car was so thick with dirt. When they cleaned it the green came out from beneath the layers of dirt like a bottle dusted from the cellar. The beautiful car was given a space in the coach house beside the carriages and landaus. Augustin used to put out his hand to it and touch its metal sides, stroking along the bonnet and the curve of the mudguard where it swept down into running board. He thought it like a fierce sheepdog stretched out there, only seeming to sleep amongst the sheep.

The young man had arrived with a friend but when the friend left he stayed on. He stayed while other parties came and went. In the heavy heat of the summer days he would drive people off between the acacias and bring them back wet from a swim in a lake or hot from some picnic in the sun. Sometimes in the mornings he came alone to the yard and took the car out and worked on it. He folded the bonnet back to work on its engine, or went into consultation with

Ilie, or lay right beneath it and wriggled out with blackened hands and a smear of oil across his cheek. The oil did not make him look dirty but emphasised the cleanness of him, his sleekness and the whiteness of his smile.

'Take a look if you like.' One day early in his stay the young man had waved Augustin over with his oily hand. It was soon after he arrived and he did not know that the boy couldn't hear him. Augustin's look seemed to show intelligence so he held forth for some time about spark plugs and pistons and carburettors, explained his marvellous engine to the stable lad. His fingers moved with precision between gleaming and greased pieces of metal, pointed and touched. Augustin's eyes widened. Such alertness was easy to interpret as comprehension. The young man bent and took the crank and started it up. Augustin saw the pieces of metal shiver into motion. He felt the vibration of the car as if it was inside him. He saw the air melting blue above the metal as it grew hot.

The young man folded the bonnet back and strapped it shut.

'Get in. I'll take you for a drive.'

Augustin had been in a car before, but the young man was not to know this. The Packard in which he had been driven to the monastery was closed so you had to put your head out of the window to feel the wind. This one was open and the wind was all about you. He closed his eyes and it seemed to him that he flew.

They went down the drive and off on a circuit of the valley. In the dip at the bottom of the valley the air was hotter, close even as they sped through it, hot about them with the smell of their own dust that they threw up on the road. In the village boys ran after them and were soaked up in the dust. Then they climbed again into fresh air and hay smell, the shadow of the car racing beneath them, the peasants standing fixed like photographs in the fields. On they went to the top of the ridge and along it. Augustin laughed at the top of his voice and the young man thought that he heard a scream and looked round but saw that the boy was happy, not afraid. At last they turned for home, taking the track back through the forest where they went slower and the air was cool and brown.

Close to home they came upon Safta walking alone with a jarful of wild strawberries she had picked. The young man stopped and Augustin got out and squeezed into the narrow seat at the back, and Safta got in the front, and turned and gave him a handful of the fruit. They drove on through the woodland and down the avenue towards the house, through stripes of light and shade. The sun dodged behind the trees, dazzling them at one moment and hiding from them the next. He ate the tiny strawberries one by one. The girl's hair flew back in dark waves towards him. Her slim brown hands gathered the tangled length of it together and tied it loosely, held the knot against the bared nape of her neck. Even when he had eaten all of the strawberries the scent of them stayed with him. He watched Safta's hands that were so close to him. They had become the hands of a woman, not those of a girl. They were conscious of themselves and their effect. He saw her face like a woman's when the hair was pulled back from it, turning towards the young man at the wheel.

The young man's name was Andrei. The car was a Lagonda. He was twenty-two and he had driven it all the way from France. He had just finished his studies and had taken the summer to travel before going back to begin his first job. He was also engaged to be married when he got back to France but he didn't mention this. At Poiana in the heat of the summer all of that seemed a world away. Almost all of his life his family had lived in France. He had not known till now how wide and beautiful his own country was, so different from the countries of Western Europe as if it magically preserved a piece of all their past. Marina Văleanu had welcomed him with vague hospitality. She had been a close friend of his mother's a long time before. Do stay, as long as you like. Treat the place as your home. And then she left him to it, and he stayed on and on. There was room in the house for that, for people to come and stay and write at a table in the library or read on a sofa, or if they liked, tinker with an engine. Every now and then the household was reminded of Andrei's presence by the roar of the car leaving or its return, heard and seen as a feather of dust across the landscape even before it reached the drive, or sometimes a fretful revving from the coach house. When he had it working he went out with the boys. Or sometimes he drove the family's big Packard – though Ilie did not like to relinquish it – and took them all on trips.

He talked politics with Constantin – and he had talked to people all the way across Europe, and this was the summer of 1939 so he had much to say. Things were serious, he said. There would be war and the world was going to change. He did not know whenever he – anyone – might make a journey like that again. When he talked in this way he acquired a gravity that the boys admired. For the space of that summer he was a hero to all the family. It was hardly surprising that Safta should fall in love with him. She was only sixteen.

It began on what was perhaps the hottest day of that July. The heat was already there when Safta woke, a whiteness in the morning beyond the window that seemed to hang over from the day before and the day before that. Usually she got up and rode but this morning even the idea of a horse was too hot, the thought of the heat and smell of its flanks and the milling flies. She heard her brothers go without her, slept on, found herself alone at the breakfast table on the verandah where dishes of fruit and bread were covered with white napkins and wasps clung to the sticky sides of pots of jam. Her grandfather was in his usual place but dozing with the newspaper on his lap. The house behind her was dim and half-shuttered. Her mother would have been up for some hours, writing letters in her study.

Andrei came in lightly so that she did not hear him. She did not know if he had come from the garden or from the house.

'There's a wonderful place for a swim. We found it yesterday.'

He did not sit but stood at the table, took some bread in his hand, spread it with honey and ate it there looking out impatiently to the valley.

'It's a bit of a way. Let's go before it gets too hot.'

'We could wait for the boys.'

'Then we'd waste the morning. We should go now before it gets any hotter.'

They got lost once or twice on the tracks until she was not sure if he would find the place again. All the tracks looked the same. But he turned and went back and at last they came over a rise and saw ahead of them the lake like dark glass, almost hidden by a silvery clump of trees. There was a gang of boys there who were swimming already, who rushed up in excitement at the sight of the car. From the far bank of the lake other boys saw, and streaked in and swam across to where they had stopped, crowding round so close that she could feel the coolness of the water on their brown bodies. The children shouted and laughed, touched the car and left wet marks on the dusty metal, barely gave her room to open the door and get out.

They swam with the children about them. There was a rope hanging from a branch high above the water. Andrei climbed up as the boys did. When he threw himself off his ripples shattered the lake.

Then Safta swam away alone to where it was still, and Andrei followed. They got out and sat for a time beneath the trees gazing out over the water.

Look at me, he said. And he pulled the strands of wet hair back from her face and kissed her.

Then they turned and swam back, swimming alongside or sometimes behind one another without speaking. The car had been all that time out in the sun. It was too hot to touch. They laid their damp towels on the leather seats, waved to the children and drove away.

They were terribly hungry from the swimming. Paraschiva had let them take a picnic from the kitchen but they could not have eaten it at the lake with all the children about them. Where they drove the land was so hard and dry that there was no need for a road. The sky was hot and wide and empty. They were driving over open country, bare as steppe. The only pieces of shade to be found lay in black crescents at the foot of the haystacks that were spaced across the fields. At last they drove up to one of these and spread a blanket on the stubble. The shade was no more than a narrow sliver, sharply outlined before their feet. The food was hot from the car, bread and salami and sheep's cheese, tomatoes, peaches. They sat with their backs to the hay and the flavours and the scents were strong. The crescent of shade shifted away from them and at first they did not notice and burnt in the sun. Then they moved the blanket over to where the shade grew longer.

There was little to be said. It was like the swimming again. She let herself float for a time and then fear overtook her. She stopped his hand before she drowned. She was suddenly shy. She packed up the picnic chaotically to cover her confusion.

*   *   *

Augustin saw it as soon as they came home. The rest of the household were perhaps too lazy with the heat to see, though it was happening right before their eyes. When she came back with Andrei that first day Augustin knew as soon as he saw the glow of the sun on her and the tangles in her hair. The car was parked askew in front of the coach house, a basket with the remnants of the picnic left on the back seat and the blanket stuffed beside it.

He went back to his work. The tack room was always soothing, its swept floor, its whitewashed walls, the gleaming leather of the saddles. The polished leather reminded him of the young man. Andrei knew now about his deafness. He didn't speak or acknowledge him like he used to, but slipped past as if he did not exist. Some people did that. They did not seem even to see a person who could not hear. It meant that Augustin saw the man with Safta as if they were alone.

He drew a new figure to add to his collection, another of his rectangular totems. This one he coloured brown with a crayon, and he licked the tip so that the colour shone. He gave the figure the young man's thick black hair; no face as it did not seem to need one, the young man's features were so regular and smooth. Often he liked to put words beside his figures as he had seen in books. Beside this one he drew two outstretched wings as they appeared in chrome above the radiator of the green car and within the wings the word *LAGONDA*. He printed the letters in clean angular capitals just as they appeared on the car. Then he had an idea. He screwed up that page and drew the figure again but now with the wings attached as if the man might fly.

They drove to a castle on a rock above a bend in the river. From the castle they could see a long way. There was the same rolling open barc country to the south but to the north they could see here and there the darker green of forest that was like a stain seeping over a ridge or like the shadow of a cloud.

Andrei put his hand down her back where the channel of her spine was like a secret beneath her hair.

'If I drove on I could drive all the way to China.'

'Can I come?'

'Your parents would never let you.'

'I'd go anyway.'

'You're too young.'

'It's dangerous over there.'

'We'll go to France then. At least there I could get parts for the car.'

They turned about, looked west the way he had come. He had left Paris in May. He had driven through snow on an Alpine pass. He had crossed Austria and Hungary where he had experienced a great storm on the *puszta*. He had the canvas roof of the car put up just in time before the black cloud that charged at him across the plain, then there was nothing he could see but the battering rain and he could not drive a yard and only huddled and sat it through like a Bedouin in a sandstorm.

'There was lightning that lit up all the land for miles.'

'I'd like to go there.'

'You will.'

'I'd like to go with you.'

He didn't answer but only kissed her and said again how young she was.

'I'm old enough.'

'I'm sure you are.'

If they had been silent that first day they went to the river, words flowed between them now. They drove on. He talked as he drove of what he planned to be. He had been studying to be an engineer. All across Europe they were building pieces of engineering that she would not believe. Architecture, viaducts, bridges. There were the pavilions he had seen in the International Exhibition in Paris, the new forms and structures. He used technical terms she didn't understand, mentioned names of architects of whom she'd never heard. He said that he was going to go to America. In America they had built a great dam across the Colorado River. There was New York. Everyone had to see New York. And in California they had just completed a beautiful bridge which was the longest bridge in the world. If there was not a war he would go to America and drive right across it on roads that ran in straight lines through the wheatfields and across the desert and then across the bridge over the San Francisco bay. Even if there was a war he would go as soon as the war was over. She listened to him talk and she didn't listen. Sometimes she was aware only of his face, his eyes, his lips, his hands that lifted again and again from the wheel as he spoke.

They bought a watermelon at the side of the road. They stopped on a high ridge. The land stretched on in all directions. He cut slices of the melon. When they kissed they tasted again the sweet juice that had spilled on to their skin.

They drove on past a peasant walking, dressed in white linen like all the peasants with a tall black hat and a scythe carried over his shoulder. The peasant turned his body stiffly like a clockwork figure to watch the car go by.

'You're living in the Middle Ages here.'

'But you keep saying how beautiful it is.'

'I couldn't spend my life here.'

'Don't you feel you should? Just because of who you are? Stay because it's your country?'

'Only sometimes. Just sometimes these last few days I think I've felt more at home here, more myself, than I ever have anywhere else.'

'That's how it should be, isn't it?'

Then he drew back into himself, became again the Paris-educated engineer. 'But things can't go on like this here. Look at the politics. The society. The inequality. The lack of progress.' And he spoke of all sorts of things she had never bothered to think about.

They were on a track going into a village. They slowed down to navigate the usual spill of people and livestock. When they left the village there were ox carts ahead of them. The day had become so hot that when the car went slow they felt they would stifle in the heat.

'To hell with this,' he said, and left the track altogether.

There was smoke rising at the edge of the forest. It seemed far too hot for smoke.

It was late when they got back. The rooks were circling in the trees about the house, louder than the crickets. It was still hot. The August nights were hot. When they came in it was hard not to touch one another. They were thirsty and went to get drinks from the kitchen. Then they walked through the rooms of the house that were empty, one then another, into the drawing room that was cool like the drinks they held.

Augustin was leading a horse in from the field. He was walking in from the drive beside the house. It was a habit with him whenever he went by to look in at the rooms that he didn't go into any more, that were so different and watery when seen through the glass. He saw through the window to a mirror and through the mirror to the room. In the room two forms moved, fused, moved away again.

As he passed the next window he saw Marina Văleanu in the room and the two in the mirror had gone. She had on a dark dress and she was standing very still, like one of the portraits on the wall.

He took the horse into the stables, into its stall. He closed his eyes and the horse nuzzled his palm, and then reached for his shirt as if there was hay in it. He took the horse's head in his hands and put his head to it and kept it there until the horse lost patience and jerked away.

It was a day later, the afternoon, the quietest time of the day. Most people about the house had gone to sleep. Usually he went to sleep like everyone else but the morning had been busy and there had been no time for him to sweep the yard. So he came out to sweep it now. He liked to keep the yard perfect. He swept until every hoofprint was gone from the dust.

When he was done he went up to the hayloft.

He saw them lying there, where they had been making love. He saw first the smooth dark skin of the young man's back, his dark brown arm reaching across the dip of her waist. He saw the shadow between them. He saw her breast, her startled nipple above the man's arm. He stood at the top of the ladder and looked directly into her eyes. She had hardly realised he was there before he was gone.

There was an ice house in the grounds, at a spot up behind the stables where the trees began. It was half tunnelled into the hillside, half mounded above it, a solitary place quite different from any other. In winter slabs of ice were brought on a sleigh and stored away in the black hole beneath the snow. And when the snow had melted, the ice remained. Sometimes they sent Augustin to fetch some for the house. Paraschiva or Stanislaw would hand him a basket, and he would avoid their eyes and put on himself the look of incomprehension he used to keep the world away. He knew what they wanted but he did not like to go there. The blackness and the cold so closed him in.

He walked that way at first just because it led away from the house. Then he saw where he had come, and saw the door that was heavy as the door of a church. He went down the ramp and pushed it back, pushed away the childish terror he always felt as the black and the chill rushed out to him. There was still some ice in there, great blocks with straw packed about them. The ice house was dark. A lantern that you could light when you needed it hung from a hook in the doorway. He knew how to light the lantern but there was nothing inside that he needed to see. The ice did not sting at the first touch. Its surface was wet. He pushed aside the straw that wrapped it and felt the ice with the palms of his two hands, then pressed the whole of his body against it for the cold to penetrate.

They did not find him until the next morning. One of the gardeners happened to notice that the door was open and went in and saw a white shape huddled at the back. The floor was made for the melt to run down it, sloping down to a drain at its centre, and half his body was wet from the drain.

She thought that she had disconnected herself from the past. She has learnt that you can do that with pieces of your life. Disconnect them. Separate yourself from the person you were. That after all is what she and everyone else is meant to be doing these days.

'I hadn't thought about Poiana in such a long time. That seems strange but it's so. You can forget that things happened, or if they happened they didn't happen to you but to somebody like yourself that you used to know.'

There has been so much between Poiana and now. An intervening life lived in tents and hospitals and makeshift barracks and later in rooms in cities that despite their apparent permanence had the same hard transitoriness to them.

'Were you there through the war? When did you leave? Did everyone leave? When I was with the army I could not imagine it touched, not even when I came upon another house like it in Ukraine, a manor like our own, built in much the same style – not grand but it had that same ease to it in its spaciousness and proportion, and there were columns at the front and the walls had been white but the stucco had cracked off leaving them bare. No one had lived a family life in that house for decades. We moved in with our wounded soldiers and despite all that I knew of the war I could not bring myself to think then that the same thing could occur at Poiana.'

Sunlight leaves the hospital garden long before the end of the day. The shadow of the buildings falls across it so that the yellow light of evening shows only in a band high on the walls, and in the street beyond the railings where people walk home from work. They have made a circuit of the garden together. They will make another one or two circuits before he goes in, keeping on the move around the limits of the space. The grey cat walks just ahead of them. Whenever Augustin comes out it slinks out from some dim corner or behind the bins and winds between his legs and walks before him.

'These things that I saw could not happen there, I told myself, as if the place was held in some capsule untouched by the war. And gradually I put the capsule away, perhaps because I could not risk it being broken. If I thought of Poiana at all, it must be just as it was, as when I'd been away at the college, and I came back and though some of the people had gone the place was just the same as if it had been waiting for me.'

This is how the other patients talk to him. She sees that. She is beginning to talk to him as they do, telling him what she can tell no one else. Finding a voice for thoughts she has hardly acknowledged to herself.

*   *   *

That last summer when Andrei was there seemed the longest summer that she had known. Endless days, long rides, nights that spun through until dawn. The drives they made, that seemed to have gone on for whole days, one merged into another. But they had been no more than pieces of days, and those days themselves just pieces taken out of that whole summer. The timelessness had to do with the fact that it was the last summer, because nothing after it was the same. The hills were long, wide, smooth as if they had been spread with a knife. The car swung up and crested them or rode along the ridges. Sometimes they drove on dusty tracks, sometimes they just drove across the open land. Once they came upon Gypsies making a road, unexpected as a flock of crows out in an ocean, and they were burning the tar and cooking above it at the same time. She had found the blackness and the shimmering heat and the smell about them almost unbearable. There were the Gypsies by the road and somewhere, some other time, there were the charcoal burners. She has them merged somehow in her memory: the heat and blackness all one, the charcoal beginning to ooze with the smell of tar. But they had stopped only a moment beside the Gypsies, to ask the way. She hadn't even got out of the car yet she had felt the heat from there and wondered if the food they cooked did not itself go black and taste of tar.

One day they took Gheorghe and Mihai with them squeezed into the car and drove east towards Russia. They crossed the Prut and drove on, and the landscape did not change but repeated itself as if it would stretch out like that for ever, the long bare slopes that ran the same way, open and featureless save where the path of a river was marked by ribbons of willow or a stream made a raw crease in the soil. It would be the same if they went on to the Nistru and into Russia, the same long flattening folds of land, the villages that clustered where it softened, the people the same only that they were Bolsheviks. In a year the Russians would cross the Nistru and there would be no difference between one side and the other. In the end they'd all have to be Bolsheviks.

'I might have left with him. Do you know that? We talked about it, driving all the way back to France. Imagine that.

'Or that was what we talked about. What he said. Was that what he meant? I can't say. I don't know now. I have no way of knowing if anything he said was true. Maybe it wasn't. Or maybe it wasn't at first but became so later. That's what I like to think, that it was true, some of the time at least. I don't really know how to remember him, you see. There's only the surface of him. The way he looked. His words. That's all I have.

'One day when we were driving we met some charcoal burners. We saw the smoke in the distance and Andrei drove up to it, just driving a line out across the pasture which was hard and dry. It was a very hot day and at first we'd thought the smoke might be the beginning of a fire, there on the edge of the forest. It seemed far too hot for burning things. The men looked so hot. They had three huge mounds burning, smoke seeping out from them, black heaps, piles of wood, a couple of caravans. There was a woman, children, a naked baby, all of them black with charcoal. The smell of the charcoal pervaded everything. It was like a smell of winter. It was odd on a day like that, smelling the winter. They'd seen us coming. They were excited about the car. Andrei talked to the men for a long time. That was just like Andrei. He always wanted to know what people did, how everything worked. You could see why he had studied to be an engineer. He wanted to know what kind of timber they used, how the logs were laid to make the fire, how many days it took to burn down. I stood about and listened, and the children came up to me. We had some sweets in the car so I went and got them out and gave them to the children. I remember I saw them take the sweets from the paper wrappers into their little black fingers and put them to their mouths. They shouldn't do that, I thought, but then I told myself it was only charcoal, it wasn't really that dirty, it was clean. I wondered where they went to wash. Andrei was wearing a light blue shirt. He looked so immaculate standing amongst them.

'I took some pieces of charcoal away for you. "Whatever are you going to do with that?" Andrei said. That surprised me.

'"It's for Tinu," I said.

'It surprised me to think how short a time Andrei had known us, how there were still so many things about me, about all of us, of which he had no idea. And how little I knew about him. Perhaps I should have paid more attention to that thought, perhaps it should have made me wary. I just saw it, and marvelled at how strange it was, and passed on. It was exciting to know that there was so much more that was unknown that I could tell him. So I talked to him as we drove, rattling away. I told him about your drawings, how beautiful they were.

'Really you see we didn't know each other very well. I couldn't even be sure if he would find your pictures beautiful.'

He was still a stranger after all. It was possible that they weren't the sort of pictures that might appeal to a stranger. Strangers looked from the outside. Tinu's pictures showed things, they were all of things, yet even when they showed the outsides of things they seemed to work from the inside. The car drove on. It was late in the afternoon and the sun cast their moving shadow across the steppe.

When Tinu drew a room he drew it empty. He drew it as it was but somehow what you saw was not the room but its emptiness. With a door you saw the opening. When he drew a pitchfork left leaning against the barn wall you saw its abandonment. How could she have explained that? An outsider might see no more than a murky sketch on a scrap of paper. Something that was too small and too inward to be communicated.

When they came back to the house Paraschiva gave them lemonade and they went through from the kitchen, through the drawing room that was cool as the lemonade.

In the mirror there she caught sight of her reflection and laughed. He had not told her that she had charcoal smudged across her cheeks. He came up to her in the mirror and tried to kiss away the smudge. Just as they separated she heard someone coming. She went on quickly, spilling the drink on to her fingers, out and down the verandah steps.

The gardener carried him out. The gardener was not a big man but Augustin was light as a child to carry. He was limp, cold, barely conscious. The gardener said that he only began to moan the moment he was touched, with a strange high-pitched nasal moan none had heard from him before. He took him up to where the sun was hot and laid him on the grass. He called for help and began to strip off the cold linen that clung to the lad's thin frame, which began to shiver as the sun struck and the blood again began to flow.

Paraschiva came pounding the ground towards her son. Her attempt to run seemed to create more awkwardness than speed. Worry for him sat oddly on her placid face. It showed in her eyes and in the tightness of her mouth, not in lines because she had none. Mama Anica hurried behind her. Paraschiva knelt on the ground and raised him on to her lap while the old woman rubbed his bare chest with brandy, put the bottle to his mouth and tried to make him drink. Then Marina Văleanu too came running. She had heard the shouts. Safta came behind her mother and saw them all clustered about him like ill-assorted holy women before the tomb.

'So cold, my boy.' Paraschiva felt his flesh like fish in her hands. She closed her eyes and tears welled from them and rolled down her cheeks.

'What was he doing there? Did you send him?'

'Of course I didn't send him. If I'd sent him I wouldn't have spent half the night looking for him.'

'Who did send him then?'

They looked one to the other. Often the boy's behaviour was inexplicable. That they were used to. This action they could not account for because of the suffering in it. They could not see what cause he had to make himself suffer.

The gardener picked him up again and carried him back, the women fluttering ahead. Safta followed slowly. She remembered that instant in the loft when he had seen them. She held the image of it, fixed, still, like a photograph in her hand. The whole household had collected now: Stanislaw who rarely stirred outdoors for anything, the rest of the gardeners; then Gheorghe and Mihai, her grandfather and Andrei together. The men had been out shooting. They carried guns and Mihai held a brace of partridge across his shoulder. Her eyes went down to the dogs, that walked pale and alert about their legs. She could not bring herself to look at Andrei just then.

Stanislaw directed the whole cavalcade back to the house where Augustin was taken upstairs and given a hot bath in the enormous bath that was like an iron sarcophagus. Some said that a doctor should be called. Mama Anica brewed a tea from herbs.

'What was he doing there?' Gheorghe asked. 'Was it an accident? Did someone shut him in?'

'It can't have been that,' said József. 'The door was open. That was why he was found.'

He might have died, they said, if he had lain there any longer.

There is a little shop on Strada Lăpuşneanu that sells magazines and books and toys and stationery, where she goes sometimes to buy him things. Yesterday she noticed a kaleidoscope in the window.

'It's just a childish thing but I thought you might like it.'

He is pleased. He takes it and puts it to his eye.

'I remembered that you had one before. It was rather better quality than this one, of course, more complex, and painted in lots of colours. Still, one can't be fussy. We should be grateful anyone at all's making kaleidoscopes these days.'

His smile is tight on his face. Even now he is watchful, tense. If only he would begin to draw again.

'I went to visit you that time when you were ill. I think it was the only time that I went inside your home in all those years. Even when we were children I never went in there. I never would have dreamt of it. It was always you who came to us. I suppose I felt bad about what happened. I didn't follow the thought through but all the same I felt responsible in some way. So I went to see you and you were sitting up in your bed, a little pale but otherwise the same as ever, only you wouldn't look at me, like when you first came here to the hospital, and you were looking at the wall. I didn't know what to do so I looked at the wall as well. It was a blue wall with that blue wash on it that all the peasant houses have – rough, dappled in the sort of way that if I was a child and ill in bed I would have looked at it and seen shapes of other things in the marks like the shapes in clouds. I always found it strange going into peasants' houses. They were so small and low, so different from the sort of rooms I was used to. Going into them was like walking into the forest from the open, everything suddenly close and dark and smelling of wood or dust. So I looked at the wall for a time and then I looked around at everything else. And it would have been just like any other peasant room, with the table and chairs and embroidered hangings by the windows, except for all your collections of things. You had such odd things. Sometimes I'd seen you pick them up but I never knew you brought them home and kept them. I didn't know how Paraschiva could stand it, except that they were all so tidily sorted and arranged. There were the drawings, of course, stacks of card and paper, neat and tied with string, and little people all along the windowsill, but there were other things, stones and pine cones and pieces of wood, and the strangest was a collection of finely formed bones that looked like pieces of armour, fantastical helmets with visors, arranged like a marching squadron, and when I looked I realised that they were just the skulls and breastbones of birds, chickens I suppose, and others you had found. And the kaleidoscope we gave you was there beside your bed. I don't know how long I stayed, whatever I thought was a proper amount of time. Paraschiva brought me some kind of fruit syrup to drink and when I had finished it I left.

'That was just after everyone went away. I should have come to you before that but I never quite got there. I think I felt bad about you, and then with each day that passed I felt bad about not going sooner, and besides, time went so fast. It was always like that at the end of a summer. The days go on like they could go on for ever and they're hot and lazy, and then suddenly they're over and everyone's going. The boys were going back to school in England. There was a great adventure planned, Andrei was going to drive with them as far as Budapest and leave the car with someone there and take the train on and see them all the way to Paris and see them off at the Gare du Nord. For a time I had thought that I was going somewhere too. There had been talk of a finishing school in Switzerland but they had changed their minds. There's no point in going abroad to start anything, my mother said. Not if there's going to be a war. We'll find you something else. She spoke lightly, as if it didn't matter, but it was like a bomb falling. I argued. I went to my father, to Constantin, but they sent me back to her. I was so angry. I shouted at her, but her voice came back smooth and cool as always. She had this way of making it seem that all these things I was concerned with were only temporal and transitory, far beneath argument.

'The last day we went mushrooming. We always did that at the end of the summer. I couldn't bear the thought that everyone else was leaving. I remember the birds. I was terribly aware of all the birds, migrating. So many of them went over Poiana, it was the route to the delta and the south. There were great flocks of them in the sky that time of year. The mushroom day was beautiful. It always was. All the mushroom days were that I remember. I didn't know that it would be the last. It was the 2nd of September 1939. Anybody would know now, knowing the date, that it was bound to be the last and that everything after it was bound to change.'

She feels that she is about to cry. He does not see because he is looking into the kaleidoscope. He looks at each pattern for a long time, as if he is bent on understanding it, breaking it up and seeing where it begins to repeat, reflect. Perhaps his mind can do that, divide and fix the shapes. Is he aware even that she is speaking? Is all the sympathy that people imagine in him no more than his passivity? And yet she goes on talking as if he understands. She wants to yell to make him hear her. Then he shifts the pattern again and she is calmed.

'We went out early, Gheorghe, Mihai, Andrei and myself, my cousin Angelica, a couple of the boys' friends. Riding where there was still dew. The sky becoming very bright. The peasants already up. Peasants up like the birds in the early morning. József had been slow saddling the horses. You weren't there. We had saddled them ourselves. Old József had to get the carriage ready to follow us later.

'Andrei and the boys were leaving the day after. There's something I have to tell you, Andrei said, but he didn't tell me. All day he didn't manage to say whatever it was.

'We rode out to a glade in a wood some ten miles away. It was a place we had come to a week or so before, just the two of us riding out there in the heat. Tall beeches, the open ground beneath them starred with white anemones, a high stillness. It was different with everyone there, all the riders and horses racing about. As if people were shouting in a cathedral. It seemed wrong. I felt separate from them all. I didn't think I could bear the day. But then Andrei came up and said something that made me laugh, and we left the horses and spread out through the trees. When the carriage came it brought the picnic and big baskets for the mushrooms we had already begun to gather. It was just like when we were children, everyone trying to pick the most, Mihai stealing from Gheorghe, squabbling over who had the best. And Andrei couldn't tell one mushroom from another. Everyone told him he had spent too long in Paris. He'd have poisoned us all if there hadn't been a Paraschiva to check them. Paraschiva would tip all the mushrooms out on to the kitchen table that evening and check every one before she cooked them. Paraschiva could always be trusted. And I think I never ate anything so good as her mushrooms, ever.

'All the morning we picked and then we came back to the glade with our baskets, and the picnic had been laid out on a great white tablecloth. Meats and breads and cheeses, salads, *sarmale*, and everything tasted a little of mushroom

because of the smell of the mushrooms about us and clinging to our fingers. Mushroom even in the wine and in the
peaches, like a taint of earth. The sun was hot through the
afternoon as in summer. All that urgency of the morning
had gone and I felt that we would be there for ever, eating
and drinking, Andrei a little way off on the grass joking
with the boys and I didn't need to be any closer to him
because he was there and I was there and we'd picked a
basket of mushrooms together and shared the touch of
them, and the tethered horses grazed and shook their tails
beneath the trees. And then it was over. József was putting
the horse back between the shafts of the carriage. The wine
was all gone. Some people were asleep, or almost asleep.
No one had talked much for a time. Everyone seemed a
little lost. We helped pack up the picnic things and my
mother and Mama Anica shook out the great white cloth
and pulled it out between them and folded it, fold upon
fold. Andrei went and got his horse and mine, and I don't
think he said anything but when he gave me the reins I felt
the leather on my fingers as if it stung. We rode off with
the others. The horses were well rested and we took a long
route, climbing up out of the wood on to the heights of the
hills then galloping down the long mown hay fields and
slaloming about the ricks.

'We were at the top of a valley, just within sight of the
house. We slowed to allow the others to ride on ahead.
We couldn't really see the house from there so much as
the trees that surrounded it, and the rooks gathering above
them. There was a cloud of dust on the road down below

that must have been the carriage, which had taken a more direct route and almost home. We turned down a track that ran along the side of the hill through the vineyards. The grapes were almost ripe and the last of the sun was on them. There's no more time, I said. He didn't hear or didn't understand and made me say it again. I wanted time, I said. I thought there was time but there isn't any. And he only looked at me and didn't say anything.

'We were coming to the first houses of the village. We had to pass through the whole village before we came to the gates at the top of the drive, and the peasants were all there at their doors or on the benches beside them waiting for the cows to come home and the sun to go down. Lots of "Good evenings" and doffing of hats. We didn't speak any more to each other. I wished that he was gone already. I thought that I could not face another dinner, another breakfast, the loud public goodbyes of the day that would follow, that I could imagine so precisely before they happened.'

'But that wasn't quite how it was. We met that night in the garden. We crept out and met under the catalpa after everyone had gone to bed. A dark night. No moon, only stars. We were out there in the garden almost till dawn.

'What was it you were going to tell me? I asked. It doesn't matter, he said. I'll sort it out. It's not important any more.

'My mother told me later. She had a letter from his mother, her old friend in Paris. It didn't arrive until after he'd gone. He had a girl in France that he was going to marry when he got back, a French girl. My mother showed me the letter and what it said.

'What was it? I asked him. Tell me. Nothing, he said. A mistake I made. I'll sort it out.

'I thought, when my mother showed me the letter, that that was what he meant, what he was talking about. I still loved him, you see.

'Some of the time that night we only lay there and felt the darkness on our skin as it cooled. I'd taken out a blanket from the verandah because of the dew. Later he ran naked as he was and got another one to put on top of us. When we slipped off it the ground was cold. We said goodbye there. We said we would meet in Paris. I'd get there somehow, soon enough. And from Paris we would go everywhere. I was so young. I thought the war they talked of would soon be over and then things would be again as they were before.'

When the Lagonda left those who saw it go noticed clouds building and predicted that Andrei would have to stop before long and put up the roof before a storm broke.

But the news came before the rain. The schoolmaster Grigorescu came pedalling furiously up the drive, the black jacket that he had put on to mark the gravity of the moment splayed like wings about him. He had heard on the wireless that England and France had declared war on Germany.

'Go after them,' Marina Văleanu said. 'Bring them back.'

Her manner was imperious. Grigorescu lifted the hand that held his hat to wipe the sweat from his brow and turned the bike around to give chase.

'No, in the car I mean.' Ilie had the Packard out ready to take the others to the station.

Her husband said the Lagonda went too fast even for the Packard. Anyhow, the boys would find out soon enough.

'Then they'll come back.'

'Why should they? They're on their way now. They should go on. England's still the best place for them to be.'

Constantin backed him up. Who knew how this would come out? If anyone could be relied upon surely it was the British. And he told his son to wait while he packed some things as he was coming to Bucharest as well. He said that since he had been in the country all summer it was time to see to his affairs, but everyone knew that the old man was tempted simply to be closer to whatever was going on.

Even as they talked it began to rain. Big drops of it at first, as Grigorescu turned up his collar and rammed his hat down and made his way back to the village, then a heavy downpour as the Packard pulled away.

Only the women were left. When the shower was over there were still black streaks in the sky above the horizon and they knew that it was raining again where the car had gone. Here there was sunshine but over there the car was swishing down wet roads with the roof up, dark with wet, and there were cities with wet streets and people beneath umbrellas that had a sheen on them like the road. And somewhere, grey armies moving. There were moments when such things seemed scarcely possible, the immediate world and the weather about them being so still, so complete. They had days again of hot weather that tried to persuade them that it wasn't September at all. The crickets sang. The afternoons were heavy, turning thoughts inward. Safta waited while her mother made plans for her to go to a college in Bucharest. She should go there, her mother said, at least until this war was sorted out. Waiting is slow in a place where nothing happens. Safta slept long, got up late and went out to ride. Each day in the afternoon she told herself she would practise the piano. She went into the long drawing room and sat before the keyboard and sometimes she did not even touch it. She sat in silence, feeling the weight of her body, hands sunk on to her lap and motionless.

Her mother came to find her. She had a letter in her hands.

'I have to tell you something.'

Blue ink, thin blue paper, an elegant looped script, all very French. She was about to read the letter aloud but she changed her mind and handed it to Safta to read for herself.

'It can't be so.'

'I'm sorry,' her mother said. 'I shouldn't have let it happen.'

She didn't look at her. She looked only at the piano, at the keys, the reflections in the polished wood.

'It's nothing to do with you.'

'I know how it is, believe me.'

'How can you know?'

'I was your age when I met your father.'

'It's to do with me, him. Not you.'

Safta imagined all the sound in the piano crashing about the space. But the room was silent, the garden soft beyond the long windows. She closed the keyboard, stood, walked a few steps, then began to run. She pulled open the doors and ran out of them, and those of the next room and ran through that, and the doors were left swinging and when she got a long way off she screamed.

Marina Văleanu went to her study. She lit the candle before the icon, knelt before it. Even by daylight the flame made the rest of the room seem to fall away. She could not at first find words for prayer. She felt for her daughter far more than she had shown. She saw herself there, her own look, her eyes, her vividness which was also a vulnerability. The perception struck her like a pain. Then she felt the influence of the holy image and her thoughts began to draw together, like lines focused through a lens. She is really very young. Younger even than I was.

When letters arrived it was the custom for them to be brought to the mistress's study before they went elsewhere. If any came for Safta from France in the weeks that followed she removed them and put them away in a drawer. She would neither destroy them nor read them. She would allow her daughter that.

When Augustin recovered and went back to work at the stables he noticed immediately how empty the place had become. For him this was just something that happened, like the weather. It did not require cause or explanation. People came to the house. People left. Sometimes they touched one another. He had begun to make a new kind of figure, that was not one flat figure alone but two profiles conjoined, single eye to single eye, nose to nose, mouths fused in a kiss. He was shy of these figures and did not stand them up on the windowsill where the other figures went but kept them put away. That was the only difference in him. Each day he got up as usual and went to the stables to take the horses out. They snorted and shook their heads as they came out from the stalls into the yard and he stroked their necks. The flies gathered at the moist edges of their eyes. One moment followed another. Life was only an indefinitely continuing series of separated events.

The emptiness deepened with the passage of time. He made drawings of hollow rooms. He drew all the rooms that he remembered inside the house, which he did not enter any more, stripped of all their things, all the pictures and curtains and furniture, with only the positions of stoves and doors and the number of windows to distinguish them one from another.

Safta went away for a period and then she came back. She looked hollow to him like the house. It was November, a bleak grey autumn. She rose early in the mornings to ride and each day he saddled the horse for her. The leaves and the colour had almost gone from the land, and she came each morning when it was barely light and took the horse and rode for a long time alone. There was mist most of those mornings. She disappeared into the mist quickly and there was no telling in which direction she went. Some days the mist had cleared by the time she returned. On others the mist held and when she rode back into the yard it was as if she had been nowhere, only he would know that she had ridden hard by the sweat beneath the horse's rug when he took it off.

When she left again there was nothing to distinguish that particular departure from any other. She might have been going only for a week or two. She might have reappeared any day but she never did.

Iaşi

In city clothes he is alien to himself. He stands like a man in a nineteenth-century photograph who has been told to be still while some mysterious event takes place, staring into the incomprehensible apparatus that is the camera.

As Adriana has brought him the various pieces of clothing he has tried them for fit but he has never worn the full rig before. Jacket, trousers, braces, shirt, even a tie. No shoes yet. He stands in socks for now with his second-hand military boots on the floor beside him. The boots have been transformed. Two days ago when she brought the shirt, Adriana brought him polish for them. She was amazed at how he went to work, brushing and spitting and rubbing. Like a proper bootblack, she said, thinking, there's a job that he might do, not knowing about all the saddles and harnesses that he has polished in the past.

He puts out his two hands to regard them, sticking out from the cuffs of shirt and jacket. He scrutinises first the backs of them and then the palms, and his arm swivels within the rigidity of the jacket sleeve. He passes his fingers down the lapels, across the buttons, along the edges of the pockets. He moves his neck this way and that against the collar of a shirt that is, despite Adriana's effort to find the right size, a little too big for him. He looks to the two women who have spent so much time persuading him into these things, doing up his buttons, pushing him this way and that.

'You look fine, very fine!' Adriana straightens his collar. She passes her fingers through his hair which was cut this morning by the barber in the yard.

His neck is bare where the hair has been cut from it and pathetically thin. When Safta looks at him she thinks of some fledgling bird caught on the ground, holding still only because it cannot fly, panic within it. Do the clothes scare him because they mean he's going outside? Nothing she can do but move gently as she would with a bird. No way to explain how much better it is that he leaves now, as soon as he is physically able, before the authorities take notice.

He puts on his boots with fumbling fingers. Takes his packet of things – pictures, magazines, kaleidoscope as well as his worn pyjamas, wrapped up in paper and tied with string – and clutches it to his chest.

Her hands softly tell him, it's all right, we're coming with you.

They leave by the main entrance. He is not conspicuous because the street is busy and there are others shambling and preoccupied like himself.

*   *   *

138

Adriana has just one room in an old villa but it is on the first floor and the proportions are generous. The door is wide and the ceiling is high. The room is big enough to be divided into two with a screen that gives a tolerable amount of privacy: a separate narrow space for him with a window looking out at the back, her bed in a corner of the main area. There is even a balcony with a heavy iron railing where they might sit out if it were not so crammed with plants.

For one person alone it is a palace. But that was because she lied and said that her son was living with her – though it wasn't quite a lie, she told herself when she filled out the form, it was only a question of time; and meanwhile there is room for this young man who must be the same age as her son and to whom she has lent his name. For now she will let the neighbours think that is who he is. It will be easiest that way. The few of them who have entered the room may have seen Ioan's picture where it hangs on the wall: a photograph taken before he went to the war, standing straight in his new uniform with his rifle held at ease to the ground. The image is not sharp. The uniform shows up more clearly than the man. It would not stretch the imagination too far to believe that this is the soldier returned. His face – all of him – is much thinner, certainly, but that is true of so many when they return. Sometimes after they have been years in Russia their families even do not recognise them.

It is normally twenty minutes' walk from the hospital, but far longer the way they choose to go. They could take a tram but they sense that he is not yet ready for trams. Better to walk. The street is so crowded that even that becomes an ordeal for him, his nervousness visible in his eyes, in his fingers clutching the packet, and in the erratic way he moves, shuffling forward, stopping, side-stepping passers-by. As soon as they can they turn off into side streets and there his pace slows and he drops behind, walking evenly but close to the walls. They go uphill a long way. In many places they pass scars from the fighting. Where they come to a place that was bombed, where there is no house but a great hole in the ground, he stalls.

Safta goes back, takes his arm and walks him on.

The villa is high on the hill in an old bourgeois district. It is a pleasant late-nineteenth-century building of muddied yellow ochre with a tin-roofed turret to one side. There is an ornate porch with stone pillars, double doors with stained-glass lights above them, a dim vestibule, stairs to her landing. He clutches his packet close to his chest and reaches out his other hand to touch the carved pillars, the door, the railing of the staircase. The villa conveys a sense of the past, history and home, even if he has never been there before. Of lives lived privately, interior space. These are things that he has not known in a long time. In the room they come to there is the smell of old furnishings well kept. There is light falling through windows on two sides, a green garden light though they are on the first floor because of the plants on the balcony and because of the trees beyond the other window beneath which his bed is placed. He touches the soft red fabric with which the bed is covered, looks out of the window where the bulbous copper roof of a church belfry shows between the trees.

'It's a fine room.' It is the best place Safta has seen since she came to Iaşi.

'I was lucky.' Adriana shuts the door behind them. 'They gave me this place because my house was bombed.' When she first got here she knew that she was lucky just to have a door, let alone the space beyond it.

In the reallocation of properties that followed the Communist takeover, the first floor of this villa, like the floors above and below, was roughly divided into three separate habitations. One was allocated to Adriana and her son. The room beside it, which is the biggest, was given to a refugee family from Bessarabia. The third room was retained by the Milescus, the elderly couple who had until then owned the entire house. Adriana has not been inside the other rooms but she has been into this one, soon after she first came there. It is an awkward room, long and narrow and running into the rounded turret space, and yet Irina Milescu said that it was her favourite. It was the room in which her daughters had slept. It had seemed spacious in those days, with just the two beds and an armoire and the curved space open at the end. Now it is crowded like a bric-a-brac shop with everything that was of greatest actual or sentimental value that the family had owned: armoires and chairs pushed one against the other; a chaise longue covered in burgundy damask; an inlaid oval table; an upright piano; lace-edged cloths on top of every polished surface, barely visible beneath the clutter of Viennese china and Hungarian jugs, lamps and candlesticks and stacks of books and photographs; and on the walls pictures stuck side by side like stamps in an album. Irina and her husband Liviu sleep in a heavy wooden bed at one end of the room and at the other they carry on a vestige of the old life. They see friends from that time and the samovar is put to boil and there are card parties at the round table in the turret.

A few pieces of their furniture still occupy the other rooms though now and again Irina diffidently takes something back that she can sell. Not from the Bessarabians – the sort of people they are, she says to her husband, so rough and rowdy, she simply wouldn't have the nerve – but from Adriana or the other tenants. There had been a large gilt mirror above the chest of drawers in Adriana's room. Irina had not known when she asked for it that Adriana would be pleased to see it go. Adriana had barely ever seen herself in a mirror of such a size before and had found it disconcerting to live alone that way with her own reflection, catching herself at all angles and unprepared: a fat old woman like a stranger passing by in her own room.

'Take it away,' she said. 'I'll be less lonely without it.'

The two women removed it from the wall, gingerly, wondering if it would have been better to have called a man to help, and rested it on the floor.

'But your son's coming. You won't be alone then.'

'Yes,' Adriana had said. Her son would be coming soon.

Irina looked at the photograph that hung on the wall beside the pale space where the mirror had been. 'He looks a fine boy.'

'Ah, but that was some years ago. He's had a hard time of it since then.'

Irina behind the wall hears Safta go and then after what seems a polite interval she knocks at the apartment. She has a cake to welcome the young man. It is the sort of act of neighbourliness that would have been commonplace in the old days but in these changed times it seems an eccentric act. As she has no oven she had had her husband buy the cake at the patisserie by the Piaţa Unirii, and she is glad to see that it is a good one, fresher than usual. He eats greedily and takes a second piece, eats every crumb that falls on to his plate.

What an odd young man he is, she tells Liviu later.

'My dear, he just sat on the bed beneath the window with the plate on his knees and ate the cake and stared. He's little and thin as a rake, not like his mother at all, with these eyes that seem to see through you. He didn't speak a word all the time I was there.'

He might have been shell-shocked, says Liviu, who fought in the first war and saw the horrors of Mărăşeşti. He remembers how it took some men, how he heard about some of them years afterwards, how they never recovered. Something had died inside them even though their bodies survived. Or then again, it might have been his experiences after. What those Russians did to him.

Liviu and Irina's children are both girls. At one time this was a disappointment to them, that there was no son, but when the war came they were thankful. Daughters did not have to fight in Russia. Whatever has happened to them since, that they were spared at least.

The first day he spends there Augustin does nothing but look about him. He gets dressed into his shirt and trousers, and then he sits motionless on the bed taking things in. He turns to rest his elbows on the windowsill and look outside. The long leaves of the chestnut tree before the window waver in the wind, otherwise everything is enormously still. Where the leaves thin out he can see the belfry, and pieces of the city down the hillside; roofs, other churches and treetops. He walks about the room. There is not much in it. Adriana had no more than a case with her when she came, which is put away now above the wardrobe, and the furniture is only what the Milescus have left her. He looks at the pale rectangle of wallpaper where the mirror had hung. On the chest of drawers beneath, propped against the wall, are a few cheap printed icons like postcards of saints. He examines each one and knows that he has seen some of the faces before. Then there is Ioan's photograph hanging on the wall. A soldier like many others but this one he does not know. He takes this photograph down and stares at it for a long time before he puts it back. Then he returns to his position on the bed. When Adriana gets home from the hospital there is no sign that anything has happened in the room since the moment she left that morning. Not a thing appears to have been changed or moved except that the lunch she had put out for him is gone and the plate also, cleaned and put away.

The second day he opens his packet of papers and magazines. For hours he occupies himself with unfolding, refolding, sorting its contents: pictures of things or people here, cut-out words there, card and blank pages somewhere else. Adriana comes back from work to see the evidence of systematic activity in the neat piles in the corner beside his bed. Good, she thinks, he is settling in. And he has rooted about and helped himself to whatever things he wants: scissors, needles, string, thread. In the days that follow she slowly gets the sense that every drawer and cupboard in the room has been gone through minutely in her absence, that each one of her few things has been moved, just so far, and put back infinitesimally out of place. It makes her a little uneasy to realise that in his wordlessness there will be no boundaries to her privacy. If he does not hear, he will see and remember more than any hearing man.

The one thing he lacks for his purpose is glue. He mimes to her what he needs. She gives him flour and water from which to mix a paste, sees that he knows already how to do it.

He begins by making a figure. He makes it the way he has always made figures, from a simple rectangle of card. This first figure he makes in Adriana's room is a soldier. He cuts out the shape from the soft grey cover of an old notebook, draws on to it a square head with a cap, buttons and boots. He adds a rifle that is actually a long splinter of wood. Because his figure has no arms the rifle cannot be held out to the side as in the photograph of Adriana's son but instead it must be stuck down the centre dividing the figure in half.

When the glue is set he stands the figure on the chest of drawers beside the icons.

Adriana doesn't know what to make of it. It is like a drawing made by a child except that it has no face. And is it meant to refer to her son? The young man sits mutely on his bed, arms crossed, regarding her. The soldier seems like a third presence in the room.

The next figure he makes is a more willowy shape. She is sure he means it to depict Irina Milescu. It is dressed in a piece of mint-coloured tissue that is just the colour of the silk dress Irina wore that time she came to meet him. And on its head he has frayed and massed pieces of red wool. This one makes her laugh.

He sees pieces of Irina through the open door, that hair of unreal auburn, her dainty shoes, the fabric of some floating dress. Adriana's bulk blocks the rest of her from view.

'Domnul – Citizen – Milescu and I don't need so much, the age we've got to. I thought you might give this to your boy.' And there is cake again or some small piece of meat left over from their ration.

One day she comes with a pan of soup, steaming hot so that Adriana has to let her in.

'There's oxtail in it. You'll have to feed him up. Get him back to what he was.'

Her eyes take in the room: the photograph on the wall, the childish figures propped up beneath it, the young man who made them sitting at the table among his pieces of paper. They have to push the papers aside to put the soup down.

'We're always here, you know. If we can do anything to help, when you're at work or if you go out sometime.'

'That's very good of you but I'm fine. Ioan's fine. He can look after himself, really he can.'

'If you have second thoughts. In an emergency . . .' Irina hovers. She has put down the soup but finds it hard to leave, still looking about her.

After she has gone Adriana takes down the photograph that bears so little resemblance to him and puts it away in a drawer. She sees the mint-coloured figure and is uneasy. Everyone in the house until now has been careful to keep to themselves.

On the Saturday Safta comes to visit and Adriana shows her the figures. They are familiar as pieces of her past, and yet she had forgotten quite how they were made.

'That one's Doamna Milescu, see, and this is my son. Do you think the others are real people too? Do you think all of them could be people he knows?'

The three of them have lunch together in the room and then Adriana goes to the cinema and Safta goes out with Tinu for a walk in the park. This will become their custom in the weeks that follow, the two women sharing his care.

They enter the park beneath a massive new statue of a Soviet soldier, a towering hero of rough-hewn stone. Each time they go he will stop to admire the statue, and each time Safta will pull him on.

Where Safta lives she is never alone. She has only a bed in a hostel roughly converted from some institutional building by the hospital. A distant ceiling, grey wasted space above, bunks packed tight on the floor, open slots between them where twenty women's privacies are exposed. It must be like that for many who inhabit this city. When they come to walk in the park they are more free, more alone, than anywhere else in their lives.

The park is full of trees. Bare ground beneath them for children to play, straight *allées* cut through for people to stroll. In June even the shade is green. They walk in step, the thin shambling man and the lively nurse. She talks and he looks ahead of him and his hands hang emptily at his sides. They pass the fountain, pass a clear space where some children are knocking a ball about. The ball lands at his feet and he runs with it and kicks it back askew, looking awkward as a puppet. The children are quick to see the oddity in him. They mimic him and flap their arms about and laugh.

She takes him on right to the end of the gardens where there are fewer people. There is a bench there that is set apart with a view out to the long blue hills beyond the city. They will come to this bench every week.

'Thank God you can see out of this city. It makes such a difference, that a city should have hills about it. You know there's somewhere else, beyond. Perhaps I wouldn't think that if I'd grown up in the city, but I didn't. I lived in Bucharest for some years, at the beginning of the war and after it. There were parks, big parks, and there were trees and flowers, but there was never a sight of hills. It was as if there was only the city and the city ran on and on and there was nothing outside it, and when it was hot in the summer – so hot and heavy and stifling it becomes there – the sense of the city pressed in and there did not seem to be any possibility of escape. Here there is always the knowledge of the hills and the forest. Perhaps one of these days I shall come for you early in the morning and we shall go to the forest. Remember how we used to go to the forest at Poiana? How well we knew it, all the paths and the hidden pools, and the places where you could climb to see out and spy on the village. You used to love it in the forest. We were secret there, just us, and you used to make signs for me, and words that I'd find written in leaves and twigs on the ground.'

She is looking ahead of herself but she doesn't see Iaşi any more. She can almost smell the dankness of the wood. It is good to go where her memories take her. A long way from the present. She does not notice the man who is approaching until he raises his hat and greets her. It is the old man she has seen on the stairs at Adriana's house. Perhaps it is because she has begun to think just now of Poiana that she thinks that he is like the sort of people she used to know, like the men who passed through the house when she was a child, who asked her name and patted her on the head and went on to see her grandfather and left a smell of cigar smoke behind them.

He has on an old mustard-coloured jacket, a straw hat with a black band. He introduces himself, kisses her hand. He knows her name. He says he knew her grandfather.

Is it possible then that he was one of the men who passed? He is very grey, his face lined, his moustache thin, his whole figure slight, diffident, forgettable. There would be nothing particular about him for her to remember.

She tells him how the family had left for England in '41 while they still could. That her brothers were there already and her mother went to join them, and Constantin went with her. He is surprised that she did not go as well.

'I was a nurse by then. I had a reason to stay. I chose to stay.'

'Ah.'

She has spoken with boldness and no sound of regret, yet regret seems to echo in the pause that follows. It is a disembodied regret that belongs neither to speaker nor listener but only to the bareness of the history about them. She does not say that she might have gone later when her father went. There were others who managed to get out after the war was over. But Liviu Milescu will know that. He will know also about those who did not leave and were arrested. So many friends, cousins, acquaintances; people like themselves. And yet neither he nor she was arrested. That is in the echo as well.

'And is your grandfather well, in England?'

'The last time I heard.'

'He probably won't remember me, but you must give him my regards . . .'

Liviu stands with his hat held in the same hand that holds his stick and they talk for a while more before he walks on. She has accepted an invitation to visit. The idea of it seems quaint, the whole encounter like something out of the past.

'They look a nice enough old couple to me. Adriana doesn't trust them but I suppose that's just because they live so close. He seems familiar, Augustin, as if I've met him before, though he says that couldn't have been possible. He never came to Poiana. There were always people like him, lawyers with thin smiles and neat moustaches, coming to see grandfather, going to and fro. I feel different when I'm with people like that. They think they know who I am but I'm not that person any more, I only seem that way. I feel like an imposter or something, someone pretending to be myself. Perhaps they'll invite me to one of their card parties now, imagine that. Should I go, do you think? He said how good it would be for them all to see a young face. They will have their friends there, the people we sometimes see going to visit them. The friends will be the same age as themselves, and they too will have known grandfather, or if they never knew him they will know of him, and they will want to meet me because I'm his granddaughter, as the person with my name that I used to be. Only I don't have the clothes to wear. No pretty things any more, nothing for a party. And Irina has so many dresses. No, I'd better not go. Really I'd be a disappointment to them, wouldn't I?

'Or maybe she'd lend me one of hers, one of those pale flimsy numbers. How funny that would be.'

All the time she has been speaking she has been looking out over the trees. The distance is unusually clear this afternoon. The separate lines of the hills can be made out, one beyond another, and they are dark with forest. As she laughs she turns to him. He always sits the same way when people are about. He has sat like that all the years that she has known him. He sits upright, to attention, like a dog with pricked ears, but perhaps this is a way not just of hearing better but of sharpening all the senses, of smelling, watching, feeling vibration. He is watching her. His back is straight and his long hands are laid flat on to his knees.

'He asked about you. How deaf you were. I said, profoundly. He said he didn't know they took deaf mutes in the army. I said I thought it was the result of an injury. I don't like to lie to them, but what does it matter? What does it matter who a person is or who they have been? Let them think what they like. We're all so many people, aren't we, nowadays? So confusing it is, I don't know how anyone keeps track. There are the people we are inside, then the people we used to be, then there are the people other people think we are. You, for example. You're at least three people that I know of: Augustin from Poiana, Ioan we gave a name to in the hospital, Ioan Adriana's son come back dumb from the war.'

He watches her face with such meticulous attention that anyone who passed would think that what she was saying was of great importance and that the man beside her on the bench was listening to every word.

'Do you think they believe it, Adriana's story? Do you think it matters if they believe it or not? It's not so implausible, you know. I saw some like that, when I was in Ukraine. There were all the obvious wounded, the bloody ones, shot up and screaming, and then there were the ones who looked all right until you went to speak to them and looked into their eyes. They didn't speak back. They didn't even seem to see you. It was as if the outside world didn't exist for them any more – or what was inside them was so much stronger and more vivid and horrific that every-thing else had just paled away. Sometimes they were only shocked or deafened and they'd come out of it after a few days or weeks. I don't know about the others. I don't know what happened to them, how they came back.'

He looks at all the pieces of her, her eyes, the arch of her eyebrows, the fluid lips, the ear that is revealed when she pushes back her hair, her moving hand, the movement in her face. Every feature remains as it was and yet she changes all the time. There are moments when the Safta he used to know flickers before him and then she goes away. Not for a moment is she fixed. He raises one of his hands and holds the palm of it flat before her mouth. He is asking her to stop talking. He wishes that she would be still.

She does not speak again until they start walking home. 'You're right. There's no reason to speak. Speaking gets us nowhere. All these people here must have words inside their heads. Swarms of words. Words they mean and words they don't mean and words whose meaning they don't know. The park's crowded now, so much fuller than it was when we came, families and children and girls out walking together and lovers and elderly couples, full of people and unspoken words. The things we could tell each other. I could tell them things that would make them cry. And how about them? There's that man without a leg. I saw him when we came in, sitting on the ground with his back to the railing and his crutch beside him, his one leg sticking out and the stump beside it with the trouser pinned up. He's come over this way now. What could he tell us? Look, he's standing there ranting at the trees, shouting at the top of his voice. His words fly up into the leaves and people stroll by and pretend not to see him or hear him. What's he saying? Best not to know. They used to rant a lot, the soldiers when they were wounded. It was the pain, the morphine, the fear. Some of them cried for their mothers. That was all right, you could feel sorry for them then, cry a little too. But there were others who were full of hate. They spoke of killing, of wanting to kill. You had to close your ears to care for them. But you did hear it and what you heard you never forgot. I know, that was the war, and it's not the war any more and nobody's fighting now but there are casualties everywhere, here in the park. It's just that you can't see the injuries any more. You can't see but they're there. The wounded, the shell-shocked, the amputees missing pieces of themselves.'

No one comes to ask who he is or take him away. He might as well be Adriana's son after all.

'Do you think that he can do a job?'

'How do we find him one, without papers?'

'How do we find him papers?'

There is still no word from Poiana.

The figures he makes are becoming ever more ingenious. Adriana knows now what sort of materials he likes to use and brings things home for him. He likes to build the figures up in layers. He sticks card to card, wraps paper around it. If it is soft card he is working with, the glue-paste makes the surfaces melt one into the other. He knows how much paste to apply to get the texture that he wants. Then he lets the body dry, and when it is dry he might dress it. He will take a piece of brown envelope as an overcoat, wrapping it around, putting the flap diagonally across the chest as the opening and bending the edges back as lapels, using a separate strip as a belt. Or he will use a piece of cloth or newspaper, or a coloured page from a magazine, or make a blue-and-white check on a piece of plain paper and stick that beneath as a shirt.

Adriana finds them comical, alive. She begins to call them his friends. There seem to be so few flesh-and-blood friends about these days.

Things begin to accumulate in his corner: the papers and scraps, drawings and materials that he might draw on, objects that have caught his eye, more matchboxes to add to the collection that he began at the hospital. All of these things are neatly sorted and stacked, some of the stacks tied with string, so that she thinks that his end of the room is beginning to resemble the back of a shop or the corner of a post office. Her own possessions in her part of the room are few. She does not acquire anything any more for herself. She lives in this place as if it is no more than a temporary measure: as if she is here only for a time, until things change and her real son comes home, and this room and this silent young man are only temporary and nothing really to do with her, but hers only by chance, for the time being. Nothing is hers but the plants on the balcony that she tends with such care. But all she has done is put in the seeds and water them. Plants are things that grow of themselves.

There was a period just after her house was destroyed when she had almost nothing and stopped nowhere at all but kept constantly on the move. She had a few things in a case that she carried with her and she slept now in one place, now in another. She had watched the battle from the forest. The civilians who had not been evacuated had fled to the forest, though the forest itself was also a scene of fighting. They saw bombardment, fires, shelling. For as long as the battle went on the city was lost in smoke and dust. And when the battle was over the dust did not settle. The late summer was dry, and every wind and movement stirred it. The civilians went back down. There were sweet and rotten smells in the rubble and sights that made her retch, so that the dust that swept over them seemed almost a mercy. She tied her headscarf about her mouth and picked through the half-ruin of her home. A whole wall was gone from it but many things were preserved in the places where they had always been, not indoors now but out in the dust-clogged open air. Beneath the bed quite undamaged was the brown suitcase which was the only suitcase the family had ever owned. Into this she put whatever first came to hand: pieces of clothing, cutlery, photographs. In those early days this was all she had. Then some time later she went back with a handcart she had borrowed and loaded it with more. She took her own clothes and her husband's and Ioan's too, and though she shook them and went to the river and washed them the dust and the war smell hung about for many months, so much so that she came to wonder if it was her mind that was impregnated and not the cloth. She washed the clothes again, smoothed her palms over them when they were folded. If laundering was all the action she could take, then she would take it. As for the rest, she lit her candles in the church and left it all to God or fate.

After a time her husband came back from the army and found her but she lit the candles again in the church as if he had never appeared. He was changed. He had no words for her nor she for him. He was not the answer to any prayer. There was no place for them to live at first but only a makeshift shelter. He seemed to blame her for this and he drank. There had always been times when he drank but now he seemed shut away in his drinking. Sometimes he came to her for impersonal sex and now and then he hit her. She could not recall at what point, whether it was cause or result of this, she no longer felt any connection to him. There was no anger in her, or love or hatred, but only disconnection. It seemed an oddity that they had once shared a son. And he would not hear her speak of Ioan. He said that he knew how it had been in Russia and that it was a waste of time to wait for him or to pretend that they were a family any more. Then he took a job with the railways. He was rebuilding lines and so he went where the lines went and worked there and lived where he worked. When the room in this house came through, she moved her clothes into it in the brown suitcase, and she moved Ioan's, but she did not take the few of her husband's clothes that he had left behind. She did not think long about the decision but merely acted as the moment prompted.

When the mute came to the hospital, all that too just came about. He needed a name so she gave him one. She had clothes so she dressed him. She had space so she took him in. She was a middle-aged woman living on her own with a few bundles of possessions and there was room in her still to be a mother. Simply having him around has filled a part of that void. When she comes in he is there like a child home from school, waiting to show her the drawings of the day. She has pinned these up as she would those of a child, on the wall at the head of his bed.

'Well done,' she says at each she sees. 'That's good, very good.'

She does not know how much effort it took him to begin his drawing. How long he had sat poised before the first scrap of paper, seated before the table with his back to the balcony and the sunlight, doing nothing morning after morning, until he put down the pencil and took up his scissors and found it easier to cut than to draw. How he would go back the next morning and lay out another piece of waste paper at first he took only waste paper, never the clean white pages they had given him – some piece of brown paper or wrapping or a torn envelope, smoothing it where it was crumpled, taking up the sharpened pencil again, fighting what had become a deep and habitual resistance against making his mark, breaking through the shells of himself until at last they cracked, one through to another, lightly as eggshells, and how he then began, tentatively at first as if drawing on eggshell, the shadow of his hand moving on the paper beside the lines as he made them.

The first drawing was tiny, made on a scrap of brown paper no bigger than a cigarette packet. On it he drew his bed in the corner against the window, the rectangle of the window and the panes across it, then the details, the lines of floorboards, the floral wisps of Irina's once-fashionable wallpaper, his pillow on the bed. Though they had given him colours he made the picture entirely in pencil, shading it until the floor was glossy and the pencil was worn down and his fingers were blackened with graphite. When the picture was done to his satisfaction, shaded dark, so small that it fitted into the palm of his hand, he folded it down to the size of a postage stamp and put it aside, then he began on a different corner of the room, until he had all four corners of the room folded together in his pocket. This miniature representation of his refuge he kept to himself like an amulet for safety. Only then did he begin again, on larger scraps but still not touching the sketchbook, and these he allowed himself to show her.

The subjects in them are once more the pieces of the room: his own bed, her bed and the doors open to the balcony, the table at which they eat, a chair pushed flat to the wall. They are repeated and sometimes they are coloured, and sometimes the wallpaper designs develop and change themselves into other shapes. They seem to her like a child's pictures at first, but they are far cleverer drawings than a child would make. He has done one on a folded strip of paper which opens to reveal the room and its reverse

162

like its own reflection, like sky and trees looking down on themselves in a lake. It is so perfect that it seems to her like a kind of conjuring.

'See this.'

She shows his pictures to Safta when she comes. She is proud like a young mother expecting a visitor to express amazement at every simple standard step in her child's progress. There is the reversing image, and another picture that was made at night, when she was on a night duty at the hospital, of the room and the long window before the balcony, and the rest of the room perfectly reflected in the window. Whenever she is at work, she says, he is doing these drawings. Every time she comes back there are more drawings.

'He's doing drawings now.' Safta is careful to say 'now', not 'again', though that is the word that comes to her lips. She is so happy to see him drawing again.

'You always thought he might be able to draw, even in the hospital when he first came.'

'I did, didn't I?'

There is a series of patterns he has made, the first in pencil and then others in colour. The patterns, like the reversing rooms, are made from folds and reflections, a pattern and its mirror image contained within a lozenge shape and the same lozenge repeated four or six or eight or twelve times in a circle, fanning out from the centre like the petals of a flower.

'I looked at them a while and thought they were like something but could not think what it was. And then I understood. Do you see what they are?'

163

'They're kaleidoscope pictures.' Safta sees it quick as a flash.

'Why then, have you seen such things before?'

Then there is a little book that he has made and stitched that is full of words. Some of the words are no more than jumbled letters and others are words taken whole and at random and copied from print: the title *Scânteia* as it appears on the newspaper masthead, the long word *internaţionale* spread across two pages, *chibrituri*, which is a favourite word as it printed on all the matchboxes.

'Does he draw anything else?'

'Only this room. Only what is before him, here, now. Or sometimes, if he has been out, the street, a shop or something, and he does it as accurately as if it is still before his eyes.'

He goes in and out as they talk about him, carrying water for the plants on the balcony. He crosses the space between the two women as if they were not there. His deafness gives him this ability, that when some task occupies him it holds his attention completely so that for its duration the rest of the world ceases to exist. So he brings up buckets from the tap downstairs and crosses the room with them as if he were in an empty yard. It is a job that he performs daily, and it is a measure of his increasing strength that he can carry the buckets full now, so full sometimes that the water slops if he walks too fast and Adriana must correct him. When he first began he was exhausted after a single trip with half the quantity of water.

'I thought there might be something he could tell us.

That he might draw where he has been, so that we could know what has happened to him.'

'Perhaps he doesn't think about it.'

'Of course he thinks. Everybody thinks, don't they? How could he be different?'

'He draws only real things.'

'He could remember real things.'

'Perhaps it hurts to remember.'

She tells Safta about the nights. She would think he was getting much better if it were not for the nights. He goes to sleep but wakes in the small hours. She knows this because she does not sleep so much herself nowadays. She hears him thrashing around and whimpering in his sleep, and then the thrashing stops and there is an intensity in the air in the room as if he is sharply awake. She can feel his thinking reaching out there in the blackness like ripples passing through water, as if the two of them are held in a black tank of water. Once he is awake the movements in his bed become more deliberate, and then cease altogether. She can imagine that he has arranged and straightened himself beneath the bedding and is lying on his back, eyes open, staring at the ceiling, only the ceiling is unseen and there are other, unimaginable, images passing through him. She herself goes to sleep again, deep under the water; often she sleeps her deepest, most reviving sleep between five and six in the morning when the blackest time of the night is over. She does not know if he also manages to sleep then.

In the mornings he is very pale. Only gradually, as the day progresses, does he pick up colour. When she is home in the daytime she sometimes finds him napping, curled on his side on the bed beneath the window, even in the middle of the day when the sunlight falls bright across him and she must reach over and draw the curtain above his head.

Safta will take him to the park this Saturday as every other.

'I think he likes it there more than anywhere,' she says. 'He likes the trees and all the green. There's nothing else in this city that he would like.'

'If they showed the sort of films they used to show, he could come with me to the cinema. I do miss those films we used to see. Gary Cooper, Marlene Dietrich. Fred Astaire and Ginger Rogers. *Roberta*, *Top Hat*, *Flying Down to Rio*. He'd love all the dancing. Or those musicals where the dancers make patterns like kaleidoscopes. Do you remember? No, I suppose you're too young. You weren't here in Iaşi then, you didn't know the old Trianon as it used to be.'

In the park Safta takes out a book to read. She will read it here and not at the nurses' hostel because the book is in French. To be seen reading French would set her apart. Even here she takes care to keep the cover flat on her knees.

This morning she went to visit the Milescus. They gave her coffee – no more than what goes for coffee nowadays, but the cups were fine and patterned with roses. She drank the coffee and made polite conversation in the cramped gentility of their room. They had pictures of their daughters in silver frames. Pretty girls; the pictures taken when they were about the age she was now, she thought, though by the look of them that must have been some years ago. She complimented Irina Milescu on her girls. They look like their mother, she said, and realised as she spoke what had not occurred to her before: that the faded Irina with her too-red hair must once have been quite a beauty. Irina picked up the photographs and handed them to Safta so that she might look at them more closely. The photographs were taken at a studio in Bucharest, softly lit so that the faces glowed. Nadia and Danuta, fashionable girls of the early '40s with restrained smiles and delicate features, long-necked, elegantly coiffed and made up. The likeness in them so clear that she asked if they were twins. Not twins, their mother said, but so close. Only a year apart. Irina took the pictures back and seemed not to notice how she clasped them to her as she talked. They had been such clever girls, she said, both of them, and so close in age. They had gone to Bucharest together. Such good jobs they had had. Such modern girls. Such a future there might have been for them. If only. Her shrug was eloquent.

'You know where they are at least?'

'Oh yes,' said Liviu. 'They get the parcels we send them.'

Irina put the photos down. 'They should have become nurses like you did.'

'That wasn't why I became a nurse.'

'You were lucky then.'

Safta looked for another subject that had fewer dangers attached. She asked about the books. There were many books in the room, a bookcase along one wall, further stacks piled up beneath the windows. There were historical works and there were novels, in French and German as well as Romanian. Liviu's books, she thought, not Irina's, and their daughters'. Borrow one, Liviu said. She chose something in French because she had not used her French in such a long time. She has never read *Madame Bovary* though she has always meant to. The book has Danuta's name on the flyleaf. She's written in the margins so she must have studied it.

* * *

She cannot concentrate, trying to read it here in the park. It is so very foreign. Not only the language. She has little difficulty with the language. That comes back to her easily. The problem is with the book, all that it is concerned with. The words flow on and she understands their meaning but they are foreign to her all the same.

In '47 when it was still just possible she had gone to apply for an exit visa. At the last minute she turned away. She looked down the street where she was, some long stone street in Bucharest, and saw the ordinariness of the crowd and saw that she was one of them. Shabby and beaten like them but this was where she belonged. Her purpose here, speaking this language. And there was someone at that time who she thought might love her, who she thought she might love. Here, not there. But the purpose vanished. They were all of them disempowered, powerless even to give meaning to themselves.

She looks up to the forested horizon beyond the city. A vague horizon, its colour neither green nor purple, its distance unknown, only she knows that there are further horizons beyond it.

'What do you think, Tinu? Is it really so different over there?'

Augustin sits beside her on the bench doing a drawing.

'Do you know that there are other places beside this one, existing now? I suppose you must. That there are other lives, all going on at the same time.'

He is using a sketchbook he has made for himself by stitching loose sheets of paper together and wrapping them about with a piece of canvas. He prefers this home-made pad to the one she bought him in the shop. His pencil presses on to the paper. His fingertips are stained with graphite.

He seems unmoving, fixed always in the present moment. And yet his drawings begin to move outside it.

She watches a picture form. *Madame Bovary* lies open on her lap but her eyes are on his picture. Only someone who knows his work already would understand that he is drawing figures. Figures on a road: black rectangles one beside the other like a row of ill-fitting teeth. But the landscape behind them is realistic, and also what are clearly carts beside them on the road. Some of the carts are pulled by horses, some by oxen, big boxy beasts with crescent horns. The loads on the carts are like hedgehogs, stuck about with things. He draws the outlines first and then goes back and puts in the detail and the things become recognisable as chair legs, bed frames, chickens, pigs. Is it for himself he is making this picture or is it a story that he is telling?

He draws the rectangles, the road, the carts. With the side of his pencil he makes the smooth grey line of the hill down which they have come. Far away on top of this he outlines small sharp black shapes that may be more people and carts. Then that picture is full and he turns the page and begins another. It would appear that this second picture is not improvised as the one before. There is a sense of composition in the positioning of all the elements – the horizon, the big carts in the foreground, the road – as if he has the entire picture in mind from the start. There is space in the centre of this picture where there was not in the last one for a bridge, raised a little out of the perspective so that all of its piers and spans are clearly visible. Beneath the bridge, a river. At this stage the picture is an accurate representation of a recognisable place; but he goes on drawing. Some whim intervenes.

He draws a cloud above the horizon and fills it with a pattern of crosses. He puts herringbone patterning on the side of a wagon, stripes on trees, diamond shapes on the grass. The picture crowds and the sense of representation fades, and then again he turns the page.

That was the way he was first to know the war, by the convoys coming down the road to the river crossing. There were to be more convoys later: armies going back the way these carts had come, armies returning, people too; so many processions.

This first one carried furniture. So did the last one, that was the Russians going home. It was more crazy, that one, richer things in it, grandfather clocks on the wagons and mirrors wrapped in velvet curtains and enormous old trumpet phonographs and landscapes in gilded frames – but it did not make such an impression on him. By that time he had become accustomed to seeing strange things.

He had sensed long before the war began that they were waiting for something to happen. He could feel it in the emptiness of the place, as if space had been cleared, people gone to prepare, before some unknown event. It was there in the deliberateness of what people did. A number of the men left, some straight away like the men from the house, others in the months that followed. When he went to the market with Paraschiva there weren't so many men in the town now either, or there were men but they were soldiers, idle soldiers but soldiers none the less, in the bars and on the streets, watching whatever was or wasn't going on.

Once or twice men in uniform came to the house. After they had gone the second time some rooms in the house were shuttered up. But the days went on, the whole winter passed, and spring came and went without change.

It was not until the summer that anything unusual occurred. Some strangers came down the drive one day asking for things. These were not Gypsies or peasants but people who were dressed in the same style as the people in the big house only they had mud on their clothes and dirty shoes. Marina Văleanu came to the door and gave them food to eat, and then he helped the women to load a cart with bedding and more food, and drove it out to a crossroads beyond the village where they met a great line of wagons coming all the way from the horizon.

He saw when he got to the wagons that they were piled high as haycarts with the contents of houses. Some were roughly loaded, bristling with chairs and tables and boxes. Others had tidy loads tied down with tarpaulin but he could tell by the lowered heads of the horses that pulled them that whatever was on them was much heavier than hay. He had never seen such traffic before so he got down and walked for a long way with the wagons coming towards him, wondering when he would reach the end. He looked into the faces of the people who walked beside the horses and drove the wagons. There were men and women and children. He went close and looked into their faces but they seemed too tired to look back at him. Not even the children smiled. He found that strange because it was a lovely summer's day and the fields were full of flowers and the children should have been smiling. He walked across that valley and up the next hill and looked down into the wider valley beyond where the big river was. The land was very green and empty except for a shimmering grey band where the willows marked the course of the river. The line continued as far as he could see, crossing the river, broken only as it passed in and out of the cover of the willows, coming all the way out of the distance. He walked back to where he had left Mama Anica and József and Paraschiva, and they had emptied their cart of all that they had brought.

July brings a stifling spell of weather. The overcrowded city attempts to disappear into itself, shutters closed, blinds down, pedestrians slipping out of the sun on to the shaded sides of the streets. In houses where people are packed too close they come and go with heads down as if neighbours do not exist, and in the nights they hear each other quarrel through wide-open windows. It adds to the tension that in these conditions, with so many crowded together, such heat and so little hygiene, vermin proliferate: rats, lice, cockroaches, bedbugs. These they blame on the filthy habits of the bombed-out or the Gypsies or the Bessarabian refugees, whatever displaced family occupies the apartments beside or above or beneath their own. Now and then things get so bad that the city authorities evacuate a house for a number of days so that it can be sprayed, and then the housed are homeless once more and see sparse possessions destroyed in the attempt to control the infestation.

The bugs do not bother Augustin greatly. He knows only the specific. He sees that they are unpleasant and his experience tells him that they proliferate in bad places where bad things happen. But they can be borne. He has lived with them long enough in the past. He does not have such a horror of them as others do since he has no sense of contagion or epidemic, of the power of vermin to spread disease. For him there is a worse, direct effect of the summer, and that is the sultry air: the sheer weight and heat of it. There are mornings when he wakes and feels almost that he has been woken by the difficulty of breathing. There is pain in his lungs and he begins to cough again.

One day he falls on the stairs. He is carrying the water for the plants and he falls just before the first turn up from the hall. When he recovers from a moment of blackout Irina Milescu is beside him, helping him upright, making him sit on a step, pushing his throbbing head down between his knees. He has the impression of a great depth of stairs, the buckets still rolling at the foot of them, water cascading down from step to step.

Irina goes in the open door of her room and pours a glass of water from the jug she has there. Drink that, she says, that'll help. No sunlight reaches the stairs and yet they seem no cooler than the rooms. The water from the buckets has spilled right down and is spreading across the tiled floor of the hall. There is a kind of coolness in that at least. Stay, don't move until you're ready. Irina rests a hand on his shoulder to still him and goes in again to fetch a mop, starts on the step just beneath where he has fallen, working from the shade into the brightness, the band of colour that comes through the fanlight.

He watches as if from far away. She looks small and fragile down there below him, frail with her halo of hair and her pale mushroom-coloured dress. She is a moth fluttering in the coloured arc of light. When she comes back up the stairs she helps him to stand. She is out of breath, the frill at the neck of her dress slightly quivering. There is a powdery smell to her, powdery like a moth. She takes a lace handkerchief from her sleeve to dab her face and a stain of powder comes away.

'You'd better come in here where I can look after you.' She takes him through the open door into her room.

'You haven't been in here before, have you? It's silly, isn't it, when you've lived here for weeks – or perhaps it's months now, I lose track. Come on, sit here on the chaise longue, you can put your feet up. I'll bring you some tea. Or perhaps it's just water you need? I'll bring both then you can choose.'

She clears some sewing off the chaise longue. He sits at first but then she lifts up his feet and he lies on it, but stiffly like a figure on a tomb. She puts a small embroidered pillow behind his head.

'You'd better stay here for now, till Adriana gets in, and I don't know what time that'll be. I wouldn't like to think of you all on your own. In case you have another turn.'

She brings the tea and the water and puts them both on a small table within his reach, pulls her own chair alongside and takes up her sewing. His eyes watch her hands for a while and then they close and he falls asleep.

Irina has the urge to stroke his head which is glistening unhealthily with sweat. There, she would say, and pass a cool hand across his brow. She has a sense, just for a moment, of wholeness, that she has slipped into a moment from an earlier life, stitching beside a silent sickbed.

She is making an alteration to a dress. She used to do this for herself. She has always had a talent for sewing but she had never expected to find herself in circumstances where she tried to make a living from it. Now she puts up and takes down hems for others according to the fashion, and cuts things down and takes things in, and spruces up old garments with trimmings and frills to make them look new. It is an occupation and it brings in a few lei but it does not focus her mind, which seems always to be falling out of the present. Like now. Like the other day when she was stitching beads on to a cardigan. A friend had brought in a fine black cashmere cardigan and she was stitching it over with pearly beads – some idea there of evening wear, of nights out in a time and a place that no longer existed – and suddenly she could not see to thread a bead because her eyes were blurred with tears. Poor Liviu saw it. He took the sewing from her with affectionate words. He is so kind to her these days. Only he was clumsy and the box of beads was spilled across the carpet, and she shrieked at him and would not let him help her pick them up. He took his hat and his stick and once he was out of the door she crumpled on to the floor among the beads and wept. She thought she had picked up all the beads but every day since then she seems to find another one glinting in some corner or crevice of a chair.

The strange young man looks out of place on her chaise longue, oddly thin, angled, foreign amongst her furnishings like a bare twig brought into a hothouse full of flowers.

She used to think that Adriana's son was dead. He was most probably dead only the poor woman would never know for sure. That seemed more terrible than anything. She told herself that she should be glad at least that her daughters could write her letters and that she could send them parcels; that they were alive and that she had only to wait. Yet there was always the other possibility, that Adriana's son might come home any day, and she was jealous of her for it. There should have been sympathy between the two of them but somehow it had seemed a division: that one had word when the other did not; that one could live in expectation but the other knew that there were years of a sentence to be served. There is no sharing pain. This much she has learnt, that a mother suffers alone. Then this shabby mute young man turned up with his gangling hands and his sharp eyes. At first she had felt pity. She was generous and brought him things. But day after day the fact had sunk in that Adriana had him there, whatever his condition. Adriana had his simple presence in the room next door. She had felt a flush of envy almost to the point of anger. She had looked in the mirror and counted the years of their sentence before her and tracked the vagueness of her thoughts, and feared that she would be old and have quite lost herself before her daughters came home.

Now she has Adriana's boy here and he is ill. Adriana is the nurse but it is she, Irina, who is nursing him. She guesses he is running a fever. She used to care for her daughters in this same room. When they were ill their eyes hazed and their cheeks flushed, and they became younger than their years and she could care for them again like babies. She would cool their brows and bring them drinks and read them stories until they slept, and when they were sleeping she would sit and watch them.

There are whispers in the street. There is someone who knows someone who knew Adriana in the past. She has heard a rumour that this man is not who he is said to be. She remembers how she saw the oddness of it at the start. There was the photograph that he did not resemble one bit; and the muteness that was not accompanied by any external sign of injury. She had thought, surely there would have been some wound? It was none of their business, Liviu said, and besides, why else would the woman ever have taken him in?

She could say why, she thinks, watching him wake, seeing an emaciated beauty in him, seeing his eyes open.

'You haven't touched your water. Come on, take a sip now. Are you feeling a little better?' She looks at her watch. 'Adriana should be back soon. I've written her a note so she knows where to find you.'

Does he understand? She thinks that he understands something.

'Liviu will be back soon too. He said he'd be back around five and it's nearly five now. He'll be surprised to see you here.'

There is an appearance of listening in his eyes. In the brief time left before Liviu comes she would like to tell him everything that troubles her, everything that she cannot say to anyone else. She would tell him how Nadia and Danuta were arrested because they were clever and spoke foreign languages and went to Bucharest and worked for foreign companies; how each of them was taken separately, on different days in different places, but so little time apart; how silently they went, how long before she heard news; how in that time she had lived with the idea that they were dead and how she could not quite believe them alive now, would not really believe it until she could touch them again. And she would tell him about the other thing, that she could not tell even to Liviu. About the men who have come to her. Twice they have come now. The first time they knocked on the door just after Liviu had gone out, and they asked only for her and not for him so that she could guess that they had watched the house and chosen that moment to find her alone. The second time they came to her in the street where they must have followed her. They said that if she helped them she might help the girls. It was up to her. Her choice. This she could tell to the mute, but she could not tell it to Liviu because she knew what he would say. Liviu was a man of principle. He would say that there was no choice to be made.

She looks into the eyes of the mute that are so cool and still. Wonders if she sees sympathy there.

In the nights she thinks about what they said. They are so hot, these nights. There's no air to breathe. And there are always voices, people about, moving, in the house or on the street. Dogs barking, always dogs. She listens to the barking of the dogs and sees the pattern of it behind her closed eyes. It's like a storm coming in. First one gust, then another, until it's blowing right across the city, a great storm of barking, but it doesn't bring rain with it, or even cool air, but only blows across the city and then dies, and then there's a silence when the night seems hotter even than before. There are too many dogs in this city.

'I hate those dogs,' she says out loud, standing and going to the window. 'Why don't they kill all the dogs? They have killed so much else. Or round them up and put them all in cages in the Bărăgan?' She can imagine a great cage – sides, floor, roof of bars – in the middle of the steppe; a million dogs barking into nothingness. 'But I suppose they don't bother you, do they?'

He's so harmless, she thinks.

If he is harmless then why should they do him harm?

Adriana arrives home at the same time as Liviu. Irina hears the two of them coming up the stairs together. She goes to the door as they reach it.

'At last you're back. I've been waiting for you. I have your Ioan here. He wasn't well.'

Adriana's concern looks real as any mother's.

'Take some coffee with us, won't you?'

'If the lad's really ill,' Liviu says, 'then he should go home.'

'No, no, take some coffee please, I insist.' Irina begins to make the coffee even as she speaks.

Liviu fumbles to help. Irina has been so unpredictable lately, a brittleness in everything she does. It worries him. There is something fey, unstable in her. They are in their own home yet she has begun to drift in it as if she does not any more belong. It worries him but he can only play along and attempt to hold her to herself. So he goes out for a walk at the same time each day and comes back, regularly as if he has been to work, as if the routine will root them, and when he comes back he brings one of the cakes she likes. Today the routine is upset and the cake will have to be shared. The box in which it comes is tied with coloured string. It takes him an awkward amount of time to untie the knot and put out the cake, and when he has done so it is clear that it is too small for the four of them, a tiny island in the centre of the gold-rimmed plate.

'He fainted. I found him on the stairs.'

'That's very kind.' Adriana says the standard phrases. 'You are very kind.'

It is true. He does look ill. His face is pale and a little shiny.

'I think he has a fever.'

'Then I must take him home.'

183

'It's his lungs, isn't it? Really the air here is not good, all that dust, the humidity, the flies. If he has delicate lungs, this is not the place for him to be. But of course you know that. Why am I telling you this? You are the nurse, not I.'

Irina hears herself trying to save him. She is trying to get her to send him away. Quickly, before anything can happen.

'Is there nowhere else that he can go?'

From the far ridge the war was no more than an ominous drab line moving along the centre of the valley. The line was angular and knotted at points like a spine. It moved so slowly, with such random halts and hesitations, that it seemed an organic part of the landscape rather than some separate entity, any entity with purpose, moving across it. That first summer the line was broken where it passed under the willows about the river but by the end of the war the willows had gone and everything was visible as on the barest days of winter.

The house at Poiana was empty by then. The rooms were swept and uninhabited as his pictures. He had seen them emptied and the dust sheets laid, the bars set across the shutters and the doors to each room closed one after the other. No one was living in the house any more, and there was just a handful of them left in the cottages beyond the yard. They dug a piece of the land, enough for maize and potatoes and vegetables. They had the chickens and a pig and a couple of cows still so that they could survive on their own. But he was all the time aware of the hollowness of the place, an echo that could be seen instead of heard. He was aware that the cause lay somehow with what passed by at the river crossing, and with the flashes that he sometimes saw in the sky.

A few times he repeated the long walk down into the valley and then the spine he'd seen from above broke up into its parts: men and machines, horses, trucks, ox carts, guns. There was dust or mud depending on the season, churned-up ground, black exhaust fumes. The first lot of soldiers wore smart uniforms like soldiers in pictures and they gave chocolate to the children who came running behind them – and once to him, so mute and birdlike among them. The chocolate was good and the soldiers were pretty, yellow-haired and blue-eyed so that they reminded him of the English governess. The soldiers who came back later from the other direction were not so pretty. Their uniforms were dirty and torn and some of them had lost their boots. These men had cloths wrapped around their feet and some had cloths about their heads that he saw were bandages but not white as bandages should be but greyed with dirt and rusted sometimes with blood. The soldiers in these columns hung their heads like stray beaten dogs at the edge of the village and he was wary of them as he would have been of the dogs. A group of them came close and sniffed about him as dogs might have done, as if he might have had food in his pockets for them, but he had nothing. He opened his hands to them like empty spoons and they snarled. After that he did not go down to the columns again.

The tanks found their way into his pictures. He could see the weight of them, the thickness of their armour, the way they mounted ditches and crushed the undergrowth, the compaction of the earth where they had passed. He drew their huge squat shapes, the turrets and the gun barrels and the great tracks; detailing machine guns, hatch-covers, handgrips, vents, the heavy metal links that made up the tracks and all the wheels that turned within them. He painted the German cross on the front of one tank, Soviet numbers on the turret of another. He cut out the shapes from cardboard and worked at making a turret and gun barrel that would swivel like the real thing. He imagined as he worked how it would feel to be the man standing with his head out of the turret, riding in such a great machine that made the ground tremble about it, swivelling the turret to point the barrel in whatever direction he chose.

Then when some planes had bombed the river crossing he came upon a ruined tank, and he climbed on to it as if it were some ruined building and found pieces of men cooked inside. He understood perfectly what he was seeing. He saw that from inside the tank was a hard and claustrophobic box, a metal trap, an oven.

The last of the family had left Poiana before any of that. It was at the end of winter or early in the spring when there was still no green to the land. There was a formal goodbye to the servants who stood in a line on the lowest step beneath the porch. The house servants wore only their indoor clothes though the Văleanus were dressed for travel in hats and furs. There was a biting wind that fluttered the women's skirts and aprons. Paraschiva wept openly. Old Stanislaw stood stiff as a soldier but with tears in his eyes. Even Mama Anica's face was very red, and a quiver ran through her as she kissed her mistress's glove.

Every space in the car was tight with boxes and there were trunks tied to the back. It was clear by all that luggage that they would be gone for a long time. Augustin saw them go with eyes that were whipped wet by the wind. They have gone to be with Safta and the boys, he thought. The children had already been away for a long time. He pictured some other house like a mirror image of Poiana. The children would be there waiting, the trunks taken in and unpacked, the family reunited. He was working indoors for quite a few days after their departure, with his mother and Mama Anica and Stanislaw, and Ileana who had come only a short time before to work as a maid, moving furniture, covering sofas and chairs with dust sheets, packing smaller things away in crates. They trusted him with this indoor work because he was so neat with his hands. He packed everything with his customary careful touch, wrapping tissue about china vases and dishes and figurines. As he packed he pictured the servants in that other house unwrapping the figurines and arranging them on other shelves: a shepherdess, a harlequin, a goddess. He imagined the rooms of that other house empty and being filled just as the rooms at Poiana were becoming empty.

There was logic and order to the work, but there was something that had happened the day they left that defied his understanding. It was so disturbing that it came back again and again before his eyes. It had no cause that he could understand, no symmetrical conclusion. If he did not push the thought of it away his fingers became hard and unsteady. He felt a terror that he would break whatever piece of china they held, some gleaming fragile cup or jug or vase smashing to the parquet floor. With an effort of will he kept his fingers supple, and nothing was broken. The crates when they were done were stacked in the hall and then later Mama Anica called the gardeners in to carry them up to the attic.

The gardeners' hands worked alongside his, holding the corners of the crates.

They were strong hands.

There was soil on them, in the cracks and beneath the fingernails.

The gardeners had buried the Lipizzaner and the memory of it was fresh on their hands.

He took a crate and carried it up the stairs.

Careful, said the man behind him, as the crate juddered and almost slipped from his grasp. Hold it there.

He caught his breath, resting the crate momentarily against the landing wall. He looked up at the portraits that were all that was left of the family, hanging unmoved above him. Then he took the weight again and nodded to the man that he could carry on.

It was he who had groomed the horse that morning, combed out its mane and tail, worked its white flanks until they shone, and brought it out to Constantin Văleanu; and Constantin had stroked its neck and nose and murmured to it close, and then mounted it, though he did not often ride now, and rode off to the wood taking his rifle slung in its case over his shoulder.

Augustin looked into the space where they had gone. It was an empty space and he did not see the horse return there, but only the small figure of the old man on foot, walking swiftly with the gun again in its case over his shoulder. The old man walked by him, not meeting his eye. He walked by and then he called the gardeners and sent them off with their spades. Augustin followed, and he sensed before he saw it what he was about to see: in a clearing in the wood, the Lipizzaner fallen on its side, hooves stuck out like chopped branches, teeth bared, a thick dark blaze of blood spreading between its eyes.

It was the first of the senseless killings. No meaning to the sight, no precedent that he had known. That the animal should be killed by the man who loved it, and that it should be buried like this. He had seen other animals killed before, but those were for eating, not for burial. There was purpose to that.

There is an image that he must make for Safta. Not the horse. She also had loved the Lipizzaner. No need for her to suffer that. There was another death of which he must tell her, but he is not strong enough yet to make the picture. The deaths and the processions press and tangle in his memory. No pattern to them, no chronology either. There are tanks, men, horses, lines of men dressed in the colours of the soil, of mud and dust; and if they were stripped of their clothes they would be pale and bare like pale stalks that should be concealed beneath the ground, covered over again with soil. And also they are like the figures he has seen on the walls of churches, the pale lines of naked men marching up and down the scenes of judgement. He does not know their meaning but he confuses in his mind those living men that he has seen with images of the dead. If he would draw them he would draw one outline merging into another like those of the naked souls passing through purgatory and hell: long faces and long limbs, the landscape shattered about them, dust, mud, craters, ruts crossing and dividing over the torn valley floor;

the landscape shattering further, cracking open, about to swallow them up.

First he might draw the jeep for her. Another of the stray events of those years. Sometime later, much later than the horse, sometime when the armies were going to and fro. A jeep that came with two soldiers in it, a driver and another man who did not drive but who he always thought of as the driver. No mistaking him even though he was a passenger now and in uniform, thinner and more sober. His jeep was dirty and snagged with grass. It drove up into the stable yard, right up to Augustin where he stood. The engine kept running and the young man shouted at him. Augustin just spread his hands wide and shrugged his shoulders.

Gone, he was telling him, they have all gone. And the young man remembered that he was deaf and understood.

Where, his hands asked.

Don't know. Only, they are gone.

And the young man took a little book out from a pocket of his tunic and tore out a page and wrote a note, while the jeep's engine was still running. Then he crumpled the note in his hand and went back to the jeep and had the driver stop the engine. He went to the steps of the mounting block and sat down there and took a long time writing a second, far longer message. This one he folded, and he wrote Safta's name on the outside.

If she comes back, give it to her.

I'll keep it safe. Augustin held the note to his chest. If she comes, I'll give it to her. I'll look after it till then.

Thank you. He was still brown and smooth, the young man, but he had become harder, like hard wood. Augustin looked into his eyes and saw the weathering in them and liked him better than he had before. There was trust in his eyes. The perfect young man was putting his trust in him.

He had tried to keep that trust. He had kept the note for years. He had kept it in his room among his papers, and when he left and went to live in the village he took it with him, and when he left the village he took it in his pocket. He would have it still if it had not been taken from him. So now he begins with the image of the yard. He must begin his story there. He draws it with the utmost precision as if he had the place before him, or a photograph of it, a sharp still shot. He draws every window and doorway, the latches on the doors, the shingles on the roof and the cobbles on the ground. He must make her see first the yard, and then the jeep, and then the young man. Only in that way will he be able to tell her what happened.

He shows it to the two women when they come in from the hospital.

'Look what he's done, Safta. It's a yard, stables. A country place.'

Safta looks at the picture over the other woman's shoulder.

'Well, what do you think?'

'It's a lovely drawing. A stable yard, like you say.'

'I think it's a real place, don't you? It must be where he lived.'

'Probably, yes, now you say that. I should think so. Or at least, somewhere that he used to go.'

'I wonder if we could find it. We might find out where he came from.'

'There must be thousands of yards like that. There will be a yard like that in every village in the country.'

'Yes, but he might do more now that he's begun. Don't you think so? He might do other pictures from memory like that. This is a breakthrough, don't you see?'

He has made the picture for Safta, not for Adriana, but Safta has given it barely a glance. He has a story to tell her and he is for a moment sharply aware of his incapacity to tell it. She is remote from him. She will not see what he needs her to see. She does not even seem to perceive his disappointment. Adriana goes to Augustin where he stands with his back to the wall and hugs him. She has come from the hospital in the heat. She smells sharp with sweat and disinfectant. The smell is not so much unpleasant as safe and functional. She takes his head in her hot disinfected hands and kisses both his cheeks.

In the days that follow he draws the yard again and again. He has found some good brown paper that takes pencil well. He draws the outlines in minute detail and then he shades them until they shine.

Adriana is disappointed that he does not move on to other subjects. Often he continues with the drawings long after the point at which she has thought they were finished. He goes on shading and overdrawing until the details disappear. Doors and openings of stables and barns become solid. Roof tiles merge with walls. The walls become so black that they can no longer be distinguished from the ground. She takes up each drawing and holds it to the light so that she can make out the outlines at least. She cannot understand what it is that he is meaning to do.

For a long time the war remained something separate, in the valley by the river. Something remote and fated and continuous. What came to them at the house was not the war but a series of stray events. Stray men turned up wanting things. They came individually or in packs. They ate and they washed at the pump and they slept in the hayloft, and left as suddenly as they came.

There was a motorcycle and sidecar, two handsome soldiers wearing goggles and shorts. They drove into the yard and the passenger stood and drew his pistol and shot a turkey. It was an ugly old male with hideous wattles that hung almost to the ground. It would have been tough to eat as leather. When they stuffed it into the sidecar and drove away the wattles streamed out like pulled guts. Paraschiva roared with laughter. Paraschiva laughed first, and then Mama Anica, going to the gate to see the motorcycle go. They doubled over cackling and Augustin came and stood beside them and laughed too, in great long peals, until the motorcycle was out of sight.

After that they moved most of the livestock out into the forest. They buried bags of flour and potatoes in pits. Other stocks they walled up in the cellar. They learnt that there was just time to hide things between the moment vehicles were first sighted on the drive and their coming in at the gate. Mostly the soldiers hesitated a moment before the house, and then went on to the yard once they saw that it was deserted. The look of absence had come to the house quickly, its luminousness gone the instant the shutters were closed. Even in bright sunlight and when the acacias were in fresh new leaf, the house beyond them looked hollow and grey and dead. The soldiers must have seen other such houses on their way, dead and emptied before them. So they paused only a second. It was enough time for Mama Anica to be ready for them. She would meet them in the yard looking older even than she was, knowing the impunity that she might gain by age and by an apparent absence of fear. Once she encountered a band of foraging soldiers with a broody hen she had just saved held beneath her shawl. It made her seem only the more hunched and grotesque. The hen was quiet so long as she kept its head clenched in the dark of her armpit, and the eggs she kept warm in the pocket of her apron. The soldiers were generally simple boys and men from villages not so different from

Poiana. The old woman scared them like their own grandmothers.

They came like animals, like strays or herds. Their physical presence was like that of animals, not only their smell but the way they moved, looked, brushed by him as if he were of some other species. They used the pump. They stripped before it to wash and their bodies were streaked with rashes from lice. They slept in the hayloft. They ate whatever was there for them to find. And the women always left a little out, the basics, enough to prevent the place being ransacked, or worse. There was corn and potatoes and salt. Eggs. Wine from the cellar. The appetite of the soldiers was sometimes astonishing. There was one soldier who swallowed twenty eggs raw. He was a big hefty red-necked man and Augustin watched in amazement as his Adam's apple moved and yolk after yolk slipped down.

Then there was a band of soldiers who came and stayed. They came at the end of a summer when everything was at its most hot and dusty, all of them stained and dusty and weary. These men were not just looking for food. They broke open the doors of the house. They went in with purpose, as if they knew the place was meant for them, and occupied the whole house and let one or two of the horses in as well.

They behaved as if they were lords. They opened up the kitchen and made Paraschiva come and work in it.

Paraschiva was a realist and Paraschiva loved to cook. So she opened up a few of her hidden hoards and fed them well. She fed them her delicious sour soups, and bacon and polenta and bowls of cream, hoping to keep them happy until the time that they would go.

They kept the shutters closed on account of the heat. The façade of the house looked as empty as before but the doors lay open to the porch and pieces of chaos spilled out: boots, rucksacks, clothing, horse manure. The soldiers did not seem to care where they slept, on the beds or the settees or the tables or the floors. They made Augustin bring them wine from the cellar and he had no choice but to go in as they said. He did not see why they had wanted the house and had not gone to the stables like the animals they were. He thought that men such as these must not have known the use of a house before. He wished that his mother would not feed them so well. He did not know as his mother did what there might have been to fear if she did not.

Even in the shuttered light he could see the damage that was being done. They were so untidy, these men, so careless, with their lumbering movements and their big clumsy hands. They had moved about the house like cattle. They had slept and drunk and eaten and vomited, and someone had defecated in the corner under the stairs. They had sat on the chairs and settees shrouded as they found them. They had put their feet up and the dust sheets had rumpled off. His fingers itched to take up the sheets from where they lay in the dirt, and shake them clean and white and put them out again. There were dark bruises on Marina

Văleanu's pale silk damasks where filthy heads and feet had rested, and in some places the fine fabrics had begun to split and tear. He took it all in as he moved through one dim room after another. He saw every defilement: marks on the walls, parquet scuffed, tables scratched, a bedstead broken, a mirror smashed, a door off its hinges, two balusters broken from the staircase. The trophies in the gun room had been shot again and again: the stag and deer heads and a boar's head shot up on the walls; a stuffed lynx taken outside for target practice beneath the trees.

They shot the lynx with their machine guns and it disintegrated in puffs of fur and taxidermist's stuffing. Augustin knew the use of shotguns and rifles but he had never seen the power of a machine gun before. One day when there was a great storm coming, and there was a wind bringing it that kicked up the dust and made everyone restless, they stayed indoors and used their machine guns on the portraits in the hall. These like the chandeliers had been left where they hung since they were too big to move to store. They had remained like the last of the family, looking on, the only inviolate part of the place and its past. Augustin had expected the guns to make holes. He had not understood that they could do so much more than make holes. They could cut right through things, one bullet following on another so close that they could cut right along a boyar's jewelled belt and slice a canvas in two. His horror must have shown on his face when he saw because it set the soldiers laughing, and one of them pointed his gun up at the chandelier and shot down a mass of pieces of crystal like a shower of hail. Augustin ran. He ran out between the columns of the porch just as the storm came in, and stayed out as hail turned to rain and he was soaked to the skin, and did not come in until it was night.

After that they teased him often. They fired their guns close behind his back and thought it funny that he went on oblivious. They found it even funnier to scare him.

He was coming from the shed where Paraschiva had milked the cow. He had a tin churn in each hand. He did this every evening, carrying the milk across the yard. On this particular evening there was a man washing at the pump. He was naked to the waist. He had taken off his tunic and his gun and laid them on the ground. When Augustin passed him he picked up the gun and shot the churn in his right hand. A fountain of white milk streamed out and Augustin swivelled to see it, just as the man fired at the second churn. Augustin saw that he was laughing like a child. He had a round baby face and a big round belly that wobbled when he laughed, and his braces hung down over his breeches. They were like children, these soldiers. They laughed like children and fooled around like children who had nothing to do, and sometimes they were cruel like children. It was nothing new to him. There had always been children who laughed at him and joked behind his back. If these ones were bigger and had guns that did not necessarily make them more wicked.

And he could escape them like he used to escape the children. There were still places that he could hide away. There was the hayloft. When he needed to be alone he went up there and watched, and one day he saw one of the village girls raped in a field. It was Ileana who used to work in the house. There was such a blue sky that day and the field looked so tidy and pretty with all the stooks ranged across it that it looked at first like a game. Ileana was running. She was wearing a white skirt like all the girls wore. Her plaits were streaming out behind. She was running and then she was trying to hide behind the stooks. There were four men spread out, hunting her down. They all looked rather small at that distance, again like children with their running legs and outstretched arms. Later Augustin found his mother looking after the girl. Paraschiva sent him away. That night Ileana was dressed up in Mama Anica's clothes and he and József walked slowly back with her to the village. She was bigger than Mama Anica but she did not look so big when she was hunched over and weeping.

The soldiers were there only a matter of days, a couple of weeks at most, yet the house when they left it seemed quite another place. It was as if many years had passed in that time. He walked through with Mama Anica, into the hall where the glass still lay like hailstones and through room after room the length of the house. Mama Anica was crying. He had never seen her cry before.

After that they moved down to the village. The girl Ileana was still crying but Mama Anica had stopped. In the village he made a cross for Paraschiva's grave. He made it out of pieces of scrap metal that he found and one of the Gypsies helped him weld it.

He had seen that they did not mean to kill her. There was no meaning to this event any more than to any of the others, only that it happened. She was cooking for the men. They liked her food and when she cooked for them they smiled at her and licked their fingers. She had been peeling potatoes, seated on a bench just outside the kitchen door, dropping them as they were peeled into a pan at her feet. She went down to the cellar for more. The big baby-faced soldier was fiddling with his gun, stripping it down and reassembling it. Augustin went to watch and the man showed him that the gun had jammed and that he was fixing it. His big sausage fingers were sure and neat when they dealt with the smooth pieces of metal and he let Augustin handle the pieces as he cleaned them. Augustin held each piece and handed it over as he put the gun together. It was satisfying how neatly the pieces snapped one into the other. Then the soldier put in a clip of ammunition and held the gun to his hip to fire, just experimentally, to check that it worked. He looked to Augustin and smiled, and as he did so he fired into the emptiest space before them, towards the ground, into a black opening that was the opening to the cellar from which Paraschiva was just at that moment bringing potatoes.

Augustin could not move to touch her. He imagined her torn in half like the portrait in the hall. And the soldiers in the yard just stood and looked. Even the air was still, weighted, impassive; as if this was nothing, all this had happened so many times before. Then one went forward and began to pick up the potatoes that had fallen on the ground in front of her, and some of these were cut apart and red. And baby face put down his gun and went and put his hands beneath her arms and dragged her out to the garden with a red trail behind her. When he had laid her down he came back for a spade and Augustin followed him. He moved at last and went behind the soldier and took the spade from him, and the soldier understood and left the young man with his mother.

The smell of earth became for him inseparable from the memory of the war. War was a thing of earth and metal, a mineral thing. It was his spade cutting through the soil.

He did not go for the priest, not then at least. In the village when someone died the priest made a show of words. There were days of mourning and procession, women in black with creases in their faces. Augustin did not know the point of all that.

When he had buried her he started to walk back through the garden. The dusk was soft. The grass was long and the flowerbeds were tangled and overgrown but in this light where there was no detail the view to the verandah was hardly different from how it had ever been. He walked across the lawn to the catalpa tree and there in the shadows he came upon one of the soldiers pissing. The man had his back to him. He was drunk. He could barely stand to piss but was swaying, steadying himself against the tree. Augustin raised the spade that he held in his hand and hit the man on the side of his head with all his strength. The drunken soldier folded over. A sweep of metal and he fell to the ground, but smoothly, not jerking as Paraschiva had done. Augustin did not distinguish the man as any particular soldier. What had occurred seemed to have occurred all within himself, not outside him. He walked on, still carrying the spade, and left that moment behind. He could do that because each moment was quite separated from the next. He went home to the cottage. Mama Anica was there waiting for him but he sent her away. He had never before spent a night alone.

The following morning as soon as there was any light Augustin returned. As he passed the tree he saw that the man was still there, still crumpled the same way. It looked quite wrong, there in the lovely garden at Poiana, even in the thin grey dawn. He moved mechanically to tidy up. He tried to put the stiff body straight, picked up the man's hat that had fallen aside and placed it on his chest. Then he pulled him into the bushes of the shrubbery. He went on to the burial place and stood for a long time gazing down where there was nothing to see but the soil that he had disturbed the day before. That was all there was, only the soil now, no past to find there.

It got light. The sun opened a yellow gash in the sky. The ground became clear at his feet: the bared soil, grass stalks, his tracks in the dew. The sun grew whole, the sky high and very pale. He was aware of some enormity and he became afraid. Instinct made him want to hide before the sunlight touched him, but he did not move. He stood still where he was and once he felt the sun then there was no point in hiding any more.

His second fear, which came to him later, was of the soldiers.

Again he might have hidden, but he did not. He went on as if drawn to whatever consequence might follow from his actions. He went back to the yard. It had changed there. The soldiers who had done nothing but hang around for days were busy, every one of them moving with purpose. He fully expected them to come at him with their guns, expected it so strongly that he could almost see it happen, he standing there with a bright ray of sunlight on him and their guns firing at him, as if it was a picture he had seen. And yet they walked by him and paid him as little attention as if he didn't exist.

He could not know that that morning of all mornings the soldiers had got the order to move on. They had suddenly become a troop again. And he didn't matter to them now. He stopped and stood there, like an obstacle in the yard, and they brushed by him. They shoved their kit into their knapsacks and put in along with it anything that was loose about the place and that they might use. He saw saucepans taken, kitchen knives, whatever stores they could find. He didn't move to take any of it back, though Mama Anica saw him through the window and was afraid of what he might do, and came out and tried to bring him away.

Just before the Russians left the soldier with the baby face came up to him. He looked worse than ever, his cheeks blubbery, his eyes bloodshot. He rolled up one sleeve of his tunic to show the watches that he wore like bracelets all down his arm.

'Have one.'

Augustin looked blank.

Some of the watches were working, some were not. Each one told a different time.

'Go on, choose one.' The soldier gestured like a salesman. 'Any one you like.'

When he saw that Augustin still didn't understand he chose for him. 'This one's Swiss. It came off a German but it's Swiss. Quality Swiss movement, works a dream.' He fastened the worn alligator strap around the youth's passive wrist. 'Now you have one of the best watches in the world.' He held it up a moment longer. The second hand ticked on and as he watched it move he began to cry.

'Take this too.' From the pocket of his tunic he brought out a picture that he kissed like an icon. The picture was gold-edged like an icon and showed a man with a braided uniform and a big grey moustache. Then he held Augustin to him and kissed him and cried some more.

Augustin just stood there like his puppet. He understood that this was the man's apology. He knew also by the smell of him that he had been drinking all the night.

*   *   *

When the troop moved off no one seemed to have noticed that a man was missing.

Augustin and Mama Anica walked through the shambles of the house that last time then they went down to the village. A few days later Augustin went back and buried the second body. He buried it where it was. All the time he worked he barely looked at it, though one glance had been enough to fix the image so deep in him that he would never be able to erase it. When he came back Mama Anica saw that he had been digging and thought that he must have been planting flowers on his mother's grave.

His cough is bad again. Adriana finds it a relief when she can be on night duty and does not have to lie there and listen to him. She comes back in the mornings and finds him already at his table working on his pictures. His face is pale and pinched and his mouth set tight. He has taken to making birds these past days. He makes them as he makes his people, out of layers of card cut and coloured and stitched together, but there is more variety to the birds than to the people. They have heads and beaks and feet and wings of different shapes, recognisably cocks or hens or ducks or geese. He is happier with the bird constructions than with the drawings he had been doing which seemed to distress him. She has encouraged him by bringing pictures of other species for him to copy, so that there is now a brightly coloured parrot and a hummingbird, and a cockatoo with a crest of fine yellow paper folded in a fan. When he makes these exotic birds he gives them to her or places them on her bed for her to find when she comes home. The farmyard birds he keeps for himself, like the country boy he is.

Irina Milescu is right. He is a country boy and he needs country air. He should leave the city. She should find a way, a place where he might go until he is better. Perhaps if he were to be readmitted to the hospital, the doctors there might refer him to a sanatorium. There are places in the mountains. Perhaps, she thinks, he would be well if he were to go to the mountains.

It is a sweltering tram ride to the centre of the city. The dust is starting up again as it does through the course of every summer. The freshness is gone from people's faces; a sheen of sweat on them; the smell of sweat oppressive. There are too many people in this city crowded into too few rooms, and not enough places to wash. Adriana has had to run to catch the tram and is sweating herself. She is afraid she will be late for the cinema. She likes to get a good seat, in the centre and close to the screen, because her eyes are not so good but also because she likes to be where she knows nothing but the picture, where she has no awareness of the black rows of people about and before and behind her. Even the tram is crowded. It is so warm, the air so thick. To cool herself she looks out of the window at the leaves of the trees and pictures Hollywood. In Hollywood everything is wide and open and new. Clean. The streets are wide and the trees, where there are trees, stand neatly on them all alike as lollipops, and the cars and people glide on ground smooth as a dance floor, and women and bellboys wear white gloves. All the films she likes best are made in Hollywood. She loves the cleanness of those films. She has loved Astaire for being so very light and clean. She wishes she might have been Ginger Rogers. Not a beauty, she has never particularly wanted to be a beauty. The great American beauties do not seem quite real to her, Ava Gardner, Rita Hayworth, Lana Turner, women who do not cook or laugh, she would not want to be one of them, she does not mind being the sort of woman who grows a little plump with age. But to have been, for a moment, Ginger Rogers, to have danced with Astaire, that would have been fine. As the tram slips down the long hill she looks out at the broken avenues and the scarred houses of Iaşi and imagines America. Sleek streets. White smiles. Bob Hope and Bing Crosby. So many places they went to, those two, clean happy places where people stepped off white liners and there were no poor and no wars but only natives with turbans or sarongs or flower garlands about their necks. Rio, Tahiti, Singapore. If only she could go to such places.

But there are hardly any Hollywood films any more, not since the Trianon became the Maxim Gorky. There are only Eastern bloc films made in Bucharest or Moscow or Prague, or Alma-Ata, wherever that might be. Nothing from Hollywood except *Rin Tin Tin*. And one she saw called *White Fang*. They show films about American animals but not the people. She wishes someone would tell her why. What harm could come from such films? No one takes them seriously. Only possibly they might be considered a little fattening, like sweet cakes.

She gets into the cinema minutes before the programme starts. There is a free seat close to the screen just beside the aisle. She walks down as the lights are put out and happens to glimpse the Milescus a couple of rows back. She sits down quickly hoping they have not seen her. The matinée is her escape. It may not be Hollywood but it is still her escape. She does not want to share a moment of it.

Liviu is going a little deaf with age. Irina has taken care to seat herself beside his better ear so that she can whisper to him if there's something he doesn't hear or he fails to catch the plot. She has perfected a sharp and penetrating whisper which her husband can hear even against the patriotic music of the newsreel.

'There's Adriana. I'm sure she saw us. You'd think she might have said hello.'

'Why should she?' Liviu says. 'The film's about to start.'

'Well we must talk to her later. I've been wanting to speak to her anyway.'

'What about?'

'The house, of course.' Irina spends the first few minutes of the film going over in her mind all the matters about which she might speak to her neighbour: the use of the shared facilities, the vermin, the noise of the Bessarabians, odd little things that have been disappearing lately. She fidgets until her husband puts his hand on hers to still her. Only beneath the gentle weight of his fingers can she at last push the tangle of thoughts aside and focus on the screen.

As it happens they don't have a chance to speak much after the film because it begins to pour with rain just as they come out on to the street, big drops of rain that soon become a heavy summer downpour. They take shelter under an awning and go for the tram when they see it coming. Others get on at the same time, all of them wet and dripping, and Adriana lets the crowd separate them.

'See. She's avoiding us.'

Adriana has squeezed herself into a seat by the window and has her face almost to the glass watching the rain.

'It's funny, her coming all alone like that, don't you think? You'd think she might have brought her son with her, wouldn't you? If he really is her son. She hides him away like some terrible secret, and comes out all alone. And he's nothing like the picture I saw. One begins to wonder.'

'He's stone deaf. Why should she take a deaf man to the cinema?'

'For the pictures. He could follow the story from the pictures.'

'You pay too much attention to these people. Let them be. Perhaps he doesn't want to go. What is it to you anyway?'

'Can't help thinking, that's all. If it was Nadia or Danuta, would you leave them at home?'

'But you have to stop thinking. It isn't Nadia or Danuta. And it's not likely to be, is it? Not till God knows when.'

It is still raining hard when they reach their tram stop. Adriana runs ahead of them – in so far as she can run, the size she is. Liviu has put his coat about his wife, who is already soaked through in her thin cotton dress. He has spoken too brutally. He understands why she has become neurotic, peevish, jealous of the world. She was not always like this. She is not herself. She looks so fragile in the clinging dress that he feels a sudden sharp tenderness for her and for the past.

When they get in she takes off her wet dress, ties a flimsy dressing gown over her slip, sits at the table in the window to drink the tea that he has made for her. In the silence they can still hear the rain. What can he say? There was the past and now there is this present that is only a waiting for the future. It goes on indefinitely. It goes on too long. They are both of them so tired. Irina's hair has dried in a garish cloud around her face. He should speak to her about the film they saw perhaps, but it has already quite gone from his mind.

They have only themselves now. All of their lives packed into this crowded room. All these things to which she clings, the pictures on the walls, the photographs of the girls. There are themselves and these things and this room, and there is a line drawn about them: all that is in the room matters, all that matters is held within the room, and what is beyond the room can no longer be his concern.

That night once he is sure that Irina is asleep, Liviu gets up from the bed in his pyjamas and puts on the small shaded lamp at the table and sits down to write a letter in the narrow pool of light. When he has finished the writing he will turn off the lamp but he will not make his way back to the bed for a long time.

He has been a lawyer all his life. It is second nature to him to think before he acts. There is a piece of his mind that is trained to watch and analyse, to judge when to pay attention to detail and when to ignore what is better not seen. Discretion lies deep in him and the habit is hard to break.

The letter does not require many words, and those that there are are controlled, considered, precise. It need only be a suggestion. A woman has someone living with her who may not be who she says he is. Since the refugee problem, movements and residence in the city have been strictly controlled. He can leave investigation to others. His writing is elegant. It may be the work of despair but it appears to be the product of a discreet and considered and calm mind.

They don't know it but they are just in time. Safta has found a doctor to sign the papers. She has leave from the hospital to take him herself to the sanatorium in the mountains.

She brings boxes to pack away his work. He is pleased with the boxes and helps to pack them, systematically, taking the pictures down from the wall and the chest of drawers, using one box for drawings, another for his friends, others for his matchbox collection and his birds and constructions, packing them tightly, smoothing the piles down with his hand, folding the boxes shut, tying string tight about them. His other things, his clothes, fill no more than the bottom of a little cardboard case.

'Don't worry,' Safta says, 'I'm going with you. We're going to the countryside. You'll like it.' Then, 'No, you can't take the boxes. Adriana will look after them for you.' His mouth sets in a thin line and for a moment she is afraid that he will not come without his work. She mimes *hurry*, looking at the watch on her wrist, putting a hand with surprise to her mouth, setting up a current that pulls him away. She gives Adriana two hasty kisses on the cheeks. 'Quick now, we must go. Quickly, or we'll be late.'

Adriana hugs him tight. For all that she has fed him there is still little more to him than bone.

The last of his presence is soon erased. The boxes are in the middle of the floor and she kneels to put them away beneath his bed. At the back there, against the skirting, she finds a paper bag that he did not pack. Inside it is one of his jackdaw collections of things: used tram and cinema tickets, a dozen shards of coloured glass, a stick of red chalk, and a pink-and-white cosmetic pot still half full of foundation cream whose colour she recognises as one he has used recently for the skin tones of his figures. One of Irina Milescu's disappearing objects. She puts the pot on the table wondering if she might find a way to return it later. From the table drawer she takes out the photograph of her son and returns it to its former place.

*   *   *

She is on the balcony when the black car arrives.

She is thinking how she will miss him. She will certainly miss him when it comes to the watering. It takes so long to bring the water can by can from the tap downstairs, and her back doesn't like the lifting any more. She has to move delicately, as she had taught him, between the plants. The tomatoes are almost a jungle in themselves, the smell of them rising heavily off the leaves as they are disturbed. She puts down the can, plucks out some side shoots, begins to tie up new stems.

The men call up to her from the street. She had thought someone else would answer the knocking at the door. Usually when there is noise or visitors it is something to do with the Bessarabians. She goes inside, goes downstairs, lets them in. Two men, neither of them hefty, but there is a blunt weight to them. She knows who they are.

They walk ahead of her into her room and poke about. She stands in the centre of the space, turning to them as they move.

'Do you live alone here?'

'Yes. No. I mean, there's only me here right now, but there is room for my son.'

'Where is your son?'

She shows them the photograph.

'He's in Russia. I expect him back any day now.'

'Then he doesn't live here.'

How is she to answer that? She pivots to face them. Her raised hands speak for her.

'What about your other son?'

'I have no other son.'

'The other son who was living here.'

'Believe me, I know how many sons I have. If you don't believe me, check with my husband.'

'Where is your husband?'

'My husband works on the railway. At Roman. I don't have the address but the railway company can find him.'

'We have information there was somebody else living here.'

'There was, for a while. But he was not living here. He was only staying. There was a patient from the hospital who had nowhere to go. He stayed here for a short time and now he has gone. If people think he is my son then they are mistaken.'

'Who was he?'

'Ask at the hospital. The TB ward. They must have a record. I think they moved him to a sanatorium.'

Going Home

He sits curled over his work on a bench in the station hall. He has the little suitcase on his knee on which to rest the paper while he draws.

He sharpens the pencil using the penknife he keeps in his pocket, keeping the point broad, slightly blunt, as he works with the side of it rather than the tip.

He works precisely, never going back to erase.

Now that they are leaving it comes easily to him. He draws the one place he can picture as a destination for the two of them. The first drawing takes the view from far in the distance, from as far away as he has ever seen it, where the house itself is not visible but only the tall trees that surround it, that can be seen on their hill from the road far away down the valley. He draws as jagged specks – yet even so at that distance they are out of scale – the rooks that he knows are there, that make their nests high in the trees, that her grandfather used sometimes to shoot from his bedroom window.

Safta sees the drawing take shape. The memory is all there in him, precise, ready to be drawn. It must have been there throughout these months in the city waiting for release. She sees the pent excitement in him. When a train comes in he looks to the platform, the stream of people, looks to her. No, not this one. And he is disappointed and goes back to his work. She had rushed him out, and now the train is late. She thought he might be afraid, hesitant at least. She sees no hesitance in him now but only impatience. How can it be that he knows where they are going. Perhaps he doesn't know. Perhaps it is only that he trusts her. That he would follow her anywhere like this, carrying his little case, just to her side but a step behind, looking confidently ahead, walking as she walks, stopping when she does, even his eyes following hers and looking where she looks. If she appears sure of what they are doing then he will be too.

Once they are on the move the jolting of the train makes it impossible to draw so he slips the page beneath his case where it cannot be seen and raises his eyes and looks out across the other passengers to the window. He does not look at the passengers themselves, only glancing at their faces in the blandest way, as if they were no more than the furnishings of the carriage. When the train stops he gets the page out again and begins to draw immediately with such quick fluent lines that it seems as if he has the picture ready, every stroke of it in his head, and it is a simple mechanical process to transfer it on to paper.

They come to a junction where they must change. The tickets Safta bought in Iași bring them only this far. She must buy new tickets, and there is another and longer wait, sitting in the sun on a narrow platform that stretches out from the small town into the fields. No one there but a stationmaster tending marigolds. Time for Augustin to make three further drawings.

He draws the drive running down between the acacias, with the columns of the porch at the end of them. This is a picture of strong verticals and deep perspective, very black and white as he draws the trees bare of leaves and does not shade the gaps between the trunks.

He draws a much softer, greyer picture of the village as it appears from before the house: the road running a little downhill, the houses scattered along the slope, the school-house with the storks' nest on its chimney, the outline of the church behind, a sketchy notion of stooks in the fields and trees in the distance.

Then, as if he had stood in the same spot but shifted position only, beginning to turn clockwise towards the house, he draws the stable entrance and the roofs of the buildings about the yard. The horizon of this picture runs on at the same height as that of the previous one, a tree that appears at the edge of one page recurring at the corresponding edge of the next.

At the next stop on the journey he will go on as if he were to continue to turn on the spot. He will make the front of the house from close up: the porch, the doors, the feathery overhang of the acacias in summer. Then he will draw the view away to the other side, to the hay fields rolling away into forest. In all of these drawings the level of the horizon will hold, as if he has kept a camera steady in his hand and turned it full circle across his memory.

At this point they leave the railway. He will make a further half-dozen drawings on the journey, in a variety of locations as they continue across the country: in the afternoon shade of trees and crosses at the roadside, in the back of a cart, in the evening on the step before a summer kitchen. The pictures home in, entering the stable yard and then the sheds and the house itself. Later when they have got there he will piece all of these drawings into a book, stitched together with end-boards made of card, and the card with holes punched in it so that it can be tied together with a piece of green wool that he has picked up along the way.

The air is thick with harvest, sun, dust. They have been walking more than half the day and though they have passed people at work Safta has spoken to no one since they left the train. For a time they rest high on a hill where they can look back the way they have come: another long valley, but almost bare of trees, long bare ridges that would be dull if they were not golden right now with harvest and if the far hills did not turn to violet under the brightness of the sky. The railway tracks run straight, north–south along the line of the valley, but the river meanders, cutting deep exposed banks from the sandy soil. They watch a train travel the length of the view; slow, long, a line of innumerable wagons the colour of rust.

A little way off a lone man stands reaping. It empties her mind to watch him. It is so long since she has been out of the city. A golden field, a man in white, the blue of the sky most intense where it touches the wheat at the crest of the hill. This man seems fixed in his work, in the rhythm of his strokes, of the stalks falling. He does not look up or around. As if there is nothing here on the hillside but the job in hand, his mind automatically measuring the uncut area ahead against the reaped area behind, his progress as steady and mechanical as that of the train. If he does not look up to check the height of the sun then he will know how far it has come by the length of his shadow. That is how it is in this heat. It is the feeling she has when they are walking, step by step up the length of the hill: that she has only to keep her eyes to the ground and at last she will be there. Beside her Augustin draws with pencil strokes that are as sure and rapid as those of the scythe.

He will not show her until he is ready. That is his way. He puts a screening arm about the page and leans low so there is no looking over his shoulder. Does he know how close they are? She thinks he does. Perhaps, like his black rooks, he knows direction.

She speaks to the sky, eyes half closed.

'I remember how it was when I left. It was winter – or perhaps not quite winter – autumn. I remember that the trees were almost bare and half the house was shut up. I didn't know I was leaving for the last time. I'd thought I would be back. But the war came and the world started to change around us. It was a time when the little moves you made became big and permanent even if you didn't mean them to be so.

'I went back just once after the war was over. I was the only one of the family left in the country by then. There was a man I was with. He had business somewhere not so far away. I told him where I came from and he said that I should come with him, and we would make a detour and see it, only the detour took much longer than we had thought it would because the roads were so bad. Some of them hadn't been fixed from the war and it had rained hard and there was still a bridge gone somewhere. I'd been seeing Paul for some time but he didn't know much about me, he knew only the nurse that he'd met in Bucharest.

'We went there and looked around. It was empty. Nobody there at all. I was surprised, that none of you were there. I had imagined you would be there always.

'We drove in the rain, through heavy summer showers that made little floods on the roads and then cleared, and when they cleared I had never seen the countryside look so beautiful. It was the year after the famine and it was amazing to see the fields lush again, everything green, great clouds with rain in them swelling above. Flowers everywhere. Frogs in the ponds. I used to love the croaking of the frogs. You wouldn't know that, would you, that it was one of the sounds of the place? I used to go to sleep to it at night. We were there in June, I suppose, early summer. That's when the frogs were loudest. We walked right around the garden but we didn't go into the house because it was locked and shuttered. If Paul hadn't been with me I'd have gone to the village. I'd have looked someone up, asked about you all. But it didn't feel right with him there. Anyway we didn't have time, the journey had taken so long. He wanted to go on, get to where we were going before it got dark. He kept talking about the state of the roads. So we just walked about the garden that was all wet with the rain and drove away. We stopped seeing one another soon after that – not for any particular reason, only that we'd both become aware of the distance between us. I remember that my shoes were wet and I took them off in the car, and he just drove and didn't say anything, and he was cross one time when we missed the way. In all the time we'd known one another I realised that there was a centre to me that he had not touched, that he had not even seen was there – the old me that nobody else knew any more, or almost no one since everyone from the past had gone, or they were going, or planning to go.

'There hasn't been anyone since Paul, no one who mattered. We went back to Bucharest and it ended, and I thought the cause was something to do with the city. It seemed a brittle, corrupted, tarnished place. People were brittle. Friendships were false, doomed to failure. Or that's how it seemed to me. In the end I decided to leave and came to Iaşi where things had been harder. As if that would give it more integrity.'

'I wrote to them in England about the house. My father had been the last person to visit it. He'd gone up at some point and taken a few pictures and pieces of furniture and brought them back to Bucharest, but then he had decided to leave the country. We'd felt for some time how the world was closing in on us, right since the end of the war, and it was almost too late by then. He came and asked me if I'd go with him. He said, didn't I see that the place was becoming a prison about us? I explained that I had thought it through and that I was staying. I had work. This was my reality. I wouldn't be real anywhere else. He asked if I wanted some of the furniture. What for? I said. Where would I put it? I could see he didn't understand at all. He got away all right of course. He had a mistress who was an aviator and they flew away in her aeroplane. My father always had style.

'He's separated from my mother now. She's in England and he's gone on to France. They're better that way. Without Poiana there wasn't anything between them any more. I think I'd always known about the other women. From when I was a child I knew that there was my mother and there were the others, and I thought they were beautiful when the house parties came. I used to watch them from the windows. There were so many windows at Poiana, and doors, rooms giving on to rooms. It wasn't a house for secrets. I used to watch the women my father brought and I wanted to grow up to be like them and wear silk and be languorous on the verandah in the middle of the night. I used to hear them from up in my room. The windows would be wide open and I would wake and hear the night outside and the men and the women talking after dinner. You know where my room was, just above. I could hear everything. I could smell the smoke of the men's cigars.'

*　　*　　*

'It's not so far from here, if I can find the right way. I don't like to ask people, I don't want to draw attention to us. That's why I thought we'd come this way, across the hills. If we went the other way we'd have to go through the town and then the village, and we might meet too many people who knew us. We should be there tomorrow. We'll take it gently. We'll walk a bit more today and find somewhere to sleep and tomorrow we'll get up early while it's cool. Mustn't let you get too tired.

'I don't know how long we'll stay there. We'll see. I just thought, we must take a look, see how it is. Just go for a day or two, then we can go on to where we're supposed to be, and nobody will be the wiser. Perhaps we'll find out where your mother is, who knows? And old Mama Anica, do you think she's still alive? She'd cure you better than any doctor.'

He folds the drawing he has completed, puts it with the others into the case, puts his pencil in his pocket.

'You're right. It's time to go on. We can't just sit around all day.'

She stands, brushes down her skirt where strands of grass have caught to it.

'We'll need to find somewhere for the night.'

She does not know where that will be, only that she wants to be over into the next valley. The lone harvester has made slow progress across the field. A couple of women are coming to gather the wheat into sheaves. She

229

hears them call greetings to one another. The afternoon is still hot and there is a long way to walk.

A cart comes alongside them as they reach the crest of the hill. The horse moves slowly even though the cart is empty. The driver has a black felt hat low over his eyes and his reins hang slack. She might have thought he was asleep only he calls out to them.

'Where are you going?'

'That way.'

'Get in if you like.'

The driver pushes the hat back and looks at them and at their cases. He is an old man. There is weariness to him. He has a grey moustache, stubble on his chin and across the furrows of his cheeks. His voice when he speaks drags like the horse.

'Going far?'

'Home.'

'Where's that?'

'Our mother's sick. We're going to her.'

And when he looks at Augustin she says, 'He's my brother. He doesn't speak.'

'Wise man,' the driver says, and tips his hat back over his eyes.

The man in the field down below is sharpening his scythe.

'Do you expect to be there tonight?'

'Tomorrow.'

'Then you'll be needing to stop somewhere. You can stop with me if you like. There's room. There's a hayloft. And there's only me there.'

'Thank you, that's very kind.'

'Looks like he needs a rest. You can go on tomorrow when he's rested.'

The horizon has turned to purple above the horse's ears.

She speaks softly. Augustin lies near her in the dark. She cannot tell if he is sleeping or not, but it doesn't matter. She hears the latch of a door opening as the old man crosses the yard to the privy in the middle of the night, hears him return indoors. Tomorrow they will be home.

'We didn't know what the war would mean for us. There was that last beautiful summer and we heard about what was happening across Europe but it all seemed such a long way off as if it couldn't touch us – or that was what I thought anyway. It wasn't our war, after all. I was so young then. Other things seemed to matter so much more. Andrei. Not going to Paris. I lived in my father's house in Bucharest. I went to a college in the daytime, a strict place run by French nuns, and then I went back to his house and in the evenings he used to take me out with him to meet his friends. He said he'd try and make up for its not being Paris. He never said anything about Andrei – I don't know if my mother talked to him, how much he knew. He bought me dresses. He took me to the opera and to fashionable restaurants. The war hadn't touched the city yet except in people's conversations and in the uniforms you saw. Everything was very fashionable. The restaurants were shiny. My father's friends wore beautiful clothes and they were witty and their hands danced when they talked. I had my hair cut and I wore beautiful clothes too and smiled at the right moments. I think he was proud of me. But I was immensely critical of them all. I was young. I told myself I was different from them. I kept looking at them and thinking how superficial they all were, he and his friends, so clever and stylish, all of them seeming to me like people in films when you know the women have been dressed just for that scene, and their clothes have never been worn for real life, and they speak lines they have been given, and the rooms they walk in have nothing behind them and everything exists only in two dimensions. I was thinking how the world they lived in wasn't true and couldn't last. And there was all the politics, the Iron Guardists, the Germans who swaggered about the city, that told me I was right.

'Beneath the surface, I was angry. I was angry all that time. I expected to hear from Andrei. I thought there must be some mistake. I thought that he would write to me at least. When no letters came I told myself it was because of the war; that normal communications couldn't be relied upon. But we were getting letters from England and from just about everywhere else. I wrote a letter to him but I didn't post it. I had to hear something from him first. I wrote other letters later and burned them.

'Once I got angry with my father. We were in a taxi coming back from a restaurant. All through the dinner I'd been watching people, hating them just for being who they were, I suppose, and not being anyone else. They used to say Bucharest was like Paris. I asked how anyone could say that. Paris to me meant culture and civilisation and reason and fairness. "Is this like Paris?" I said. "Is anything here like Paris – apart from a few boulevards and an imitation Arc de Triomphe? It's all fake, isn't it? I don't think it's really like Paris at all. Look at the Gypsies. Look at all the poor people on the streets. Look what's going on here. This place is full of lies." I don't think he knew what to say to that. He didn't really know me very well. I don't think he had any idea what I was talking about.'

'In the break from college I went home. It was to be the last time but I didn't know that then, only that I was already disconnected from it. I made the train journey alone. The landscape was very bleak. It was cold and wet and all the dust of the summer had turned to mud. The car that Ilie brought to pick me up was spattered and dirty just from the journey to the railway station.

'There was a bitter edge to the wind. Such bitter winds we used to get there, that blew down from Russia. Perhaps it was the wind that made the place seem so empty, driving people indoors or into grey huddles. The villages smelled of cabbage as they always do that time of year.

'I remember Ilie said that he wasn't going to be our driver any more. He was joining the army. Who'll drive us then? I asked. He said József could drive. I thought József was too old, and anyway he was the groom. József knows how to drive, Ilie said, and there was you. You wouldn't be joining the army and you could do József's work in the stables. I said I supposed there wasn't much work to do any more. That's right, he said.

'Until that moment I don't think I'd ever considered the possibility that Ilie or any of the staff might want to do anything but work for us. Now I noticed him, noticed that he was still young, not even ten years older than me, and strong. And he knew about machines. Of course he would want to go and fight in the war, if – when – the war happened. I should have seen that. Coming back from being away I was starting to see things differently. It was as if I was seeing the place from the outside for the first time.'

The hay in the loft smells sweet. It takes her back. There are things of which she has never spoken to anyone, of which she will not speak even to a deaf man in the dark.

Her mother came out to the porch to greet her. There was a commotion of dogs about them as they kissed, racing out and surging about their legs, that made the meeting easier.

'It's good to see you.'

'Good to be home.'

Their kisses barely touched.

When they went into the house the dogs' feet skittered on the parquet. She bent down to them and fondled their silky ears and let them lick her face. The big tiled stove was burning in the hall but the other rooms were cold.

'I thought it a waste to heat them,' Marina said. 'Just myself here, rattling around. I have my study warm, and Ileana's lit a fire up in your room, but now you've come we should get her to put a fire somewhere else. Where would you like it, do you think? In the drawing room perhaps? But perhaps that's too big. I don't know where you'll want to be.'

'Let's think about it in the morning.'

She went up to her room. She sat on her bed for a long time before she opened her case. She thought it was a dead room. She could feel how the room had been shuttered all the time that she was away; how it had been without light as well as heat.

As she went back down the stairs the Weimaraners got up again from their place on the rug before the stove. They were bored by the lack of people, the lack of hunting that resulted from the lack of men. Come, Spitzy, Heinz. She put on her coat and hat and threw open the doors, ran after them as they rushed out towards the trees.

At dinner they sat like two icons regarding one another.

'How are things in Bucharest?'

'Just the same.'

'But how about you? Are you enjoying yourself?'

'Yes, everything's fine.'

'Where did you have your hair done?'

'A friend of father's took me.'

'It's lovely like that.'

'It's how everybody has it nowadays.'

'And you're wearing make-up.'

'Do you mind?'

'Just so long as you don't wear too much, at your age. No need to look vulgar.'

'Of course not.'

'You're not eating much. Don't you like Paraschiva's food any more?'

She was so cool, her mother. There was something still and carved about her, as if she was a fine piece cut out of marble and you knew before you touched her that she would be cooler than her surroundings. And because of that you didn't touch her or tell her things, and she became ever cooler and more still.

Her mother wanted everything to do with Andrei to be over, never mentioned again. But it wasn't all over. Safta could never have told her that. It was still no more than a suspicion, an intuition within her, and she didn't dare to speak it even to herself.

In the morning she woke early and went riding. She rode a long way, through the woods and away from the village, away from everyone. The ground was still heavy from the rain. On the tracks the horse's hooves sank deep in mud and she could do no more than walk. On the open hillside she kicked the horse into a gallop. She rode on for miles and the land stretched endless before her. She rode on until the horse tired. She felt that she could have gone on and on until the feeling in her was pounded away.

When she got back Augustin was waiting on the block by the gate. She could see that he had been worrying about her. She had always been able to read his face.

He came to hold the horse.

'It's good to see you, Tinu.' She meant this when she said it more than anything she had said since coming home.

No, she thought. He is deaf and mute. He can have no sense of my confusion.

She washed her hands under the pump and went in through the back door to the kitchen rather than round to the front of the house. Mama Anica was there and Paraschiva with her sleeves rolled up and her hands dipped in flour. You got up so early, Paraschiva said, I thought you'd be hungry when you came in. The ride had made her hungrier than she had been in days. Paraschiva had made thick polenta pancakes and she had put out bread, cheese, pork, sausage, whatever was left over from the day before. She ate a piece of everything except the pork which she felt she could not stomach. Paraschiva was kneading dough. She watched Paraschiva's arms that were so strong and brown working the dough on the board. She felt her own strength coming back to her. How was it in the city,

Paraschiva asked. Paraschiva had never been to a city in her life.

'It's the city. Lots of buildings and cars and trams, and people in suits and hats.'

'You'll be missing fresh food, if you've been in the city. There's some lovely soured cream, in that bowl on the sideboard. Take some of that with the pancakes. I don't suppose you get any of that over there.'

Paraschiva took more flour in cupped hands and sprinkled it over the mound of dough.

Of course they have soured cream in the city, Paraschiva, she was going to say. People bring it in straight from the dairies. Women like you come in from the countryside every morning and bring in fresh cream and cheese and fruit. Thousands of them. They bring vegetables and spread them to sell on the pavements. Walnuts. Garlic in endless ropes. Vast baskets full of flowers. There is more choice than you could imagine . . .

She was going to say something like that but when she went to pick up the bowl it slipped from her fingers to the floor. Her two hands held still for a second as if they kept the bowl in their grip even as she gazed down at the cream spilling about her feet. And she threw herself down on the chair and cried like a child.

'Oh you poor girl,' Mama Anica exclaimed, seeing the meaning in it.

She was sitting with her head on the table crying, and beneath her a white pool of cream and blue-flowered shards of china. The old woman reached over and stroked the hair that was so tangled from the ride, pulled gnarled fingers through and smoothed it, stroked her quivering shoulders and her back.

'How many months?'

'How do you know?'

It's like that, Mama Anica said. Sometimes when a woman was pregnant the muscles went like that, inexplicably, things just slipped away. She had seen it before. She had felt it herself, the strangeness of it. There are things like that that you can sense, she said. You can sense it in the skin of a woman, in the smell of her, in the way her feet are planted on the ground.

Paraschiva began to mop up the cream. She had laid a piece of linen over the bread and put it to rise, all in her own time, no urgency to anything, and only then had she taken a cloth in her hand and bent her sturdy form down over the floor. When she was done she shifted back on to her heels and asked if she had told the young man.

Mama Anica made up a tea. Mama Anica knew things, people believed that. Women came to the back door and Mama Anica sent them away with cures. Safta had thought it little more than superstition, because they were ignorant and because Mama Anica was old – she had been old as long as anyone seemed to have known her – and had lines on her face that made her look wise.

She did not know what went into the tea, only that it was dark and bitter, but Mama Anica would not allow her to sweeten it with honey. She said that honey would stop it from working. Safta drank the tea as she was told. In the nights she woke with cramps. She could not be sure that the tea was the cause. She told herself she didn't really believe in it. If it worked so well then why did Paraschiva not make use of it when Augustin's father had deserted her? Then she started to be afraid. Her thoughts carried on and asked, was it that it only partly worked, Paraschiva being so big and strong? Was that why her boy was born as he was? She spent much of the nights awake and when she slept she had dreams of snakes that gnawed at her, snakes with teeth and the skeletons of snakes on the bank of the lake where she had swum with Andrei. Then Andrei was there and he said they could not be snakes because snakes did not have those kind of bones. Or perhaps they were only the skins of snakes, dry and white, and the snakes had slithered out of them and away. She got up in the mornings and drank the tea again and then she went out and rode. She had Augustin saddle up the Lipizzaner. The horse had not been ridden in weeks and was very fresh. She rode recklessly. The rain held off and the ground hardened but there was mist that on some days didn't clear and she rode out all the same. She wanted to know nothing but the wind on her face and the smells of the earth and of the horse's sweat. One of those mornings, out there on the hillside out of sight of anyone, she fell. The horse tripped and she fell hard on to the ground and rolled, and lay stunned on the grass and felt the shudder of the impact inside her. The horse came back to her where she lay and after a time she remounted and rode home. She had bruises on her arm and on her hip but no other visible injury.

The bleeding did not happen until she got back to Bucharest. She was very afraid. She had to confide in someone so she spoke to the woman who was her father's mistress at the time, who seemed to be the sort of woman who would understand such things. Ramona was sympathetic and discreet, and took her to a doctor to get her checked. The doctor said that miscarriages occurred quite commonly at that time in a pregnancy, particularly in a first pregnancy when a girl was as young as herself.

It was not long after that she decided to become a nurse. Because, she said, the war was coming.

Her father was angry with her. She did not know if Ramona had spoken with him. 'You don't know what you're letting yourself in for, my dear Safta,' her father said. 'It's not a world for girls like you.'

'Why not?' she said. 'At least I'll be doing something with my life.'

There was a row and she moved out of his house. She wrote a letter to him and she wrote separately to her mother saying that she would be on her own now. For a time she did not even tell them where she was.

She wakes at sunrise. Lies still with her eyes open and watches the light increase and give definition until everything at last has outline and colour. Knows that she is in this place, this one moment and no other. Then she sleeps again.

By the time she comes down Augustin is sitting on the step making a drawing and the old man has put out a breakfast for them on the table beside the summer kitchen.

'He's quite an artist, your brother.'

'He's always done that.'

'Is it a real place in the picture?'

'I think all the places in his pictures are real. Sometimes he adds things, things that I don't understand, but the places are real.'

'Would he draw this place?'

'He might.'

'Ask him.'

She shows Augustin what the old man wants. She cannot predict what he will do. Usually his drawings are generated within himself. He draws what he wants to draw and she does not know if he will work to order. But he seems to agree. He looks around him for a while with his eyes narrowed, studying the place. It is a place worthy of a picture, the little farmstead at the edge of its village, the road below, a track coming to meet it down the grass of the opposing hillside. He chooses his view and sets to work, and once he has started on it she cannot hurry him. She sits, and the old man sits and does not go to his field, and there is the sound of Augustin's pencil between them and sometimes the toneless humming that comes from him as he works.

They don't get on the road until late in the morning. It is already getting hot.

'That was good. He liked your picture very much.'

She can see that Augustin is pleased with himself. He is proud of the picture and the man has paid him for it with food. He walks briskly for an hour or two with his case tight under one arm and the bag of food over his shoulder. Then they stop for a rest and he takes out one of the drawings he had made of the house the day before and starts another drawing on the back of it, sketching the land before them.

'No, you can't do that now. We should keep going if we're to get there tonight.'

She stands in front of him, picks up the case, holds it out to him, but he does not rise. He goes stubbornly on with his picture, outlining the track they are to walk, a line of stooks like statues on the horizon, a single oblong cloud in the sky. She walks off, bluffing him as she would a small child, but has to come back as he has failed to follow, throws herself down defeated on the grass. She has known no one in her life so stubborn. It is not possible to make him aware of time. She has always known that in him. For him there are only moments, each one present and immediate, but no sense of the hours and days passing; no continuity, before and after. There is some kind of instinctive clock in him that used to make it possible for him to surprise them all by turning up for meals punctual to the minute, or to the stables when he used to work there, but it operates only as he chooses. He cannot be made to conform to time beyond that.

'Come on, Tinu. Put it away and get up. We really need to go.'

His eyes pass between paper and landscape without meeting her own. His mouth that never speaks holds its horizontal line.

'Have it your own way then.'

She plucks a grass stalk, strips it and puts it between her lips. It is so long since she has been in the countryside.

'I suppose we shall be there tomorrow. Or the next day. Or the day after that.'

Only this matters: here and now. It matters that the weather is fine and that they have the food that the old man has given them. She takes off her shoes. They are sturdy nurse's shoes, not bad for walking in but it is good to take them off. There is a stream a little way off. Barefoot she walks to it across the grass, puts her feet into the shallow water and feels the mud between her toes. It clouds

245

the water so much that her ankles disappear. She wades further, hitching up her skirt, bends when she comes to where the stream is clear and throws water over her face and hair.

She knows the way across country from here. They are within riding distance of the house. She will remember, if not too much has changed. There is a place in the forest where they could camp, if they don't reach it today. She doesn't know how long it will take on foot. It occurs to her as they start to walk again that it is possible that they are already on land that her family once owned. They might camp on what used to be their land, and get up and walk the rest of the way in the morning on what used to be their land. The thought is odd, after the years she has spent sharing cramped rooms in overcrowded cities. How could anyone ever have owned so much land?

Augustin's eyes are sharp. He sees it before she does and points it out: the long white house like a faraway ship, still catching the sunlight though the valley below has already fallen into shade. They approach through the trees. It is good, she thinks, that they are coming from the direction of the forest because if there is someone inside the house they will not be seen. At the edge of the trees where the garden used to begin but where now there is wilderness, she stops. She pulls him back beside her just as he is about to step out into the open. He shakes his head, indicating that they can go on. For the first time, he leads the way. It is as if he has been here recently and knows what they will find. That's it, she thinks, seeing it suddenly. He has been here. He must have come here before he came to Iaşi. So is it empty then? He knows that we will find it empty. All of the windows are shuttered save one, where the shutter hangs away broken. There is no movement. There is not even a track among the weeds on the driveway to show that anyone comes there.

It looks more than empty. It looks hollow. It will be dark and dead inside like a dead and hollow tree. For a moment she is afraid. She sees that the walls are not so white now that they are close. The white is stained, streaked in places almost to the colour of the bark of the acacias. But the leaves of the acacias are green as ever. The shade beneath them has that soft quality of acacia shade. And there are dogs slinking out from the porch. Some of the dogs have the paleness of Weimaraners.

The dogs bark at them. She walks forward, speaking gently, calling their names. But she cannot expect Spitzy and Heinz to still be alive. These dogs are only mongrels though they have elements of the Weimaraners in them. One thin black cur has the Weimaraners' yellow eyes. She braves the ghostly eyes and it lets her pass.

The porch has collected leaves over the years, a debris of leaves piled into the corners. Leaves all along the base of the door. The right-hand panel has a sign on it stating that the property has been expropriated by the state. She puts her hand to it, to the heavy brass handle. She knows it will be locked. It seems scarcely possible that she could just walk in after all these years. She turns the handle, puts a hand against a panel and pushes, just in case. The dogs have come in close behind her, as if they trust her to open it, as if there will be something for them inside. She turns around and shoos them away. Nothing for any of them but dried leaves.

'Tinu?'

He has gone. His case sits on the porch step between the columns but he is nowhere to be seen.

She steps out, looks across the grass, then back at the house. She walks around the side of the house towards the stable yard. The stables have burned down. There are only black and broken ruins. The cottages where the servants had lived have walls intact but their roofs have fallen in. She climbs over rubble and debris, round to the garden side of the house. There, the shutters are open along the verandah. The further ones are opening even as she looks. The shutters are being thrown back, the windows behind them opened and catching the last of the light.

'Tinu!'

She runs to the verandah steps, along to the last window.

He is there, inside the house, laughing, throwing the window open. She climbs in. His laughter is rare but when it comes it is like bells, resounding through the empty rooms as he runs away. She chases after him, door after door, room after room, seeing the evening light come in down the length of the house, churning up a golden trail of dust. All the way she hears his laughter. Then she runs ahead of him back to the hall and up the stairs. She takes one side and he takes the other, opening all the windows in the bedrooms, shocking the rooms with air.

They come to the nursery last. He stops, panting. There is the map of the world on the wall. She gathers herself and looks about. He is coughing. All the dust has made him cough. There is so much dust and it has lain still for so long. She wonders when the house was finally abandoned. Who was last here.

'You knew how to get in. Where did you get in? The dining-room window? Show me.'

When he has recovered they walk back down the corridor past the open bedroom doors. She goes more soberly now, looking about her, down their footprints on the stairs. Though the rooms are empty of furniture her ancestors remain on the walls above the hall, torn in their frames. There is the smashed chandelier dangling remnants of crystal. So the Russians came through. That much she might have predicted. But someone else has been here. In the dining room, against the wall, lies a straw mattress. A few other things show some more recent and solitary occupation of the room: a bucket that must have brought water, an empty bottle, some old newspapers and dry sticks for kindling on the floor beside the stove.

'You?'

He shakes his head.

'But you knew the way in.'

The catch on the window has been broken. The window must just have been pulled to and wedged; and the shutter also, not barred, so that it will have been blown open and broken in a gale. Who? How long ago? She can learn nothing from the dust on the floor that is now so messed with their prints. She has an idea, looks at the newspapers by the stove. There are Russian ones as well as Romanian, and the most recent are dated from 1947. But whoever lit the fire might have found them already in the house. She opens the door of the stove. Ash. What did she expect? There is no telling how long ago a heap of ash was burnt.

'Let's not sleep here. Someone's been here before us. I don't feel right about it. But the mattress is good. I wonder where it came from anyway? Not from here. Whoever it was must have brought it. Maybe it came from the ruins of the cottages by the stables. Let's take it, move it somewhere else.' She has him help her pick up the mattress and carry it along the enfilade of rooms. 'The green drawing room, let's put it there. It always used to be such a beautiful room, so cool. It was green like the shade of the trees, only cooler, with the draught from the windows on both sides. And there were the mirrors, remember? Long mirrors in gilt frames that made the room seem to go on for ever. They're gone now but you can see the shadows where they hung.' The room is all the greener with the growth of the wisteria. The plant has grown into a jungle right over the far end of the verandah and has wound its tendrils all the way to the windows of the drawing room. In another year the leaves will cover the glass. The light inside will be like light underwater.

'Wait, let's sweep it first. I saw a broom somewhere. But let me do it alone. This dust is not good for you.' She runs to the doorway by the kitchen. Comes back with an old broom, begins to sweep the boards, softly as the dust rises. She sweeps a corner. Pulls the mattress there. She goes on sweeping and the dust runs in a wave before her. She will not let him back in the room until the dust in the air has settled.

In the meantime he has climbed out of the window on to the verandah. He has found a couple of cane chairs there, where they were about to be engulfed by the wisteria. They are grey with age and there are breaks in the cane but they are more or less serviceable. He has brought them one by one and set them just before the window. There is a wooden bench. He has pulled that in place as well. He brings their cases. Then the pile of newspapers from the dining room. 'We shan't be needing a fire yet,' she says, 'it's so warm.' But that is not what he has brought the newspapers for. He takes the pile apart and squares it, and places it neatly beside his case on the wooden bench. Then he takes out his pencils and places them on top.

'Look what I found, on the floor just beneath the window. I thought it was just a blown leaf but it's not, it's a dead bird. A sparrow, see.' The small brown bird is tiny in her hand. 'Do you think it came in the window? Then it would have been the last time it was open. It flew in and then the window was closed and it was trapped, and it must have happened quite recently because it's not decayed at all; the feathers, all of it, perfect. Or I suppose it could have come in some other way, through a chimney or a hole in the roof or something, and then it would have found the window and died there because that was the only daylight that it could find. Here, maybe you'd like to have it to draw.'

She lays the bird beside his things on the bench.

'How long do you think we can stay here? I only thought of coming here, I haven't thought beyond that.' She can feel tears rushing to her eyes and does not know why she should cry in this moment when she is happy. 'It was just that we needed to be here. We had to get out of Iaşi. It was making you ill. You'll be better here, I know you will.' With the tears clouding her eyes she strokes his thin face. She pulls him to her and hugs him harshly. 'Don't worry. I'll make a plan. I'll find someone you know, find somewhere for you. If I can't find anything else, then you can go on to the sanatorium after all. Tomorrow I'll go into the village. We'll eat the last of what that man gave us and then I'll have to go tomorrow to find some food.'

Even after the war was over he kept on making soldiers. He cut them out of any old scraps and drew their uniforms on to them, tunics and belts and buttons, the caps on their heads and the wrappings they wore instead of boots. They were made without the care that he had usually put into his figures, without variety. There was just enough detail to identify them as Russians, no more than that. He made them and left them behind him wherever he had been, until one day Mama Anica decided to collect them up and destroy them. She went about and picked them up from the floor and the chairs and the tables and beneath his bed, and placed them together like a pack of cards. She went to Augustin with the pack in her hand.

'That's enough,' she said. 'You've done enough of them now.'

She made him hand her the soldier he had in his hand that moment, which he had cut out but on which he had not yet begun to draw.

'Are there any more? Let's see in your pockets.'

There were a couple crumpled in his trousers. She smoothed them and added them to the pack.

Then she went to the stove and opened the door and fed them to the fire.

'There. They're gone now. No more soldiers.'

They were living up by the big house again, he and Mama Anica and József and Stanislaw. For a time they had all that they needed. They had kept the vegetables planted, and there were the hens they had hidden and the cow that József had brought back from the forest. No bees any more as soldiers had burned out the hives. They seemed all right while the old men were with them. But all across the countryside folk were hungry and on the move, and József took it into his head to go back to the village he came from, in the Székely land across the mountains. Then Stanislaw also began to speak of going home. He had a sister who would take him in. He hesitated a long time before he left, mumbling with the shame of deserting the house where he had served so long.

One morning Mama Anica decided that they too should go. She thought that she had heard wolves in the night. The dogs themselves were becoming like wolves. They were running as a pack with the strays now that they had to fend for themselves. She could no longer be sure that they would be any protection.

They travelled like the others they had seen before. They took with them only the little that they could carry and lived however they could along the way. Sometimes they travelled in company and sometimes on their own. An old woman and a mute were no threat to anyone. They were not part of a convoy like the first war refugees but pieces of a more random and fragmented exodus. People were taking off individually or in little groups, like scared birds; rising and scattering, moving on, settling for a moment and then scattering again, keeping only to the constant of a direction south. Just as surely as those others before them, they were driven by the war. People went on being driven by the war long after the war was finished, because of the hunger that followed on from war. Where the war had passed, animals were taken and fields were not planted. After the war had gone there was hunger.

It was the time of year when the birds flew north. Augustin looked up into the sky and saw high above them the flocks of birds flying in the opposite direction, following the same migration routes they used each year, flying north as those below went south.

He had no idea that the land could stretch so far or be so empty. Once or twice on the road they passed through villages that seemed to be entirely empty. Most times they were just sparsely populated, some houses and yards abandoned, others lived in, and the people who lived within their gates might come out and offer what little they had, if only bread or maize or salt. Between the villages the fields ran wild. Thistles, oats, wild flowers and the reseeded remnants of previous crops of maize tangled beneath a year or two years' dried growth of grass. It was good that Mama Anica knew what there was to eat in them. She found leaves, mushrooms, roots. She dug up the fat roots of burdock and ground thistles that boiled into a starchy pulp. Sometimes in the fields there were craters, and the trees that ran along the road were broken off, and he knew that there had been fighting in that place.

The south was flat. The hills had gradually stretched themselves out. The land was flat and the road ran straight between fields that were once more tended and controlled. Villages were strung loosely along the roads, avenues of unbroken trees and houses and wells, everything low beneath the great breadth of sky.

The people there were meant to take in the refugees. An old woman and a slightly built mute youth were no threat to anyone on the road but they were not much use either. It was a while before they found a place, and then it was only a room in a ramshackle house at the edge of a village with a rough peasant couple and a gang of filthy children. The moment Mama Anica moved in she cleaned the room they had been given, that was along the yard from the main house. Then she cleared and swept the portion of yard before their door. She swept that space every day thereafter of every leaf and chicken dropping that landed there. It was an expression of her separation from the family in the house. The man was brutish, callous with his animals and taciturn with people.

The woman was heavy and sullen. Mama Anica heard them sometimes when the man came back drunk from the bar and knew that the woman had cause for her anger. These people could be trouble, she saw, but she could not guess the form that the trouble would take.

The summer passed. They worked the length of narrow fields that seemed to stretch to the horizon. They hoed baked soil in straight lines, rows of tomatoes and peppers and onions, the uprooted weeds wilting fast on the ground behind them. Augustin was a good worker. There was wiry endurance in his body, and he had persistence. He would close his mind to everything but the blade of the hoe on the soil and the day would pass. Sometimes he would pause a moment to stretch his back and he would see the woman watching him. She was heavy and coarse but she had soft eyes like a cow's. He bent to the hoe again and forgot her.

When the work was done he would sit in the shade of the vine on their side of the yard and take out whatever paper he had found and start to draw. At first this was hard as the children gathered about and jeered at him. They laughed all the more when he wrapped his arm about his picture and turned his back so that they could not see. They shouted behind his back to make him turn and, when he did not, they roared louder, and if he did not hear then in the end he sensed their presence, and he looked round and saw their vicious little faces with the big shadows of the vine leaves falling across them. Mama Anica came out and scolded them. In Poiana any child would have been broken by her scolding, but here in this other place she seemed to have lost her power. They went on with their staring and their taunting until one evening Augustin flew into a rage. He grabbed the child who was closest, who happened to be the oldest boy, and beat him hard. The boy was hurt, and worse, he was humiliated. He kept his distance mostly after that.

Augustin drew the kind of things he had always drawn. The room they lived in. The saucepans in the summer kitchen. The rest of the place. The land that was just a dull line beneath the jutting fingers of trees. The big road that went through the village though the village itself seemed nowhere; the trucks that went along the road so much faster than the wagons. And he drew the signs that had sprung up at the entrance to the village and the banners that hung down from the big two-storey house at its centre: red signs with white words and white signs with red or black words; and the same words appeared again in newspapers and on pages stuck to posts and walls. He liked these new words that were printed in a variety of typefaces, bold block capitals, oblique, chunky, standing sometimes on their shadows. There were human figures that went with these new strong words that were like real people but bigger and stronger, with square jaws and outstretched muscled arms, standing tall against the sky. These he drew also. There was a bold and graphic beauty to them that he sought to imitate.

Mama Anica saw the drawings and was glad that there weren't any more soldiers in them. At the shop in the village she bought him chalks in a variety of colours, extra red ones as that was the colour he had begun to use most. She did not worry about the meaning in what he drew. It wasn't as if she could read the words herself but she appreciated the way that they were formed.

Mama Anica was asleep in their room the night that the woman first came to him. It was a fine moonlit night, so light outside that there were shadows along the floor of the yard. Augustin had not gone to bed at his usual time but sat out late in his place beneath the vine and watched as thin blades of cloud passed across the white disc of the moon. The night was exceptionally bright and to him in the yard there it seemed exceptionally still. There was a wedding party going on at the other end of the village but he knew nothing of the noise and the dancing. From where he sat the village might as well have been abandoned. When the gate was opened it surprised him to know that anyone was around and awake.

It was the owners of the house stumbling home. It was clear to him that both of them were drunk, but from the way they clung on to each other you could not tell which one was the drunker. They went to their room and lit the lamp. Augustin sat in the dark and saw the room become bright. He watched without guilt. There was never guilt to his watching of others. He saw the man throw himself down on to the bed fully clothed while the woman undressed. He saw the lamp go out. And then after a little time the woman came out again into the moonlight. She had only a shawl about her. He could see her nakedness beneath the shawl. It gave him such a shock to see her that he thought she wasn't real. She was an apparition, some blown-up and monstrous figure from a dream. She came right up to him and she was hot. He could feel that even before she touched him. She was hot and she smelled of drink and already she smelled of sex. She spoke words that he could not hear. Crude words. She was swearing about her bastard of a husband passed out on the bed.

She came to him again. In the day he looked for acknowledgement from her but there was none. Not once again did her eyes meet his. He knew because of this that it was wrong. She was using him like a thing. He looked back with revulsion at her heavy face, her body when she was working in the field, her thick legs spread apart, her breasts that hung down and swayed as she bent to pick tomatoes. He began to avoid her, working away from her at the far end of the line, shutting himself inside his room, ensuring that she could not find him alone. He had some idea of punishment. He punished himself by working harder when the sun was higher. One evening he made a figure of her. There was obscenity in the figure. He made her naked as when she came to him, pink. He made her out of a piece of soft card that melted with the pressure and the sweat of his hands. It started to come apart and he crushed it into a ball, threw it away.

He could not know that there would be a consequence to his rejection.

He has a page before him. It is a page cut square from a newspaper, a background of dense columns of type. It is the sort of page on which it is usually easy for him to make a picture. Yet he does not know how to begin what he now wants to draw. He makes a line, makes another beside it, shades, cross-hatches. When pictures come to him usually the lines suggest themselves, one after another, the elements falling into place like pieces of a construction, piecing together into the final form. For this particular thing that he has in mind no satisfactory form emerges from the lines he makes. He turns the page over and starts again.

Prison was blackness. Whiteness. A box where there was only darkness or light. When it was dark there was nothing: no knowledge of anything existing beyond the door, nothing but the sensations of his body, cold, hunger, the touch of the walls, of his rough blanket – grey, he would remind himself that the blanket was grey before the light went off, that the walls had been white but were scored with grey; he would deliberately recall the form of each thing within his reach (all of them things of right angles and flatness and without colour) in an attempt to fill the void. Then when the light came on again it was a light so bare that there were no shadows or depths. And still, nothing beyond the door, nothing outside the box.

When he was first brought in there were doors and passages; a bleak high space with metal staircases and landings; doors along the landings, rows of doors. They made him climb two flights of stairs to the upper landing. He walked so tentatively that the guard hit him from behind and pushed him like an animal herded towards a pen. When he looked down to his feet he could see through the diamond pattern of holes in the metal grid to the lower landing, and through that to the floor such a long way below. He repeated the memory to himself time and again so that he might fix himself in some exterior reality: the sequence of doors, passages and stairs and landings. He held to each image like a man holding on to the edge of a cliff, but in time all of them dissolved like dreams and he felt that he was falling, and he kept on falling until the door was opened once again and he was taken out and back along the landings and down the stairs and through the passages and doors, and outside into a yard where he saw that there were others like himself walking in circles – or rather in squares, walking a straight line and turning at the corners. All of the prisoners had faces that were very pale. There was a covering of snow on the ground, not where they walked but in the centre of the yard that was like an island between them, and the faces of the men were white as if they had taken on the reflection of the snow. It could not be the reflection of the sky. The sky above was a grey rectangle that had less light in it than the snow.

He takes other pieces of newspaper. He draws door, walls, bed, blanket, bucket. He draws a box from the inside. Then from the outside, as if he looked down on it from some distance above. He screws up each drawing when he has done it and throws it away.

He understood at the time that it was the drawings that were his crime. He understood and yet he didn't understand, because no one had showed interest in his pictures before – not strangers anyway, not peasant women or villagers or men from the town, like these big men in long coats, who crowded into his room and then left, leaving the door locked against him. Three of them returned later with boxes. They went inside and again they closed the door. When they came out the boxes were filled with all of his papers. Every piece of paper from the room was gone: the pictures he had pinned to the walls, the figures he had lined up beneath the window, his stack of home-stitched books, the stacks of unused paper as well, all the scraps and labels and receipts he had collected, the schoolbooks the children had let him take when they had finished with them, the old newspapers and magazines and pamphlets and election flyers. Even Mama Anica's icon was gone, and hardly any of that was paper. It was made almost entirely of tin.

He saw them carry the boxes out, three full boxes, each one as much as a man could carry on his own, to the waiting car. The boxes were too tall for the boot to shut on them so they opened a passenger door and put them on the back seat, two of them piled one upon the other, the third in the centre. He went to the door of the room that had been his home. Everything in it was overturned, thrown across the floor. There was not a space clear on the floor, and the walls were bare, bald as eggshell. Bare, white, smudged, stained, they were like the shell of an egg that has lain forgotten on the henhouse floor, that he would not want to pick up because of its smell if it should crack. He closed his eyes to close out the sight but that did not stop it from cracking.

A hand gripped his shoulder. He was quite passive under the hand. His head was full of the foul smell. They took him to the car. There was barely room for him on the back seat, crammed in beside the boxes. The three men sat together in the front so that their shoulders and heads were like a wall before him. He looked to the side, out of the window. At the gate of the house, Mama Anica was an old crone crying, and the woman stood there sullen and knowing with her children beside her and watched him go. He noticed that they had arranged themselves in a line in order of height as if for a formal photograph. They had all of them been husking maize when the car arrived. In the open barn behind them he could see the mountain of yellow cobs and a buff litter of husks. In other yards and barns, as the car passed along the road, the same image was repeated. It was a grey day and the yellow of the maize was strong.

The car drove on out of that village. The road was straight and after a while another village spilled along it in the same way as the first. Every place looked much the same in this landscape and in every place there was maize. Then at the edge of a town they turned off to a large low building that must previously have been a manor, not so beautiful as Poiana but it had a fine red banner and a star over the front door. They took the papers out first as if those were all that mattered, left him in the car with the driver who did not watch him but only leant on the wheel and smoked. Later someone else came and took him into the house, but by a back entrance and down to a cellar where there were other prisoners, a crowd and a stink of men pressing against him.

He didn't know how much time had passed in the cellar, only that he was hungry. They took him upstairs into the room that had once been the dining room of the house, with a long table and faded rose damask curtains still at the windows. He had hoped there might be food but there were just his drawings laid out on the table and a man standing behind it.

He did not pay the man much attention at first. He had eyes only for his pictures that were so neatly arranged there on the polished wood.

There were some of his cut-out figures. There was one they had chosen that he had made with a handsome uniform, gold buttons on it and gold epaulettes, and it had a bushy moustache and a military hat with stars, and there was another that had a head shaped like a tank.

There was one of his books, that he had stitched together and covered with red card. It was one that he had made with care, made like a real book inside, with pictures of men and lines of writing beneath the pictures, and red frames around them made from strips of the same red card. The faces of these men were like real faces because they were copied from photographs. They were the four men he saw all over the place in posters and newspapers and in frames on walls and above doorways. Though the figures he drew from life or from imagination were no more than totems, when he copied from a flat page he could make a good likeness, and these faces were instantly recognisable in their line of nose and eye and eyebrow, and the shape of each grey beard or drooping moustache. The words also were real words that he had copied from pieces of print, random words that caught his eye: *ȚĂRANI, nu credeți!*; *TRAIASCA.*

Then there was the wall newspaper. This had been a large-scale work for him on which he had laboured for days on end. He had modelled it on the wall gazette that stood outside the House of Culture. The base was as big as an actual sheet of newspaper and he had coloured a border around it and was gradually filling it with smaller items and notices, some of them images of his own, some cut out from print: items of solid script, cartoons, photographs, headlines. *CETĂȚENI luați* SOARELE. The symbol of the sun that had been everywhere on posters at the time of the election. B.P.T. PCR. *JOS BURGHEZIE!!! JOS CAPITALISMUL!!!* Then, JOS MUNCITORII. And across the page in a bold red diagonal like a banner: *MOARTE CRIMINALILOR DE RĂZBOI.*

It was his work. All of these things were his work, put on view in this alien place. He walked the length of the table. He went from one item to the next, remembering how each one was made, seeing it anew, familiar and yet strange at the same time, observing details as he had not seen them before, noting where something was wrong or should be added or taken away, what he should not have done, what he might have done instead, where white space might yet be filled in the wall newspaper. He studied them all with an artist's compulsion. There was a little booklet that he had covered in white linen on which he had chalked a landscape – he had been pleased with that – and above the landscape that same symbol of the sun, but the chalk had become smudged and besides, they had placed it the wrong way up. How careless they were. They had put the sun underground and not in the sky. Didn't they see? He reached out to pick it up and turn it round, and as he did so he noticed the man again. He had almost forgotten that the man was there.

It was one of the men who had arrested him. He was not unfriendly to look at, a chubby-faced, balding man. He looked like a peasant really, as if he was not quite used to his city clothes. He had big crude peasant hands and a brightness to his eyes that Augustin did not at first interpret as anger. And he was shouting. Augustin was used to the look of people shouting. People always shouted when they discovered he couldn't hear, and it distorted their faces. It made them look hard and sometimes frightening but he had come to understand that usually they meant no aggression. In such circumstances it was his habit to withdraw, to hang his head, put his eyes to the floor. But this man came closer when he did that and shouted all the more vigorously and slammed his fat hand on to the little linen-covered book. Augustin looked down at the hand. He could tell how close the man's face was to his without looking up. He could feel the anger coming off him now, and he determined, stubborn as he was, to look down and stand his ground. To take a step back would only give the man more power.

His interrogator called him a saboteur, a counter-revolutionary, an enemy agitator. The more the interrogator shouted, the more the man came to hate him. This prisoner might be mute, the interrogator thought, but he was intelligent. He could see that in his eyes, which were cold and quick and clever. That humble downcast pose did not convince. He pulled up his head and slapped him hard. The eyes stared into his for a split second and then looked down again. A silent hooligan, that's what he was. A vagabond, a subversive, a danger to society.

He picked up a piece of folded paper from the table. It was the picture Augustin had been given by the Russian soldier, that he had folded down to fit inside a matchbox and had carried with him the four years since Paraschiva died. The interrogator took it in his thick fingers and folded it out again and again, and finally smoothed it flat on the table top.

'Look at this!' He slammed the table again with his fist.

The paper was much worn with handling. The gold border was torn. Parts had been scribbled over with flying words in Cyrillic script. Other parts of the image were worn away. Even so, any fool could see who the man was in the picture.

'Where did you get this?'

The interrogator had never known a subject so still before him, so apparently implacable. A subject who did not even look at him, as if he were not in the same room. If he were to look at him, deaf or not, then surely he might read the questions on his lips? He called over the guard who stood by the door, had him hold the prisoner's head so that he could not any longer look away, hit him each time he closed his eyes.

'Where did you learn to write Russian? Who taught you this?'

They had had the Cyrillic words translated. Some were crude, obscene. Augustin had learnt them from the things Russian soldiers had scratched on the walls at Poiana. Others he had memorised long ago, from icons and icon-ostases and painted skies in churches. Those words the interrogator recognised for himself from his own past. They were holy words, names of saints and angels. They called to mind his peasant mother's piety and his own superstitions, which remained in him even in these changed times. How could this supposed mute use such words to deface a picture of Stalin? This was not just counter-revolution. This was a double blasphemy.

There was no sense to any of it. The interrogator's anger. His pictures that he drew so privately, that were only for himself, exposed for all to see. Himself, exposed. No sense to this event, or the next or the next.

Down to the cellar.

Up again.

Another place.

Another interrogation room, the pictures again displayed.

Where he was taken in a transport, his pictures must also have been taken, handled by other hands, packed away in their boxes, re-sorted, rearranged according to systems other than his own.

He learned to be no more than an object, like his handled and folded and re-folded pictures.

To keep his head down, hands limp to his sides. To stand always in the corners of rooms, against the walls.

Not to look up.

And not any more to draw.

To get to the village Safta takes a route out through the overgrown garden and orchard and through the fields, directly to the priest's house on the little rise of land beside the church. She wants to be seen by as few people as possible and hopes that she will not be recognised by those who do see her. She is so much older than when she was here last, so much changed. But the priest's wife knows her as soon as she opens the door. 'You're just like your mother,' she says. 'I would have known you anywhere.'

The priest's wife herself seems to have aged twenty years in the last ten, the priest also. He is feeble now and white-haired though she remembers him bushy-bearded and robust.

He says that he sent a reply to the letter she wrote him.

'Where did you send it?'

'To Iaşi. To the address you gave.'

'I didn't receive it.'

A touch of fear in that: where letters do or do not go, who it is that reads them.

'There was nothing in it. Nothing that could matter. I said only the little that I knew. That Paraschiva died in the war and that the boy went south in the famine. A lot of people went then. The old woman went and the boy went with her. Many of them didn't come back.'

'What happened to Paraschiva?'

'Only the boy knows, if anyone does. It was when the Russians were here. They were living at the house. I didn't put that in the letter. There's a grave in the forest, not far off. We helped him get a cross made. The lad was very withdrawn after that.'

'And Mama Anica?'

'She was one who didn't come back.'

There is a moment of silence. She looks away from him and out of the small window, down past the church to the village street. There are not many figures on it at this time of the morning when most people are out in the fields, but there are chickens, and geese wandering along the banks of the stream, and a couple of old women spinning on a bench. Anyone would think nothing at all had happened here.

She asks about the house.

'The Russians did most of the damage, then it was abandoned. One night someone set fire to the stables. That was around the time of the expropriations. There were some acts of arson like that. On one of the other estates the peasants burned the forest. What a foolish thing to do, to burn the landlord's forest once he doesn't own it any more. We could see it in the distance. It went on burning for days. The stables seemed only a small thing after that. And God was kind. The fire didn't touch the house. That was luck, that there was no wind that night. There wasn't anybody trying to save it. Since then it's been locked up. Nobody has a use for a house like that nowadays.'

'No. I see that.'

'But you mustn't stay there. Somebody will see you.'

'We'll not stay long. Only a few days, for Augustin to rest and recover a little. He's been very ill.'

'He was ill when he came here in the winter.'

'So he was here? I thought that he was.'

'My wife tried to make him stay with us but he wanted to find you. He wrote your name. I didn't know that he could write.'

'He can write a few words, that's all, and my name is one of them.'

'I'd heard that you were at the hospital in Iaşi. It was important to him to find you.'

He's lying in the grass looking at the sky. She had expected to see him where she had left him but the verandah is deserted and his papers screwed up on the floor. She goes back into the garden to look for him, almost stumbles on to him hidden in the long grass.

'Look what I've got. This will keep us fed for days. And the first of the plums are ripe in the orchard. I tried one. There are masses of plums.'

She kneels down beside him and shows him what she has in the bag the priest's wife has given her: bread, sheep's cheese, sausage, vegetables from their garden. She breaks off the end of a loaf and takes a bite from a tomato. It's so ripe that she has to lean away to eat it so the drips don't fall on her blouse. Then she throws herself back on the grass with her arms wide. Her hands reach into the stalks. Her grandfather's lawn, how high it has grown. She thinks of him walking there with his pale dogs.

'Do you remember the lawnmower? Perhaps it's still here somewhere. I wonder what they've done with it. Remember how grandfather had that lawnmower shipped out here? He wanted the place like England. He wanted a lawn in stripes like they had in England. But nobody could bear to use the thing. My mother said it made a hellish noise and wouldn't let anyone start it so long as she was in the house. Ilie was the only person who was trusted to work it, but he thought it was beneath him. He was a driver, he said, not a gardener. Then some piece of it broke. Perhaps Ilie broke it himself to save his dignity – either that or one of the gardeners sabotaged it – and grandfather had to send all the way to England again for the part. You remember all of it, don't you? You were always there, watching.'

She rolls over and looks into his eyes. 'I sometimes think you see everything.'

She is solemn now.

'The priest told me about Paraschiva. I'm sorry. Did you see that too? I think you did, didn't you?'

He is not looking at the sky any more but watching the sun and the clouds passing in her face.

She bends close, putting her two hands to his cheeks.

'If only you had words for what you've seen.'

Later in the day he sits again at his drawing table on the verandah. She sees him get down to work with great seriousness. She wonders if there is some memory that the house has stirred in him, some memory perhaps of his mother. It has become clear to her that the drawings are his way of sorting and securing the world about him. If he has no words, she thinks, then at least he has these pictures. And when, as now, he makes such earnest steps at preparation, cutting out his pages, sharpening his pencil, arranging himself just so, closing his eyes in concentration, she thinks that he must have some project of importance in mind. She starts to move away from him to give him space, moving quietly even though she is aware that her noise cannot disturb him. There are still nightmares in him, she knows that. Perhaps the drawings will draw his nightmares out.

He looks at her directly, pulls her back, points to the second chair. She must sit there while he works. She had assumed that it was for himself that he was compelled to draw. The difficulty he is facing at this moment is that these drawings he wants to make are not for himself but for her.

He draws a gateway standing in a field. The field is wide and flat and there is nothing planted on it but the arch of the gateway, which has lettering along the top of it – spelling nothing – and stars.

He draws a group of low rectangular buildings. They are arranged in straight lines along a grid. Each building has many small windows. There is a high fence around the site.

'Poor Tinu,' she says. 'How could they do that to you?'

He draws line after line of slim rectangles with square heads on them, masses of identical totem figures one beside and behind another.

He draws another of the figures, but larger, on a separate page. When he comes to the square outline of the head, he pauses. He looks thoughtful. Then inside the square he draws what appear to be wings. The wings are somehow familiar but she can't think where she has seen them before.

He draws the wings again, but as they appear on the bonnet of a car. He has remembered the car precisely, the pattern of the radiator, the straps and vents on the bonnet, the curve of the running boards. It is the Lagonda. She sees that. Then the figure must be the driver of the Lagonda.

'But that's Andrei, isn't it? I don't understand.'

He holds the pencil over the drawing, looking intently at her, willing her to see.

'It can't be Andrei, not if it's what I think it is.'

So he takes another page, draws the camp gates again and stretching from them three rings of barbed wire fencing, watchtowers spaced along the rings, so many barbs between each tower, all very clear and orderly. In the centre of the rings he repeats the winged figure.

'Andrei went to France before the war. I saw him go. How could he be in a camp?'

He draws a second, smaller figure beside the first. He puts a cross where its mouth should be. He points at himself and at the figure.

'It's you, with Andrei.'

This is where he starts to tell her. He has bungled the chronology. He tells her about the camp but he has failed to tell her about that earlier time when the man came as a soldier to Poiana. And now that he has begun here he does not know how to go back and show her what was before. He can only go on, ahead from this beginning.

Safta puts out her hand to his that holds the pencil, stalls it and looks into his eyes. She has never seen him make so much effort to communicate anything before.

'He came back. Is that what you're telling me? Can you be sure?' Perhaps he was mistaken. 'But I know that he went to France. He went to France and he was going to be an engineer. When the war ended he would have become an engineer. There, not here. He didn't want to be here.'

Augustin is stubborn. He wants to go on drawing. Gently he moves his hand away from hers. He takes up another piece of paper.

She watches his drawing hand that is so nimble and expressive, his other hand that lightly secures the edge of the page; the lines that form, all of them small lines, delicate, slowly massing.

She dreads the image that will appear. When his pencil becomes blunt he sharpens it with a few deft strokes of his knife, goes back where he left off. You don't have to do this, she wants to say, not for me.

There is so much that he would like to tell her, now that he has begun. He would like to show her how it was. The flatness of the land. How bare it was, cleared of trees and anything that grew; the soil black, drying in the sun to fine black crumbs like cake, soaking up the wet when it rained to become heavy black mud. How at the edge of the land there was the marsh, and this they were burning away until it was as bare and black as the land. Men went out and set light to it and he could see it burning, the smoke rising from it in the day and a flat red line in the night. And where the land and the marsh were cleared, they were digging a river through it.

He came there at the start of the summer. It was not too hot then. The heat and the mosquitoes did not get bad until later. In the first moment of arrival he was glad simply that he was outdoors, in a world of colour. He could see in an instant the difference between the men who like him had just come from prison, whose faces were so pale that there was almost a blueness to them, and the men who already belonged to the camp, whose skin was dark and brown. He did not know what he was coming to, or how soon he would come to hate that huge bright sky.

She tries to go. He senses it and looks up immediately. She must stay until he's done. She sits frozen again in the chair and closes her eyes. Beyond the scrabble of his pencil she can hear the hum of the afternoon passing, the crickets, the calls of the swallows that fly above the lawn. Whenever she opens her eyes Augustin is still drawing.

His next picture shows the digging. There is the black land, flat to the horizon, and then there is the line they are cutting through it, the heaps of soil on either side. It has been surveyed and marked out as a straight line, all neat and tidy, but the work is not tidy at all. What he draws is chaos. The inanimate things are chaotic in themselves: between the huge ditch that is the base of the digging and the high sides of the banks, the random heaps of tipped soil, of rocks and timber, the jumble of hoists and wagons. And these are only the background to the figures he must draw. The flat ground and the banks alike swarm with figures, but these cannot be standing figures of the type he usually makes. Every one of them must be in motion, at work. He remembers how it was: how they had to appear to work even if they did not work, incessantly, how it brought punishment to be seen to be still. Of necessity these figures he draws must be more complex than any that he has drawn before, broken into more parts, jointed so that he can make them stoop, dig, bend, contort. This whole drawing must be more complex than any that he has ever made.

Safta sees the marks appearing on the paper. He draws swiftly and with intensity. The strain in his fingers is clear. He is pressing hard and the marks come out very black. The drawing becomes harder to decipher the more he adds to it. The figures begin to spill everywhere, down the banks and across the floor of the ditch, among the rocks and trolleys and wagons. She has a notion of an antheap disturbed, the ants all on the move, racing in different directions. The little thin figures, with their broken bodies and their oversize heads, are more like ants than people. And yet they are people. She sees that all of them are holding tools – shovels, spades, pickaxes – and that above them all, high on the top of the bank, two straight figures hold what appear to be guns. In the space of sky, which is the only remaining space in the picture, he draws the arm of a crane. The clarity of this image – the straightness of the interlocking lines – is almost reassuring after the furious mass of pencil strokes below.

She is beginning to guess what is the purpose of this extraordinary scene of labour. The crane is the link. Everyone has seen the propaganda images in the newsreels and newspapers. A canal that is the great project of the nation, a thing of glorious music and banners and marching workers. A marvellous construction done by brave men pulling levers of gigantic and wonderful machines. Bulldozers the size of houses, diggers with giant shovels tipping boulders into the marsh. Far away in a field, hands press down on a detonator and great holes are blasted out of the ground, fountains of rocks and dust blown into the sky, the explosions going off in sequence as in a battle. But in Augustin's drawings the work is done by men alone without machines.

He puts his pencil down. He is worn out.

'I think I see. May I take the picture?' She puts her hands out to it.

He nods.

The paper trembles as she holds it out into the low sunlight. Some of the drawing is so dark and dense it needs to be brightly lit before she can make out the detail. She feels a terrible pity at what she sees.

'You've done well, Augustin. It's an amazing picture.'

Then she says, 'But that's enough. Isn't that enough for now?'

He has taken up his knife and is sharpening the pencil to begin another drawing.

He knows that he would not have survived if it had not been for the driver of the Lagonda. He was already ill. He would never have been strong enough for the work.

He did not recognise the man at first. That summer he had spent at Poiana he had been so young and handsome, even that time he came by during the war. Now he was just a prisoner, thin, filthy, shaven-headed like everyone else. That was something about the camp, that after a time there was no one who stood out as an individual, nothing distinguishing about anyone. Augustin had noticed this man only because of the work he did, which was different from that of most other prisoners. Sometimes he carried papers about with him or stood and unfolded sheets of plans. The plans had the sharp clean identity to them that the man had lost.

One day he was coughing badly. The camp was where he began to be ill. He was at the diggings and he was bent over coughing and the man pulled him over. The man knew him for who he was and even remembered his name. He spoke it and Augustin read it on his lips. Then the man spoke for him.

He was sent to the doctor and put in the hospital for some days. When he came back he was given work with the horses. He thought that the man must have told them how good he was at working with horses.

The man spoke for him and now he must speak for the man.

He makes the Lagonda figure again, but this time he makes it lying flat on the ground. It is hard to draw. His fingers are shaking.

How can he draw movement? He has never drawn movement. All he has drawn in the past are static forms: rooms, landscapes, standing figures. Even these ant figures he has drawn building the canal are not moving in the drawing but static, each one of them caught in a still piece of motion, in its specific pose, as in a photograph. They are the closest that he has come to drawing movement but they arc not moving.

He must draw the bank again, the walls of the canal and the heaps of extracted soil and the workers. Then he wants to draw the whole bank in motion. This motion should be rushing, like water.

The summer was over. They had had some weeks of cool when the work went smoothly and well, and then there came days of torrential rain. The chocolate soil, that crumbled so easily and was so treacherous, made its trans-formation to treacly mud. He had never seen such mud, coating every man and every surface, making deep ruts where the carts clogged so that the horses could get no trac-tion and slipped in their traces. And it went on raining. All the vast grey sky was emptying itself on to the land.

The man was standing at the base of the canal when the bank started to shift. A whole section of bank cracked away suddenly from the rest, and flowed down, the scram-bling workers carried on it like debris, even the guard who had stood at the top and the dogs that were with him.

Augustin was holding a horse by the head, trying to lead it on. The horse shied as the land moved and he was thrown down. For a moment all his conscious attention was for the horse, though he felt the land shuddering about him. He scrambled up, steadied the horse, and only then did he see. The man was gone. He had been at the bottom of the ditch, and he was gone altogether. Pieces of other men, heads, arms, legs, stuck out from the mud. Some of these men were alive, and were brought out black and shiny as eels.

Safta does not see the movement in the picture but only the static fact: the horizontal figure and the heap of earth. 'Andrei died. You met him in the camp. And he died in the camp and was buried. Is that what you're telling me?'

They sit with the drawings on the table before them. The light is going. Soon she won't be able any more to see what he has drawn.

He has put his hands to his lap, folded one into the other. His eyes are on her, his face very close. It is a strange face because you can see the youth in it and yet it is old at the same time. You see the fine structure of the bones, no flesh on them; the heart shape pale and vulnerable beneath the dark mop of his hair. His eyes are taut even in the dusk. She senses the knowledge coiled in them.

She speaks again. 'Is that it? Is that what you're telling me? But you know you can't just tell a person something like that and leave it there and say no more.'

She has a need to move. She stands up and then he stands too, awkward, knocking the table so that the drawings fall to the floor.

'You have to tell me more. You have to make it clear.'

Her voice has begun quiet, as ever when she talks to him, even and uninflected as if she were speaking to herself. Now it begins to rise, sharp like a blade.

'Oh Tinu, don't you understand? Don't you see?'

At last she cannot bear his silence any more. She takes hold of him and shakes him. She holds him with her two hands, pinning his arms to his sides. She wants to shake the words out of him, out of his body so tight and dumb, that seems to be all bone, no flesh but all dumb bone. She shakes him so hard as if it would make him snap.

And then lets go and falls against him, and his body softens and he raises a trembling hand to stroke her hair.

After a time she looks about her.

'Look, it's almost dark. The dark comes down so swiftly now. Those are bats flying over the lawn now, where just a few moments ago I thought there were swallows.'

She has cried and stopped crying, and still he strokes her hair.

Her words come slowly, drawing back into themselves.

'Do you know, I thought I saw him once? If this is true, what you have drawn, if I understand it correctly, then perhaps I did. But it was just for a moment, from a distance. It might very easily have been someone else. That happens, doesn't it? That you see someone's back or the shape of them, or the way they walk in the street, and you think that it's someone you used to love; but then they turn or you get up close and you see they're not really like that person at all. It was in Ukraine. I was at a field hospital, not far behind the front. I went out to meet some ambulances coming in and I saw this man standing beyond the next tent with his arm in a sling, just his back first and then the side of him; and then the ambulance driver opened the doors and began unloading a stretcher and there was a poor boy on it in screaming pain. I saw to the boy, saw to it that they gave him a first shot of morphine, and when I looked again the man had gone. I was so busy. You cannot imagine the chaos that there was: no time to think or act for yourself, everything frantic, the smells, the cries, the movement, so intense. I let the moment go. It was just a fragment of all that was happening. I didn't think about it at the time but later it came back to me. And then I told myself that it was only a passing resemblance, some memory that had floated up. I was so tired in those days. Sometimes one was so tired that one just went on mechanically and one's thoughts quite separated themselves. The pieces of one's mind separated and came together at moments in unexpected ways, and there was no point trying to make sense of them. What was so special about the way that particular man stood? At that distance? Any number of men might have stood that way.'

And what if it had been him, would she have gone and spoken to him? She doesn't know. There was so much that

286

had happened in between, so much that had been put away that she could not open — least of all in that place where there were already too many wounds.

'What could we have said to one another anyway? Everything had changed. I was changed.'

This night, for the first night since she has been with him, he does not appear to be disturbed by his dreams. It is she who is disturbed. She remembers the past so intensely that it seems to be about her in the house. The moon lights the walls where the mirrors hung. It is almost as if she can see them. They were old mirrors, framed in gilt. They seemed to have a slight tint to the glass, that flattered everyone in them. Or that was what her grandfather used to say. He said that he had been to a famous tailor's in London who had just such mirrors that flattered all its clients. Her mother said that it was just an effect of the soft light that filled the room in the daytime, that came in filtered from the verandah on one side and the acacias on the other. She sees her mother gliding in through the double doors, deliberate in her walking like a ballerina, going to the green sofa. Sees her father in the room as if there were two of him: the man he was and his reflection in the mirror of which he was always aware. She thinks of Andrei. Augustin thought he was still important to her. She would have said only a day before, only that morning, that Andrei wasn't important any more. He hadn't been important for a long time. But once Augustin had an idea he fixed on it. She had held his hand back from drawing. She had wanted to tell him that the past was past, even if his pictures made it present. It wasn't necessary to work so hard to tell her something that she didn't need to know.

Didn't he understand about the past? She had thought, perhaps you needed words for that, to pack time away, to file and classify events and sort them into history. Words made it possible to say: this happened then. That is finished. Here is now.

But it isn't so.

The windows to the garden are wide open. The moon must be full though out of view behind the house. Under its light the grass has become smooth lawn again. The catalpa has grown huge since she has been gone, a dark cumulus shape making a squat cumulus shadow. There used to be a bench beneath it, a white bench of iron cast to look like twigs. Even then the branches hung down so low that when the tree was in full leaf the bench was almost hidden from the house.

Not only then but now, here in the dark.

The smell of mushrooms on her fingers.

They rode without speaking through the village in the evening and the peasants doffed their hats.

The lake. A time before they had so much as touched one another. Beneath the trees, a long flat dive, the brown length of him. He challenges her to race but keeps himself just within reach, the water taut between them, she all the time catching up yet knowing that it is in his power to pull away.

His brownness. His blue shirt. She has the image of his hands as he drove. They said they would drive across continents. Did they mean it or was it only the words carrying them onwards? There is his face, the profile looking ahead, the elation on it that might be happiness or might be no more than the impact of the wind.

Is she to believe in him again, all of a sudden, on the basis of a drawing? She saw the drawing form, line by line. She watched the movement of the pencil, listened to its friction on the paper. She followed the lines as they came together, gaining density, forming, transforming. The lines were nothing in themselves. They were nothing until they were interpreted, some process of intelligence and intuition turning two dimensions into three, representation into reality; and all the while there was the other reality of Augustin working away and humming through closed lips. Still they are no more than lines and yet they have become meaning, story, fact. And the story lies out there on the table where Augustin left it. Before they came in he had picked the drawings up from the floor where they had fallen and laid them back on the table and placed a stone on them to hold them there. In the morning they will be there in the light again for her to see.

They are driving in the darkness. They drive into black space with the headlights of the car lighting a white funnel before them. No sky, no horizon, but only the lit ground like liquid running on and falling away. They head on into the land as if it is a vast dark sea. They ride the swell of great waves, slipping down into the long troughs between. Gradually they go deeper and deeper until the land subsumes them. It has pulled them down into itself and they are drowned.

That was how Augustin drew him, not so much buried as drowned in earth.

She has slept only in snatches. Some time deep in the night she wakes. The moon has climbed higher and shifted its light across the room. She thinks she has heard a sound in the house. The night is very still. She listens for the sound to repeat.

Augustin sleeps on unaware. The shifted light falls across his face but it does not wake him.

She sleeps another stretch – or perhaps it's only an instant. Black sleep this time, no pictures. She wakes again sharply. Someone is moving around inside the house.

She hasn't heard the dogs barking. If the dogs have made no noise and yet someone is there then perhaps it is because they know the intruder.

Without making any noise herself, she goes to the windows on the side of the drive. She has kept the shutters on that side closed in case anyone should come by. She opens one of them a crack.

There is a cart there, a couple of horses and a foal. One of the horses whinnies and the foal goes close to it beneath the acacias. Then she hears a man's voice. She cannot make out what he is saying. She is not even sure of the language. The dogs run down the steps and behind them comes a man. Only one man, and it seems to be to the dogs that he is speaking. He is a small man, his movements quick and precise. He has a wide-brimmed hat like a Gypsy. He takes something from the cart and goes back into the house. Probably he is only a Gypsy.

She has nothing with which to defend herself. There is not even anything in the room with which she can wedge the door shut. She moves softly as if she was in a night ward, through from the drawing room into the next room and to the half-open doors of the room beyond. The man appears to have no suspicion of their presence. He seems to be settling down for the night. He must have noticed the loss of his mattress but he has put a blanket on the floor where the mattress was. She creeps back, pulling each pair of doors to behind her. Lies down again beside Augustin. She is back in the present. Her ghosts are gone. The room is just a room. The house is only a collection of empty rooms that they share with a stranger.

The man is up early. She watches as he draws water for his horses. They are good horses, better than she would expect of an ordinary Gypsy. And he takes good care of them. She sees him feel for some injury on one of the mare's legs. He takes a packet from the cart and begins to prepare some kind of dressing. She had hoped that he was preparing to move on but it seems that he is planning to stay longer. She thinks he will not go so long as the mare is lame.

She opens the shutter fully and shows herself.

'It's a big house. There's no reason why we shouldn't share it.'

He is older than she had thought in the night. Small, wiry, quick, but his moustache is grey. Bow-legged, weathered. He comes to face her where she stands at the window looking down at him.

'I know who you are,' he says.

He makes coffee. He has already made a camp fire outside. He seems to have everything he needs with him on the cart, even tin mugs for the two of them. He hands one to Augustin who is shy as he always is with strangers.

'He's my brother. He doesn't speak.'

'Drink?' There's a bottle of *pálinka* on the seat of the cart. He holds it out to her.

'No thank you. My brother won't have any either.'

'You're one of the family, aren't you?'

'Why do you think that?'

'Your looks. And why else would you be here?'

She doesn't answer.

'I shan't tell anyone.'

She wonders if she can trust him. There is something odd and free to him, unpredictable.

'My name's Elisabeta, Safta. And this is Tinu.'

'István.'

'You've been here before.'

'I come past now and again. I travel a lot.'

'What do you do?'

'I trade horses. I knew this place years ago, spent some time here.'

'When was that?'

'A long time ago. A long time before the war even. I brought a horse here from Transylvania.'

'The Lipizzaner.'

'A fine horse, really fine, that one. What happened to it?'

'The *Moşier* shot it.' She speaks of her grandfather as the squire, letting herself slip for a moment into a word from the past. 'He could not bear for it to go to Russia with the cavalry.'

'I'm glad that it didn't go to Russia.'

Augustin has put his cup down and gone to the horses.

'He's not really your brother.'

'Not family, no, but almost like a brother. He's deaf and dumb but he knows horses. He used to work in the stables. He loved your Lipizzaner very much.'

The foal comes to Augustin's outstretched hand as if it has always known him.

'I think that you knew his mother.'

'Who was his mother?'

'Paraschiva. She was the cook, here in the house.'

'Paraschiva. I remember Paraschiva.'

'She never married. She brought Tinu up on her own. He was born the year after the Lipizzaner came.'

Does he understand? He considers Augustin, who has the mare nudging his back now as he strokes the foal.

'The lad has a way with horses.'

'He was born with it. Horses like him. He likes them. He is happier I think with horses than with people.'

'And Paraschiva?'

'She's gone. We came to see if we could find her. Someone told me she was killed when the Russians were here.'

'I shan't be here long,' he has said. 'Just a day or two, then you'll have the place to yourselves again.'

He has put the horses to graze on the lawn and gone off on foot. Now that he is out of sight Safta does not trust him. She will not be at ease until she sees him return alone. She considers whether they should leave themselves while there's time but cannot think where they might go.

When he comes back at the end of the day he brings a chicken. It is newly killed and she guesses that he did not buy it. He makes a fire. Plucks the bird and cuts it into pieces. Puts them to cook. He also has peppers and tomatoes.

'You two can share. There's more than I can eat.'

Safta has gathered a basket of plums from the orchard. She brings that and the last of the bread the priest had given her.

'Tell him that I'm sorry about his mother. Can you tell him that? Tell him that I knew her once.'

'You can tell him yourself. He'll understand that much.'

*   *   *

When István has spoken – with his hands as much as with his lips – Augustin considers him for some time. It is rare for him to look at a stranger so directly. Then he nods, and stands up, lifting his hand to tell them to stand as well. He wants them to follow him. He leads them out at the side of the house, through the yard. The cellar door lies open at the foot of its steps; there are bullet holes in it but they have no meaning for anyone apart from himself. He walks the way the big Russian dragged her, out from the yard and across the grass. Everything is so overgrown that it is hard to find the place. It was at the edge of the wood but the wood has moved in towards the house. He looks for a tree that he recognises, a big beech that stood out from the wood. He thinks that he finds it at last, but it is changed. While the other trees about it have grown this one has lost a great branch that lies broken on the ground before it. From this point he begins a close search, parting the grass with his hands where it is long.

'What's he looking for?'

'I don't know.'

'It's getting dark. Soon we won't be able to see a thing.'

The moon will not rise till later. The twilight will soon be as dense as one of his drawings. Safta starts to work through the grass herself. He must think he's close or he would have given up by now. Her hands find a piece of metal standing out of the ground. A metal hood with a cross beneath it. She kneels to part the grass.

'It's her grave.'

Augustin is kneeling on the ground beside her pulling away the grass.

'The priest told me he buried her himself. Nobody knew anything about it till she was already buried.'

István stands a little back. He has taken off his hat and holds it before him.

'It's too dark now,' he says. 'We can come back and clear it properly in the morning.'

István takes the scythe from his cart and goes to the grave alone soon after dawn. He stands before it and sharpens the scythe, then works with short crisp strokes, beginning around the cross but moving out to mow a neat rectangle over the area where her body must lie. In daylight he sees what the cross is made from. Strange boy. It's all scrap from the war. The hood is beaten out of a battered and rough-cut sheet of metal that still bears a few traces of khaki paint. The cross itself is two round steel poles that could have been parts of an aeroplane; the ends of the horizontal bar finished with brass cartridge cases and the vertical bar, which is broader, with a slender brass shellcase. Just above the central joint a strip of tin has been attached and her name beaten out from it. Above the name, the pinprick outline of a bird with outstretched wings. He passes his fingers across it as if he would feel it fly.

When he has done he puts the scythe back in its place on the underside of the cart and goes to check the mare. Easy now, let's see how you are, my lovely, is that still tender now? He murmurs to her as he feels down her leg. The leg is relaxed beneath his fingers, all the way down. There is no longer the tightening in it that was there when he touched it before, that indicated hurt. Her lameness is almost gone.

Unseen within the house Safta watches him with the horse. He is very gentle. There is lightness in his fingers. All of her life – ever since she was of an age to hear the gossip at least – she had thought that he must have been a bad man, Augustin's father, the man who abandoned Paraschiva. She had looked at Paraschiva who was so palpably good and wondered how she could have made such a mistake. Now she thinks, it was no mistake. It would have been his lightness that attracted her, that same quick touch. Paraschiva herself was so placid, heavy, slow. You could not imagine permanence in such a connection. Paraschiva must have known from the moment she saw him that it would be in his nature to take off, some morning like this one, clear away with the mist. And if that was so, if she knew that, then the child was her way of holding a piece of him. For an instant Safta has a physical sense of how that would have been. It comes to her like her own pain.

'Will you go today?'
    'No, not today. She's still a little lame.'
    'When, do you think?'
    'One day, two. I don't know. We'll see.'
    'Where will you go to?'
    'Back to Transylvania. To my village.'

'Have you been away long?'

'Just a month or so.'

Later he has his questions for her.

'What will you do?'

'I have to return to Iaşi.'

'And him?'

'I don't know. I know that he needs to be out of the city. There's a sanatorium. I was meant to take him there.'

'He doesn't need a sanatorium.'

'No.'

'He just needs air.'

'That's why we came here.'

'You can get somebody to take him in. The priest in the village who gave you the food.'

'I don't know. He is old. His wife is old. And they're afraid.'

'Do you think he can get by without you?'

'He seems to survive. He must have looked after himself all these years. He got himself through the war. Then he was in a camp. He got himself through that somehow. He's stronger than you think.'

'I could take him.'

'You?'

'Why not? He's good with horses. He can be useful.'

'He doesn't have the right papers.'

'I can manage that.'

*　　*　　*

The moment of parting lies close. They know that they cannot remain unnoticed for more than a few days and yet they live as if they will be there indefinitely.

István cuts wood and they light the stove in the kitchen so that they have more than the camp fire to cook on. They find pans and utensils scattered about the place, not only in the big house but in the ruins of the cottages as well.

One day they heat water and carry it through to the bathroom, and one after the other each of them takes a bath in the great iron bath. Safta looks at herself in the mirror and sees how wild she has become. She combs out her hair with a care it has not been given in many days and washes it, and washes the clothes she has been wearing and lays them out to dry on the bushes in the sun.

Augustin takes a big round basket to the orchard and fills it with plums. There are many and of many kinds, plums and greengages and little golden mirabelles. He brings back one basketful after another and tips them out on to the kitchen table. There are empty preserving jars on the shelves in the corridor beyond the kitchen, dark high shelves where they have survived unnoticed and unbroken. He takes them down. One or two have spiders dead inside them. How the spiders lived and grew so huge on air within the empty jars is a mystery.

Augustin washes the jars and leaves them upturned to drain. He spreads and sorts the plums, then packs them into the jars. Some jars he packs with fruit all of one kind; others he packs in tiers of different colours. The plums look beautiful pressed against the cleaned glass.

'But we have no sugar.' And Safta knows she is no Paraschiva, so expert at making preserves.

Augustin brings out Paraschiva's old copper pan from the floor of the larder. Then he goes to the yard, takes a pickaxe and goes down to the cellar. Safta lights a lamp and follows him. There is one last hoard that was walled up in the time of the soldiers, hidden behind a heap of rotten crates and wine flasks. He strikes in two places before he finds the right spot, where the wall that he and József so hastily laid caves in easily. 'Bravo, Tinu,' she says, 'you really are a marvel,' and helps him to pick away the bricks and the soft mortar. There is a rack of wine – not their own home-grown wine whose barrels have long been emptied, but imported French bottles bearing the names of famous chateaux – and tins containing salt and flour, and sugar. 'Eureka!' She pours a white stream of sugar into the water in the pan. And if she has so much sugar then she will make jam as well. She has never done such a thing before; she has barely in all these years had a kitchen of her own. She sings as she watches the fruit come to the boil. Lifts off the scum as it rises. There used to be some fine precision in the making of preserves, she recalls, Paraschiva knowing as if by instinct the sweetness demanded of the syrup for a particular fruit or the moment of a jam's setting. Safta has no mind for any of that. She sings to herself and for the length of another song or two she watches the ruby geysers seething in the pan. That'll do, she thinks then. (Knowing all the time how little it matters. It is not after all as if she is stocking up for seasons to come. She is living within this

303

interval, without time, without requirement for the fruit to last; standing thus over the hot stove for the purpose only of the present moment and the illusion of a future.) She takes a cloth in each hand and lifts the heavy pan to the side. 'No,' she says, holding Augustin back as he brings the first of the jars. 'It's too hot. We have to wait and let it cool just a little. If we poured it this hot the glass would break.'

There are pears also in the orchard, early French varieties that they pick from espaliers that have formed strange and misshapen trees. A single vine has grown unpruned into a jungle but yields translucent grapes which he presses into juice.

On those hidden shelves at the back of the cellar István discovers an ancient bottle of Tokay. They drink it the last night on the verandah by the light of a dozen votive candles he has stolen from the church.

They leave together. Augustin sits up beside István on the cart. Safta rides the mare. She has taken to riding these last few days, wandering bareback over the hills. At first Augustin did not like her to leave him at all but he has got used to it. He has been happy to occupy himself without her. When she has come back she has seen the new draw-ings that he has been making, that often mix the present and the past together: the house furnished as it was but the garden wild; or the old stable yard that is now a burnt-out ruin precisely as it was, and István's cart — recognisably his cart crammed with all his nomadic possessions – coming in at the gate.

Through the earliest hours of the morning they travel together until they come to a paved road. Here she dismounts. István takes the horse and ties it to the cart. He lifts out her case and a big basket of fruit and places them at the roadside.

'You stay with István. You are going to the mountains.' She gestures towards the west. 'I'll come and see you.'

She kisses him goodbye. She has planned her goodbye in advance, told herself that she must not show any hesitation. If she were to hesitate it would open him to doubt. She must be firm, sure, restrained.

From his pocket he produces a present wrapped up in a piece of plum-stained muslin and tied with string. So he has known all along that they were going to separate. How could she have thought she could keep it from him?

The two men get up again on the cart and István hands Augustin the reins so that he can drive. From deep in the back of his throat he makes one of those sounds with which he communicates with horses. The cart starts away with the mare and the foal running alongside.

She does not have long to wait for the bus to take her to the town and the railway. No part of the return journey takes much time. The watching down the road. The bus materialising after so few moments of emptiness from the direction in which the cart had disappeared. The bus journey itself. It is market day in the town and the bus is packed. She has only the edge of an inner seat, a broken view out to the road. The woman beside her has a goose on her lap. They pass a cart, two men on it and a bay foal running alongside. She looks back compulsively as if to see the mare as well even though she knows that this is not the way they have gone. Then there are more carts appearing off tracks or out of nothing in the open land. Many of them run with additional horses or with foals. She asks her neighbour if there will be frequent trains to Iași. The woman shakes her head. She wouldn't know. What cause would a woman like her have for going to Iași?

The trains are not frequent but there is one leaving a mere ten minutes after she comes to the station. She buys her ticket and gets on to it breathless, hungry. It is as if she is winded with the transition. The train moves fast, throwing the landscape away behind her. The days at Poiana are receding from her with the land, too fast, losing their perspective, beginning too soon to merge with the distant past, the other memories from before. She opens Augustin's gift.

It is a book that he has made in secret, of drawings of the house. He has drawn each room in turn just as it used to be, furnished and with pictures on the walls, all in pencil, all with that duskiness that is in his drawings which means that you must look hard into them to see each form and minute detail, and she believes it is all there: teacups on a tray in the drawing room, her music laid out on the piano, her grandfather's pipe and his newspaper folded on the verandah. He has put everything back as it was, pieced it all together for her to take away, precise memories of the rooms that are lost. On the cover of the book he has drawn the view of the garden from the verandah, this too as it was, with the lawn mown and the bench beneath the catalpa and the border full of flowers, and above them he has written a remembered word: *août*. This had been a favourite word of his from the early days of their lessons, that he loved to draw for its shape, for its roundness and the hat of the circumflex above it, and also for its connection with himself. It is not August any more, it is September, but she holds the sense of August about her.

She wraps the book again in the cloth and puts it away in the basket with the fruit. As soon as she gets to Iaşi she will take the fruit to Adriana. Adriana will have worried that she has been away so long. She will share the fruit with her. She will say that they met a man who gave the mute a job that he could do, and took him to the mountains where the air will be as good for his lungs as that in any sanatorium. That will be close enough to the truth. One day the two of them might perhaps take a trip to visit him.

It will not even be dark by the time she arrives. She had expected it to be dark, for more time to have passed between the one place and the other, for there to have been some palpable change to the day. She left – they all left – Poiana in the early morning and it is late afternoon when she comes into Iaşi, in the same degree of light. The station hall is crowded and full of noise. She walks out swiftly with her case in one hand and the basket in the other. She does not at first take a tram but walks on for some time until she is free of the crowds.

In the morning she will go to the hospital. She will make some excuse for her extended absence. Then the old routine will return. The shifts. The daily tasks. The only facts will be the things that she does each day. The city. Her work. She will leave the past to itself.

Such beautiful fruit. They sit before a cloth on the floor in Adriana's room and unpack the basket, doing the work that Augustin had done at Poiana so few days before. Some of the plums are bruised. Adriana takes these first and cuts out the bruises and the stones and puts them into a pan for jam.

'You'll have to come and help me eat it as I'll be alone here now.'

She has the juice from the plums shining on her fingers.

'I have news,' she says.

Safta's hands fall still. This news will demand stillness of her.

'I know now.'

'How do you know? Did you get a letter?'

'A film. I saw a film about Stalingrad. I knew then that he could not have survived. It was a message to me.'

It was only a film, Safta might say. Adriana knows that she might say that. She knows that herself, perfectly well. She knows that the soldiers she saw in the film were real soldiers. She read that in the newspaper. The tanks and the guns were real, the Russian ones and the German ones which were captured in the battle, and the aeroplanes. The soldiers were actual veterans acting as themselves. Ones who survived. Only it will not be helpful to say that.

The film showed a battle on a scale that she could not have imagined. Even though she had read all the facts in the newspapers when it was happening and afterwards, all the facts, the statistics and the casualties. Though she had seen with her own eyes what happened in Iaşi and what happened to the wounded who came into her hospital, and multiplied all that in her head a thousand times. Alone in the dark with the rows of people about her silent as if they did not exist she understood it for the first time as she saw it on the screen. The vastness of it, the sheer numbers of aeroplanes, tanks, guns lined up across whole wide hillsides. She had never imagined such great space or such destruction. Such fighting – on the steppe, in the snow-filled trenches, on the ice on the Volga, in broken houses up staircases floor by floor. So many bright and eager young men, and she could see their faces, their courage and the shock in them when they were killed. The audience was entirely silent. She might have been alone and yet she was infected by the spread of emotion. And the music had such power. She like the rest was carried away by the music, forgetting even who she was, who was who, which side was which and which was hers. Silently inside herself she was cheering for the Russians, then weeping for the Germans. And the Romanian division to which her Ioan belonged was, they said, annihilated. They named his division in the film and the name brought her back to reality.

When the film ended the whole audience held there until the last white word had faded from the screen and the curtain fell across it. When they went out there were tears on many faces besides her own. She walked a long time in the streets. At last she came to a church. The door was locked but there was a kiosk outside with candles burning. She went to it and took a candle for Ioan, lit the candle and said a prayer. There were two sides to the kiosk: *Vii* and *Morţii*, two trays with water in them reflecting the flames of the candles. For the first time she placed Ioan's candle in the tray for the dead and not the living.

'I'm so sorry.'

'As I said, I'll be on my own here now.'

'Yes.'

'I thought I might offer. It's just an idea, I thought of it just now. You might live here if you like. You'll have more space than in the hostel where you've been.'

Safta has started on the plums again, passing her fingers lightly over their bloom, pulling out the stalks then slicing them in half and stoning them before they too go in the pan.

'Thank you, yes, that would be wonderful, for a time at least.' Then she says, 'Do you have enough sugar? We'll need a lot of sugar for jam. I can go tomorrow and get some more.'

István sings as they pass through a great gorge. A good thing, he thinks, that the lad is deaf. His singing is not something to which anyone has ever liked to listen. He bellows a song at the top of his voice for the satisfaction of hearing the sound come back at him. The cart goes slowly. The horse has had to climb a long way. They wind between high bare walls of rock. He sings ever the louder and the walls of the gorge amplify the song, bouncing the echo of it back again and again before them. When his voice runs dry he takes another swig from the bottle that he keeps propped against the footboard. It is a vintage Dom Pérignon. He has all that was saved in the cellar stacked in the cart, the pick of Constantin Văleanu's choice vintages alongside the plum preserves. Each time he drinks he hands the bottle on to Augustin who begins to drink as he does and sees what he is doing and opens his mouth and begins to keen, just for the feeling of it. The voices of the two of them resound like those of a dozen madmen through the ravine.

They camp high. They build a fire against the cold up there. When they wake they must drink some *pálinka* to face the day. It is his own *pálinka*, that he made himself

311

the last winter. It is much rougher than the champagne but effective. Sometimes István holds the reins, sometimes Augustin, but the horse can find its way and the way is down. There is really no need for a driver.

'So I have a son for my old age.'

Augustin looks blankly.

'A son. You.'

Augustin's face breaks into laughter that falls away down the mountainside.

'Yes, I know, it's a joke. And I wonder if they're any more of you about? István's sons, eh?'

But Augustin has forgotten him. They have come round a bend and there is a great landscape that suddenly draws all his attention: a long golden view into Transylvania. He has seen so much in the past few days, sitting up high in the cart with the land passing so slowly all about him. He has done no drawing but he has stored away image after image that he will be able to draw in the days that follow. Before this view, the mountains. The gorge. Between the gorge and the last climb into the mountains, a slender valley. They had stopped there beside a dark-coloured lake that had stumps of trees sticking out of it as if a whole broken forest had drowned in the water. He was not to know how it was formed, by a natural landslide that dammed the river and flooded the valley; and how the stumps of the trees had stood bereft in the water since long before he or even István was born. To him the broken trees looked sinister and raw like the work of men, not nature. It had made no sense to him. He could not understand why the soldiers had attacked the trees.

ACKNOWLEDGEMENTS

I would like to acknowledge two inspirations: the work of the artist James Castle and Patrick Leigh Fermor's introduction to Matila Ghyka's *The World Mine Oyster*.

Then I would like to thank all those who helped with the research and with my attempts to get things right: Mihaela Teodor, Tibor Kálnoky, József Rózsa, Marie-Lyse Ruhemann, Sherban Cantacuzino, Dana Codorean-Berciu, Laura Vesa and Kati, and the friendly children of the Project at Hârja.

I must also thank Alexandra Pringle, Mary Tomlinson, my agent Broo Doherty, Ariane, and David, as ever.

A NOTE ON THE AUTHOR

Georgina Harding is the author of two novels: *The Solitude of Thomas Cave* and *The Spy Game*, a BBC Book at Bedtime; and two works of non-fiction: *Tranquebar* and *In Another Europe*. She lives in London and the Stour Valley, Essex.

A NOTE ON THE TYPE

The text of this book is set in Granjon. This old-style face is named after the Frenchman Robert Granjon, a sixteenth-century letter cutter whose italic types have often been used with the romans of Claude Garamond. The origins of this face, like those of Garamond, lie in the late fifteenth century types used by Aldus Manutius in Italy.